INSPECTOR FRENCH:
FATAL VENTURE

Freeman Wills Crofts (1879–1957), the son of an army doctor who died before he was born, was raised in Northern Ireland and became a civil engineer on the railways. His first book, *The Cask*, written in 1919 during a long illness, was published in the summer of 1920, immediately establishing him as a new master of detective fiction. Regularly outselling Agatha Christie, it was with his fifth book that Crofts introduced his iconic Scotland Yard detective, Inspector Joseph French, who would feature in no less than thirty books over the next three decades. He was a founder member of the Detection Club and was elected a Fellow of the Royal Society of Arts in 1939. Continually praised for his ingenious plotting and meticulous attention to detail—including the intricacies of railway timetables—Crofts was once dubbed 'The King of Detective Story Writers' and described by Raymond Chandler as 'the soundest builder of them all'.

Also in this series

By the same author

*with other Detection Club authors

FREEMAN WILLS CROFTS

Inspector French: Fatal Venture

COLLINS
CRIME
CLUB

COLLINS CRIME CLUB
An imprint of HarperCollins*Publishers*
1 London Bridge Street
London SE1 9GF
www.harpercollins.co.uk

HarperCollins*Publishers*
1st Floor, Watermarque Building, Ringsend Road
Dublin 4, Ireland

This paperback edition 2022

1

First published in Great Britain by Hodder & Stoughton Ltd 1939

A catalogue record for this book is
available from the British Library

ISBN 978-0-00-855409-5

Set in Sabon Lt Std by Palimpsest Book Production Ltd, Falkirk, Stirlingshire

Printed and bound in the UK using
100% Renewable Energy at CPI Group (UK) Ltd

Contents

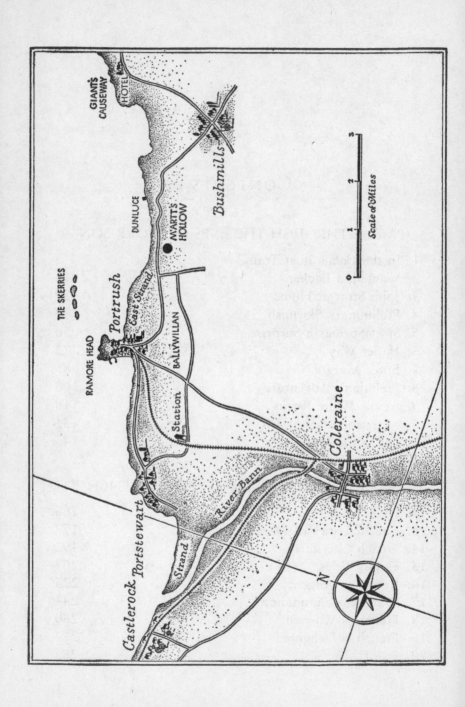

PART I

Through the Eyes of Morrison

1

In the Calais Boat Train

It was while acting as courier to a Boscombe Travel Agency touring party that Harry Morrison first met Charles Bristow.

Morrison was normally a clerk in the firm's head office in Lower Regent Street. Usually he spent his time arranging for other people the enthralling journeys he so much longed to take himself. He was well acquainted with the world, and particularly with Europe, in what might be called a theoretic or paper fashion. Asked the route from Copenhagen to Constanta or from Archangel to Archachon, he would say before ever opening a book: 'Oh, yes. The best way is via such and such towns and it will take you so many hours.' He was as much at home with a Continental Bradshaw as the normal Englishman is with Test Match scores, and always carried in his head the sterling equivalent of the principal currencies of the world.

Harry Morrison had been intended for the diplomatic service and had gone to Cambridge from a good school. But before he had taken his degree his father had died, leaving, instead of the expected fortune, debts which

practically wiped his legacy out, the result of secret specu-
lation. His mother was also dead, and at the age of twenty
he found himself alone in the world, with his future
dependent on his own efforts. Foreign travel had always
been his dream, and he now moved heaven and earth to
get a start in the Boscombe office. His good French and
German and his smattering of Italian and Spanish had stood
to him, together with the fact that he had been to certain
of the Alpine winter sports centres and knew some of the
the ropes of Continental travel. That had been five years
earlier, and since then he had put his whole soul into his
work, so that if the chance of foreign service should occur,
he should be in a position to seize it.

Now in his five-and-twentieth year, this chance had come.
Captain Holdsworth, one of the couriers, had fallen ill, and
there was no understudy to take his place. Morrison was
asked if he could undertake the work. His answer needn't
be recorded.

He was to conduct a party of seventy to Lucerne, see
them settled in their various hotels, and then go on to
Marseilles to meet a small but more select cruising party
and convoy them home. It was rather a job for him, but
he had copious directions from Holdsworth, as well as a
stout heart and a high courage.

He had managed with less difficulty than he had expected;
indeed, as they left Paris on the return journey, he was
congratulating himself that he had made a success of the
trip. His easy manner and his obvious pleasure in what was
happening had not only seen him through, but had made
him mildly popular with both sets of travellers.

Charles Bristow was a member of the second set, the
cruising party. Morrison had come specially in contact with

4

him over a suitcase which had disappeared during the transit across Paris, and which Morrison had triumphantly rescued as it was being borne away by an alien porter. Later in the Calais train the two had begun to chat, and it was then that Bristow dropped the remark which was to change the whole of Morrison's life, and lead him, as a crime reporter put it afterwards, into the very shadow of the gallows.

Morrison was passing down the swaying corridor when Bristow hailed him.

'Jolly good getting that suitcase,' he said. 'How did you twig the porter had taken it?'

'Orange label caught my eye,' returned Morrison, pausing at the door of the first-class compartment. 'Some people don't like to have tourist agency labels on their luggage, but'—he smiled—'they have their advantages.'

'Swank, that objection,' Bristow pronounced. He held out a case. 'Cigarette?'

'Thanks.' Morrison helped himself.

Bristow moved a paper from the opposite seat. 'Chap sitting here gone to lunch,' he explained. 'Won't you sit down or a moment?'

The compartment was empty save for a man sitting on the same side as Bristow. As he glanced up momentarily from his paper, Morrison was conscious of a pair of dark, suspicious eyes and one of those thin-lipped mouths which suggest a trap. A man of force of character, he thought idly, though probably not wont to be too much handicapped by scruples.

He dropped into the corner seat and a desultory conversation began. After the weather, the crowd on the train, and the chances of a smooth crossing had been duly dealt with, Bristow became more personal.

'Interesting job, this of yours,' he essayed. 'You've not been doing it long, I imagine?'

Morrison smiled. 'That's rather a blow,' he declared. 'As a matter of fact, it's my first trip, but I thought I was doing it as if bred in the bone. What has given me away?'

'Nothing against the way you've done it. If I may say so, we've been jolly well looked after. It was something else. You were enjoying yourself too much.'

Morrison laughed outright. 'And why shouldn't I? I'm fond of travelling: foreign sights and sounds and all that. Just the very feel of another country thrills me.'

'Just my point. When you've done the journey x to the nth times, you won't be so thrilled over it.'

'I won't do it x to the nth times. Long before that I'll be taking our clients round the world. Canada, the Rockies, Rio, India, the Far East. Lord, what wouldn't I give to see it all!'

'I envy you,' Bristow declared with a half-sigh. 'I wish I was as keen as that about my work.

'The very names of the places draw you,' went on Morrison unheedingly. 'Java, Borneo, Surabaya, Krakatoa, just to mention one corner of the world. Can you hear those names and not want to go?'

'I know: I've felt the same. Do your people do much of that? What I call big cruise work?'

'More than any firm, I think. We have three round-the-world trips running at this moment. And it's seldom we've less than two.'

Bristow grew more serious. 'I'm interested in that, he explained. 'Not that I could afford it myself. This little cruise to the Greek Islands is about my limit. But I'm interested in an abstract way in big-ship cruising.'

'Some people say that to read the folders is half the fun.'

'There's something in it. But I've often felt that the mere being on a big ship at sea would be a treat to a lot of people.'

'You mean apart from the places they call at?'

'Yes. Given reasonable weather, I think a lot of people would go cruising just for the sea and the ship alone, irrespective of where they were being taken. 'We do advertise that side of it; all the agencies do.'

'You mean deck games and sun and swimming-pools?'

'Yes. The life of the sea. Even the eleven o'clock soup has its advertising value.'

'I include all those things, but even more I mean the sea itself: the fresh wind, the salt on one's lips, watching the waves, even the gentle roll of a big ship. There must be a lot of people who would delight in it.'

'I expect you're right. A lot of people would probably try it if they could. But there aren't many who can, you know. Big-ship cruising is expensive.'

Bristow had grown more serious still. 'Suppose,' he went on, 'you could give big-ship cruising on moderate terms, how do you think it would go? Could you fill a ship? And would it pay?'

Morrison was surprised at the other's eagerness. 'I think you could fill a ship if your rates were low enough and if one could book for short enough periods, But I question if it would pay.'

'You mean the running expenses are so high?'

'Yes, that and the overhead—depreciation and so on. It's been tried, you know.'

Bristow's face fell to an astonishing degree. 'Tried?' he repeated. 'I didn't know that. When or where?'

'Well, several lines do it or have done it. The Booth Line, for instance, have a heavy trade between Lisbon and South America. But they start from London. From London to Lisbon they are running comparatively light. They can therefore offer cheap and excellent trips between England and Lisbon.'

Bristow seemed slightly relieved. 'Ah, yes,' he said, 'but that isn't quite what I meant.'

'The same thing happens with lines going to the East. They pick up a number of their passengers at Marseilles or Toulon or Genoa. They can offer cheap trips between home and these ports.'

'I hadn't thought of that.'

'Yes, it's done in several parts of the world. And the very cheap fares pay—but only for one reason: because you've already provided the heavy items: the ship, the fuel, the staff. Practically all that these fill-up passengers cost is their food.'

'Yes, I see that,' Bristow returned, speaking as if a load had been removed from his mind. 'But it's not quite what I meant. Those are small ships and they take people abroad, even if it's not round the world.'

'The Booth Line ships are not very large, but some of the others run up to twenty thousand tons. I don't know that I'd call that such a small ship.'

'I meant even larger than that: the big North Atlantic ships. What was really in my mind was big American liners cruising round the British Isles. That has never been done, has it?'

Morrison smiled. The idea seemed fantastic. 'Not exactly. Some of the big cruising boats—I'm not sure that it wasn't the *Arandora Star* herself—have done short local Whitsuntide or August Bank Holiday trips. For instance, I remember one to Kenmare—or was it Bantry?—for Killarney, you know. A three-day trip between their ordinary cruises.'

'And they paid?'

'Oh, yes. Full up as a rule.'

Bristow moved uneasily. 'That's not,' he pointed out, 'exactly what I had in mind. Suppose you had a big Atlantic liner cruising round Britain—continuously. Up and down the Channel and the Irish Sea, and perhaps about the Scottish Islands. Keeping in sheltered water and calling every day or two to take up and set down. What do you think of that idea?'

Morrison's surprise grew. Bristow was taking the conversation dead seriously. 'I never heard of that being done,' Morrison admitted cautiously.

'What I had in mind,' Bristow continued eagerly, 'was an hotel which moved about: a floating hydro if you like. People could go to it for a couple of days, a week or a number of weeks, just as they do to hotels. Well, there's the idea. What do you think of it—from a financial point of view?'

Morrison hesitated. He glanced round. The man in the opposite corner had dropped his paper and was composing himself to sleep. They had slacked for the curve at Amiens and now the platform slid past the window. The conductor showed for a moment in the corridor. The line narrowed and they went under a bridge.

'I don't know that I could form an opinion,' he said at last. 'I should think if there was money in it, someone would have done it. Let me have some more details. You spoke of cheap fares. What does that mean? How cheap?'

'I don't know,' Bristow returned. 'That would have to be

worked out. I would suggest all one class, and things to be run on the lines of your popular excursions to Lucerne or Blankenberghe. Everything plain, but comfortable and good. Plenty of deck space for games and so on. I should hope to keep the ship full for the season.'

Morrison gazed vacantly at the fields and copses as they hurried past the window. 'Tell me,' he asked, 'is this a serious matter? Have you some actual scheme in your mind?'

It was now Bristow's turn to hesitate. He looked searchingly at Morrison, then spoke more confidentially.

'I don't mind telling you that I have; a very definite scheme. I've even got a name for it: Home Waters Cruising Limited.' He glanced at his now slumbering neighbour and still further lowered his voice. 'I believe there is money in it, big money. But, like all these schemes, it would take money to develop. And that money I haven't got. I want to interest someone who has.'

Morrison laughed. 'You don't suppose I have, do you?'

'You may not have money, but you've something else,' Bristow returned seriously. 'In fact, you've two things. First, you have a knowledge of the tourist business and particularly of cruising, and secondly, you have—or I presume you have—access to the heads of your firm.'

Morrison shook his head. 'I'm afraid I haven't access enough to persuade them to charter an Atlantic liner for cruising round the British Isles.'

'No; I didn't suggest that. That's not my plan. But leave that for the moment. I want some technical help in the matter, which I think you could give me. You'll excuse me'—he smiled crookedly—'I don't know anything about you really, but from your appearance and manner I feel I can trust you.'

'I hope you can,' Morrison retorted drily.

Bristow nodded. 'I may say now that I didn't start this conversation merely to pass the time. I did it to lead up to this question: Would you be willing to give me that help? It's not very polite, but I admit I'm asking you because no one else will listen to me.'

Morrison grew slightly uneasy. He didn't want to become involved in anything doubtful. Was Bristow telling the truth, or was it merely a trick hoary with age? Enter Mr X. 'I have an admirable idea, which only requires a little capital to become a gold mine. Will you put in the capital? You will? Excellent!' Exit Mr X. and the capital.

And yet as Morrison studied the other's appearance he did not think it that of a swindler. Bristow was a big man, six feet tall or over, and, though not stout, was muscular and strongly built. He was of the Nordic type, with a long, rectangular face, a high forehead and a strong jaw. His nose was straight and his clean-shaven mouth was firm. He was fair, with light hair, blue eyes, and what official documents call a fresh complexion. There was a general look of decision and competence about him, as if he would be slow to make up his mind, but when once this was done—from an exhaustive weighing of all the available evidence—he would carry out his decision in the face of heavy odds. He did not look too kindly, and Morrison imagined that he might be unpleasant if crossed. However, when he smiled his face lighted up and its somewhat hard lines disappeared. It was certainly, thought Morrison, the face of an honest, if a hard man.

'That's rather a large question,' he answered. 'What help do you want?'

'Before we begin to talk business,' Bristow returned, 'I think we should know something more of each other. I'll start. My name is Charles Bristow and I'm thirty-two years old. I'm a solicitor; junior partner in the firm of Bristow, Emerson and Bristow of Fenchurch Street.' He handed over a business card. 'I've had the usual education, which I needn't go into. I'm not married and I live in rooms in Hampstead. If there's anything else you want to know to establish my *bonâ-fides*, ask it and I'll answer you. If not, tell me the same about yourself.'

To Morrison it seemed like a game. However, he was interested and there could be no harm in going so far.

'My name is Harry Morrison,' he returned, 'and I'm a clerk in the head office of the Boscombe Travel Agency in Lower Regent Street. I'm not really a courier, and I was only sent on this job because of illness among the regular staff. I'm twenty-five and I've been in the office for five years, having been twice promoted in that time. I'm not married either and I lodge in Acton. Anything, else?'

'Just one thing before we get down to it. I want your word of honour that you'll keep all this confidential.'

'I promise,' Morrison returned without hesitation.

'Very well. What I want is this: a statement of the cost of running a big ship. I want it divided into two items: first, interest on the cost of the ship with depreciation, and, second, the actual running. This latter would include fuel, food, stores, wags and so on. Then lastly I want the probably daily rate we should have to charge to make the thing pay. Can you get these out, approximately?'

Morrison was not sure. The charges his firm paid for big liners were not divided under the required headings. However, he knew clerks in the shipping offices and he might be able to get the information. The fares he could work out for himself.

But he was not sure whether he ought. It would mean a lot of work, and if it were a thank-you job, it would not be worth his while. Then some of the information might be confidential. Bristow looked all right, but, for all Morrison knew to the contrary, he might be acting for some other tourist firm and merely want to learn some of the Boscombe's secrets. There was no proof even that he was a solicitor. Morrison felt that until he knew more, he should not commit himself.

'We would, of course, want a proper agreement before you did anything,' Bristow chimed in, having apparently read his thoughts. 'You would want to be sure, first, of my *bonâ-fides*, and, second, that you yourself would be paid for your trouble. Now, on the first item I shall tell you my idea, trusting you to keep it to yourself. That should meet that difficulty. On the second, I'll offer you alternatives. Either I'll pay for your labour at an agreed rate, or else I'll offer you nothing now, but a much larger sum if the idea should come to anything.'

This sounded reassuring, and Morrison decided to go a step further. 'If you care to tell me your idea,' he said, 'I repeat my promise to keep it to myself.'

'Good enough,' Bristow nodded. 'I'll tell you.'

Like a skilled narrator, he paused to whet his listener's interest and enhance the value of what was coming. In spite of the speed of the train, it was comparatively silent in the compartment. The roar of the wheels on the rails, with the underlying rhythm of the passing joints, was muffled in the well-sprung coach with its sound-insulated walls and floor. For a moment none of the three occupants moved. Bristow sat with an eager expression in his eyes, Morrison awaited developments with a certain doubt, while the man in the further corner still slept unconcernedly. Bristow glanced at him searchingly; then, satisfied, he leant still further forward and resumed.

'My tentative estimates—which I am not sure are correct—tell me that the cost of the ship itself is a heavy item in the cruising balance sheet. Take a great liner of, say; fifty thousand tons, and put her present-day cost down at two and a half millions. Say, she has a life of twenty years. That would mean about three hundred and seventy-five thousand a year for interest and sinking fund alone. Suppose we cruised for six months in the year and carried an average of two thousand passengers. Then each passenger would have to pay a hundred and eighty-seven pounds towards the cost of the ship, or over seven pounds a week. Am I correct so far?'

Morrison calculated on the margin of a newspaper. 'I think so,' he agreed.

'Now here's my idea. I happened to be in Southampton recently and I saw the *Berengaria* leaving for the Tyne to be broken up. The papers said that she was sold for a hundred thousand. There's another big ship, the *Hellenic*, lying there waiting to be sold for the same purpose. Now, why not buy her and fit her up for cruising?'

Morrison almost gasped. 'But, good Lord, you couldn't!' he exclaimed. 'They're done, those ships, for cruising: worn out: finished. Their plates are thin. Isn't that the reason for them being broken up?'

'No, Bristow returned, 'more frequently it's because they're out of date. But don't worry about that. Suppose they *are* done for the Atlantic traffic. Remember that thrashing at full speed through winter storms in the Western Ocean is one thing, and summer cruising at half speed in

14

sheltered waters not more than thirty miles from land is quite another.'

'Would you get a certificate?' Morrison asked dubiously. 'I doubt if the Board of Trade would grant it, or Lloyd's either.'

'I've enquired into that. I'm told they would: for that limited work. But leave that for the moment and consider costs. The ship is bought, say, for a hundred thousand. Another hundred thousand is spent in overhaul and decorations. That is, she costs two hundred thousand instead of two and a half million.'

Morrison shook his head. 'That sounds right enough, but there's one thing you've forgotten.'

'What's that?'

'The two and a half million ship will last twenty years. Yours at two hundred thousand won't last five.'

'I think she'd last twenty under the conditions I've named—always in sheltered waters and never at more than half speed. There are plenty of steamers forty years old and more still plying under such conditions. However, let's take ten for argument's sake. I make interest and sinking fund forty thousand a year, or say, fifteen shillings a week per passenger. That's a saving of nearly six pound ten per passenger per week.'

Morrison figured again. 'That's correct, so far as it goes.'

'Then there's fuel. I don't know what the oil would cost for running her at full speed, but I'm told about fourteen thousand pounds per week. Now I estimate my scheme would save sixty-six per cent of this. First, if you run her at half speed, you save a lot more than half the fuel, and then on this cruising she'd lie a lot at anchor. There'd be stops during the day for shore excursions, and at night where beauty spots lay close together. Say, however, you only saved nine thousand a week: that would be four pounds ten per week per passenger.'

'Good God!' Morrison exclaimed, overawed by these figures.

'Then, of course, the working of the ship would cost less. With the easier conditions, I should hope for a small saving in both deck and engineering staffs. I'd carry only about half her complement of passengers and that would mean a big saving in food and stewards. Then, again, the food would be simpler and cheaper. I don't know what these would come to, but say another pound per passenger per week.'

'You mean a total saving of some twelve pounds per passenger per week?'

'Yes, but it's not quite so good as it looks. There are items on the other side. Harbour dues, for instance, or, alternatively, the hire of tenders. I'm only speaking very approximately.'

Morrison felt that Bristow was wrong to limit the number of passengers to be carried, but before he could say so, there came an interruption. A little group of people appeared moving along the corridor, an early contingent from the first lunch. One of these, a flamboyant-looking woman, was talking vivaciously. 'Ach, no!' she said in English as she passed the compartment, 'I must have the monkey!' She moved on and her further words were lost.

The incongruous phrase, thrust into the serious discussion on marine transport costs, struck Morrison. Involuntarily, he stopped to listen. Evidently their fellow traveller was similarly affected. Morrison, glancing across the compartment, happened to notice him open an interested eye, look at the speaker, close it again, and remain motionless as if still asleep.

A little qualm of doubt passed through Morrison's mind. Had the man been awake long? Had he heard Bristow's scheme?

Morrison did not think he could. Bristow had not spoken loudly and the man was the whole length of the seat from him. The coach, admittedly, was running silently, yet even the best coach makes a fair noise at seventy miles an hour. No, it was all right. Nothing could have been heard.

All the same, Morrison noted again the label hanging from the suitcase above the man's head: A. N. Malthus, 777 Jordan Square, London, W.8. He wondered if they should continue their talk, but as it happened the decision was taken from him. The man whose place he occupied arrived from the first lunch and he had to move.

'You taking the second lunch?' Bristow asked. 'Then let's carry on there.'

But the restaurant car was crowded, and though they sat together, they could no longer speak in private. And after lunch Morrison's duties claimed him. It was not till an hour later, on the deck of the Canterbury, that they were able to talk again, and then there was only time to fix a meeting in London for the following weekend.

2

Wanted, a Backer

It was on a Monday that the Greek Islands cruising party returned to London, and at intervals all through that week Morrison thought over the strange interview the journey had included.

He was impressed with the case Bristow had made. While remaining pessimistic about the ship's certificate, he had no doubts as to the tourist side of the affair. The popularity of the piers at seaside places—the nearest approach to large ship cruising that the average man could achieve—proved that the scheme would meet a real need. If Bristow could produce his ship, he, Morrison, could fill her.

The more, indeed, he thought over it, the more profitable the scheme began to appear. It was overheads that killed the great steamship lines, and here there would be comparatively little. Only the ship herself would be needed. No great sets of offices would have to be maintained. The existing tourist agencies would do the booking, and the purser's rooms on board would accommodate the clerical staff.

On the other hand, the scheme had obvious drawbacks. It was hard to believe that, if it contained no snag, someone wouldn't have already tried it. Then existing tourist concerns and seaside resorts would see in it a rival and do all in their power to damn it. It would, moreover, be extraordinarily vulnerable. Tom would say to Dick or Harry: 'I thought of going on her, but I can't forget she was sold for breaking up. Tell me in confidence, old man, do you think she's safe?' A hint of that kind would grow like a snowball. Or someone might be put up to state baldly that the ship was dangerous, knowing that a slander action, even if unsuccessfully defended, would in itself achieve the aim.

But during this week Morrison had not only ruminated; he had acted. First he had enquired about Bristow. He had found a clerk in the office of his firm's solicitors who knew a member of the staff of Bristow, Emerson and Bristow, and at the cost of a film and supper he was able to put his questions direct. From these it emerged that the man he had met in the train really was the firm's junior partner, and that he bore very much the character Morrison had imagined. Bristow, as seen through his subordinate's eyes, was clever and efficient, good at his job, determined and decent up to a point. 'He's alright if everything goes his way,' the young man explained, 'but if he gets crossed, he's the very devil. But he's straight enough, if that's what you want to know.'

This being the point at immediate issue, Morrison decided to go ahead with the costs, trusting Bristow to pay him a reasonable sum for the work. He also determined to make a few enquiries about Malthus, the man who had been asleep—or awake—in the train. He could check him up in the various books of reference, and perhaps might find someone who knew him.

19

Getting out the costs proved a bigger job than he had expected, and he had to bribe with theatres and dinners certain other acquaintances—this time from shipping offices—before he could get his information, However, what with this and the figures he found in his own firm's books, he was able to prepare what he believed was a reasonable statement.

The figures were impressive. If they were correct, there was a fortune in the scheme. Morrison began to wonder whether chance had not brought him his great opportunity, and he determined to make himself so useful to Bristow that he couldn't be done without.

It was therefore with something of excitement that on Sunday afternoon he presented himself at Bristow's rooms in Hampstead.

The house was of a good type in a good neighbourhood and Bristow's sitting-room, a large, front, bow-windowed chamber on the first floor, was charmingly furnished. 'Oozing with money,' Morrison thought, as his host waved him to an armchair and offered cigarettes and whisky. Bristow was civil, though not effusive. 'Glad to see you,' in somewhat dry tones was his highest flight of cordiality, and he went on at once to business as if he considered time spent on social amenities was wasted.

'Well,' he began, 'you've thought over what I said in the train? Do you feel like helping me—for an agreed consideration?'

Morrison restrained his urge to reply, 'Such is my desire,' and instead answered that he had already got out some figures.

Bristow seemed pleased. 'Good!' he pronounced. 'Then before we go into them, let's fix up an agreement. I've drafted two: I said I was going to give you an alternative.' He crossed to a desk and picked up a couple of papers. 'Both start with a secrecy clause, and by this'—he held up the first—'I agree to pay you for your time at whatever rate you consider fair.'

'And the other?'

'By the other,' Bristow returned, 'you agree to put in whatever time you can without any direct payment. If the scheme proves a failure, you get nothing. If it succeeds I promise you twenty per cent of my net profits up to a figure to be agreed on: I suggest five hundred pounds. I may add that if the thing really clicks, there'd be a job for you if you cared to take it, though this wouldn't be guaranteed.'

'I'll take the second,' said Morrison.

For the first time a trace of enthusiasm showed in Bristow's manner. 'That's fine,' he declared warmly. 'I'm delighted. Very well: read this, and if you're satisfied, we'll sign.'

Morrison read the second paper carefully. He was no lawyer, but his job had brought him some knowledge of agreements. In spite of its legal language, the document was clear.

'I'll sign,' he decided.

'Fine!' Bristow repeated, rising and ringing the bell. 'I have it in duplicate and we'll go straight through with it.'

The maids being out, the landlady was impressed as a witness, and in five minutes the delighted Morrison had in his pocket a document which under favourable circumstances would give him a legal claim to £500.

'Now let's go ahead,' went on Bristow. 'What figures have you got out?'

'Very encouraging they are,' Morrison returned, opening his notebook. 'If your figure for the ship is correct, I think

21

the scheme would be a good proposition. In fact, I think it would pay extremely well.'

'You do?' exclaimed Bristow with evident satisfaction.

'I'm sure of it. First, take your figure of two thousand passengers for six months of the year.' And he plunged into the details of his statement. These agreed largely with the figures Bristow had put up in the train. They discussed each point from every angle, then at last Morrison straightened himself up. 'Very well,' he said, 'that leads me to fares.'

Bristow took a deep breath. 'Ah!' he exclaimed 'Now you're getting to it. What about fares?'

Morrison was keenly enjoying himself. 'I think,' he pronounced, 'that you could offer a fare that would keep her filled. I make it about nine pounds a week *and*'—he raised his hand as Bristow would have spoken—'if you increase the number of your passengers to three thousand, as I should advise, that nine pounds would come down to about seven.'

'Seven pounds a week!' Bristow repeated excitedly. 'Good Lord! If we could do that we're millionaires. What does that include?'

'Everything but shore excursions.'

'Everything!' Bristow's eyes goggled. 'Why man alive, we could easily get eight pounds a week or more—much more, I should think. If you're right that would mean a pound a week per passenger profit: say'—he figured rapidly—'nearly eighty thousand a year!'

Morrison grinned. 'That's what I made it,' he agreed.

Bristow got up and began to pace the room. 'I thought there was money in it,' he declared, 'but I never thought it ran to anything like that. Say it was only fifty thousand a year! I can't get over it!'

'It mightn't work out quite so well in practice,' went on the less exuberant Morrison. After all, he didn't hope to get fifty thousand, but five hundred at most, 'There might be unexpected repairs wanted, and the ship mightn't last as long as you think.'

'But, damn it, man, if she lasted four years we'd get our money back. And if she lasted five we'd make a pile. We needn't worry about her lasting.' He gave a whistle, and picking up the whisky, poured a couple of fingers into each glass. 'We need a drink after that,' he declared. 'I feel all bowled over.'

They had their whisky, and then for a couple of hours they worked, checking calculations, weighing probabilities, estimating unknowns. They made some slight amendments, but in the main Morrison's conclusions stood.

'Bless my soul, I can't get over it,' Bristow said as at last he threw down his pencil and sank back in his chair. 'How is it the thing hasn't been done before?'

Morrison shrugged. 'Makes you feel there must be a snag somewhere.'

Bristow nodded. 'That's what's bothering me. It's too good.'

He seemed frightened by the vastness of the promise. He sat staring before him for some seconds, then with a little gasp went on:

'It's easy enough to see our next step. We must get the two hundred thousand to start the thing. How are we going to do it?'

What they wanted, Bristow considered, was a rich man who would put in the whole sum in return for a fifty-fifty share in the profits. He preferred an individual to a syndicate for many reasons. Negotiations would be easier, less formal, more elastic. But he had already approached without success all the rich men whom he knew.

'It's not so easy as it sounds,' Morrison pointed out. 'No one could be expected to consider the scheme without examining all these figures, but if we showed them to the wrong man he might easily buy the ship for himself and leave us out in the cold.'

'I fancy I could guard against that,' Bristow declared grimly. 'However, the first thing is to find the man. I suggest we think over it until next Sunday, and if we've no luck we'll then consider the syndicate.'

'Right,' Morrison agreed. Then, as an afterthought, he touched on the Malthus matter, which at intervals had given him a little uneasiness. 'Something I forgot to mention to you. Do you remember the man in the carriage When we were talking?'

'Yes; he was asleep.'

'He wasn't asleep—at least, not all the time.'

Bristow sat up. 'What?' he almost shouted.

'You remember some people came past and a woman said something about a monkey? I happened to glance at him just as she spoke. He opened his eyes and looked at her and shut them again.

Bristow swore. 'Then, damn it all, man, he might have heard what I said!'

'I doubt it.'

Bristow grew more upset. 'Of course he could! It was a silent-running coach. Why in hell didn't you mention it before?'

Morrison was getting annoyed. 'How could I? There was no opportunity, as you know very well. Besides, I didn't think it important.'

'No opportunity! A word in the corridor and we might have found out who he was!'

'I did that myself,' Morrison retorted in slightly sulky tones.

Bristow made a gesture of exasperation. 'Damn you, Morrison! You're hard to live up to! Who was it?'

Morrison turned over the pages of his notebook. 'Mr A. N. Malthus, 777 Jordan Square, W.8. He seems to be well off; is believed to have no job, but goes to races and does a lot of cruising.'

'Cruising? Hell, how did you find all that out?'

'I saw his name and address on his suitcase, and I checked him up in the directory. He's not in *Who's Who*. As he was travelling abroad, I wondered if we knew anything about him, but his name wasn't on our books. I asked a friend of mine in Butler's, and he knew him all right. He had dealt with them for years.'

'Any special reputation?'

'Pleasant spoken, but too sharp to be quite wholesome.'

Bristow seemed unreasonably upset. 'I don't like it,' he repeated. 'I was a fool to talk in a place like that, but I was sure the man was asleep.'

'But what matter?' persisted Morrison. 'It's not likely he'd steal the idea.'

'It's not likely perhaps, but it's possible. What did you think he looked like, Morrison? You sat opposite him and could see him better than I.'

Morrison reassured him, though without much success. 'It just means,' Bristow ended up, 'that we must get our money and an option on the ship as soon as possible.'

All the next week the problem remained in Morrison's mind, and then on the Friday an incident occurred which led to a new development.

On that morning Morrison was called into his manager's room. Mr Alcorn was a pleasant man, on good terms with his staff. He was writing as Morrison entered, but he looked up, grunted, 'Here's Stott on the warpath again,' pushed a letter across the desk, and buried himself once more in his correspondence.

Morrison took the letter. 'The wanderlust is again upon me,' it read, 'and this time I want to go somewhere new. I'm sick of all the usual tours. What do you advise? You know where I've been for the past few years, and also that I will neither take violent exercise of any kind, nor rough it in order to visit out of the way corners of the earth. Will you send someone down to talk it over?'

John M. Stott had for some time been one of Morrison's *bêtes noire*. A man of about seventy, he was small of stature, red-faced and choleric in appearance, and possessed at moments of stress of an unpleasantly rough tongue. He lived alone with his butler, house-keeper and chauffeur in a charming house near Windsor. He was undoubtedly rich— to Morrison his wealth seemed fabulous—and he was a good friend to the house of Boscombe. He liked sea travel, as represented by patronage of the largest and most luxurious liners, and every year he gave the Agency the pleasure and profit of arranging some still more extensive tour. Three months of the previous winter he had spent on the liner *Silurian*, 34,000 tons, doing a world tour at a quoted price of 800 guineas. This was his most expensive holiday to date, though its cost was not unduly above the average.

It was an idiosyncrasy of Stott's that he would never call to see people if they could be made to call to see him. When, therefore, his urge for travel possessed him, a representative of the Boscombe Agency found it convenient to attend at 'St Austell', the charming villa near Windsor. Formerly the managing director himself had gone, but latterly the dirty work had fallen to Morrison. This was due to Morrison's successful handling of another job. Stott's neighbour, the Earl of Bullen, had called at the Agency about a complicated shooting journey through Syria, Transjordania and Iraq, and been so impressed by Morrison that on his return he had sung his praises. Stott, always ready to defer to a peer of the realm, demanded Morrison's aid when the time came for his next tour. Once again Morrison gave satisfaction and from that date Stott became his special charge.

'Well,' said Alcorn, putting down his pen and throwing his letter into the 'out' basket, 'where shall we send the blighter this time?' Alcorn hated Stott, who had always treated him as a not very superior servant.

'The trouble is, sir, that's he's been everywhere,' Morrison pointed out; 'everywhere that there are big liners and restaurant cars and *de luxe* hotels.'

'What about improvements and developments since his last visit?'

'I tried that last year and it didn't work. If you suggest his going back to a place, he always says: "Damn it! I was there three years ago, or five or whatever it is."'

'I know. A lot of people before Stott have wanted new worlds to conquer. Then what about a new vehicle of travel? A private yacht or plane?'

'He doesn't like the air, sir, but a yacht might do the trick. What about crossing Europe by water in a super-launch?'

'Too humdrum. He must be able to prate about his originality. What about that South American river: the Parana, isn't it? A super-launch to explore the Chaco where the fighting was, and those forests someone wrote about a few years ago: Something Hell, I think the name was. A good book, I remember.'

Morrison smiled. 'You've hit it, sir. Blue Star to Buenos and then up the Parana or whatever it is, until he gets too sick of it to go further. Back to Buenos and across the continent by *de luxe* express to Valparaiso and home by the Canal. I believe that's the ticket.'

'Very well. Go down and try it on. And if he turns it down, ask him what he'd prefer.'

So it happened that Morrison, after a rapid though intensive study of what the British Museum had to say on the Chaco, turned the bonnet of the firm's small Ford westwards. It was a charming autumn day and Morrison was in the best of spirits. He gazed about him with approval. The leaves had not yet begun to come down, but they had turned every conceivable shade of brown and russet: all spectacular and delightful. The sun shone brightly, though its light was already a little thinner than in full summer. Morrison congratulated himself as the last vestiges of Town fell behind and he came to what was indubitable country.

It was just as he was approaching the gate of 'St Austell' that the great idea shot into his mind. Stott! Wasn't Stott the man he had been looking for?

Stott's enemy, to escape which he had planned these colossal tours, was, Morrison believed, nothing more nor less than boredom. What the man wanted was not a trip or a cruise, but an interest. He had too much money to work, and he was no sportsman. He had often told Morrison that the thought of poking a ball about with a golf club or billiard cue made him ill. He neither fished nor shot nor rode to hounds. It was true he was a bridge player, but one couldn't play bridge all day.

But if he wanted an interest *and* a cruise, how more perfectly could he have both than through Bristow's scheme? If only he could be interested, the thing was as good as done.

He could live on board in the most luxurious suite—indeed, if he wanted it, he could have a whole deck reserved for himself and his friends. He could be made chairman of the venture, which would pander to his pride, while presiding at frequent staff conferences would give him an interest and he could kid himself that he was running the entire affair. Certainly Stott seemed to be their man!

Morrison ran past the gates of 'St Austell' to the Post Office in Windsor. There he was lucky enough to get a through call to Bristow. A possible backer! Should he put the thing up to him?

With Bristow's reply drumming in his ears and his heart beating slightly quicker than usual, Morrison headed the Ford back to 'St Austell'.

3

John Stott at Home

Stott's house was long and low, built of reddish-brown bricks and tiles, mellowed not with chemicals, but by age. It gave an extraordinary impression of peace and stability, as if nothing could ever disturb its serenity, standing there with its creeper-covered walls, its surrounding lawns and gardens and its background of great elms and beeches. Perfectly appointed, it might have been chosen as a sample of the English country cottage at its best.

Marshall, the butler, greeted Morrison with becoming gravity. 'Mr Stott's expecting you, sir,' he declared. 'He's in the garden. Will you come this way?'

The master of the house was lying in a deck-chair in the shadow of a patriarchal elm, a giant among trees, with a cigar in his mouth, a book on his knee and a glass of whisky and soda at his elbow. He did not move as Morrison appeared, though he greeted him civilly enough.

'I expected you before lunch,' he said. 'However, now that you've arrived, pull over that chair and help yourself to a cigar and a drink.'

Morrison did as he was told. 'I wanted to have some proposals to submit to you, sir,' he explained, 'and I had to look various points up. I hope you'll approve the result.'

'Well, go ahead and let's hear.'

Morrison opened with a graceful tribute to the profundity of his host's knowledge of the world, geographically as well as sociologically. He indicated that organised tours were no longer capable of giving satisfaction to so experienced a traveller, and, moving by easy stages, at length reached the suggestion of river exploration.

Stott, obviously taking the flattery as his due, made no reply to this, but sat obviously waiting for more.

'We thought that you might care to hire a motor cruiser, sufficiently large to have comfortable cabins for yourself, and, if you desired it, for friends. In this way you could go where you wished at your own time and independent of steamer schedules.'

'I've done a lot of rivers, as you know,' Stott replied, 'and I can't say I found them very interesting.

This was not exactly promising, but Morrison knew his man. 'I can well understand that, sir,' he answered diplomatically. 'But, if I may say so, I think that was because you travelled by tourist steamer—not always very comfortably, I'm afraid. I was going to suggest a waterways tour a little off the beaten track.'

'Where?'

'Well, what about the Northern European countries? Say, Norway, Sweden and Finland to start with?'

Stott pointed out with some force that there was little of Norway, Sweden and Finland that he didn't already know. Morrison, however, was just getting into his stride. He suggested a more ambitious programme: across Europe from

31

the English Channel to the Black Sea. This also Stott turned down with contumely, as the police say, together with similar suggestions about the U.S.A. and India. With skill, Morrison finally worked round to the Chaco scheme.

'There *is* one other proposal,' he said hesitatingly, 'but I scarcely like to mention it, as I don't think it would appeal to you. It's to go out by Blue Star Line to Buenos Aires and then take a private cruiser up the Parana, through the Chaco, where the fighting was. But I need hardly talk about that. I feel sure you wouldn't consider it.'

Stott rose to it as Morrison had hoped. 'And why shouldn't I consider it, young man? It seems to me the first sensible thing you've said today. Tell me more about it.'

Morrison threw off as casually as he could the information he had amassed at the British Museum. Stott listened silently and at first seemed favourable to the scheme. But as he learned the distance he would have to go and the character of the forest through which he would have to pass, he grew less enthusiastic. Finally, he turned it down with a complete lack of ambiguity.

Morrison wondered if the time had yet come to attempt his *coup*. He thought so, but, to keep his conscience clear, he decided first to put Alcorn's question.

'Then, sir, is there any other proposal you would prefer? As you know, we should be only too glad to get out details.'

It was when Stott declared pithily that to make proposals was Morrison's job, not his, that the young man felt that zero hour had come. He went to work craftily.

'I wonder, sir,' he began deprecatingly, 'whether you would care to get in on this new home waters cruising idea? It's novel enough and you might enjoy it.'

Stott glanced at him shrewdly, 'Never heard of it. What is it?'

'Well, it's really confidential, sir, and perhaps I shouldn't have mentioned it. A friend of mine is mixed up with it and that's how I happen to know. It's proposed to try cruising in home waters with big ships. You know the Hebrides, of course?'

'Been to Oban and Skye and so on long ago,'

Morrison's heart leaped. 'Ah, yes, sir; very pretty and all that,' he admitted condescendingly. 'But it's not what I mean. The outer islands are the thing; at least, so I've heard. But the snag is that you can only see them by going in small steamers. Very comfortable, of course, but not what you, sir, are accustomed to. Now, this scheme is to bring these islands and other interesting parts of our coast within the reach of the traveller who knows what's what.'

'Why didn't you suggest that for the motor cruiser?'

'Because of the sea, sir,' Morrison returned with admirable presence of mind. 'It can be rough there. Still, the motor cruiser might be the best way, if you didn't care for the idea of the other.'

'Why shouldn't I care for it? What's the hitch? What are you beating about the bush for?'

Morrison made a deprecating gesture. 'Sorry, sir, but I'm afraid I haven't made myself clear. The scheme is not in operation yet. In fact, I understand the company is only being floated.'

'Oh.' Stott looked unpleasant. 'Money wanted?'

'You'll naturally think that's what I'm after, sir, and, of course, if you became interested, it would be fine for my friend. But it was really yourself I was thinking of, as a passenger. Would you care for a trip of the kind?'

'I might.'

'Then we could keep that in view. Of course, there is the other side of it that you suggested. If you chose to put some money into it you might find the scheme an interest: to have some control, for instance, and perhaps a complete deck reserved for yourself and friends. It would certainly be novel.'

'And what would you get if I came in?'

Morrison was careful to avoid showing indignation. 'Nothing, sir, if you came in. But—between ourselves, if you please—I'm hoping for a job in the new company.'

Stott did not answer, continuing to stare questioningly at the other, and Morrison presently continued: 'Please don't think, sir, that I'm asking you to invest in it. It simply occurred to me that, as you were out for a novel cruise, you might be interested to hear the details.'

'Well, I suppose I'm for it to that extent. Go ahead.'

Morrison realised that he had reached his principal hurdle. 'I'm afraid, sir, I've told you all I know myself. If you're interested you'd have to see someone in the affair. I dare say I could bring down my friend, if you cared to meet him.'

Stott looked harder at the young man. 'Looks damned tricky,' he said threateningly.

Morrison smiled. 'I'm not such a fool as to think we could get you to do anything against your will, Mr Stott.'

Stott grunted. 'Huh! You know that much, do you?' He paused, then went on: 'Who is he, this friend?'

'His name is Bristow and he's a partner in a firm of solicitors, Bristow, Emerson and Bristow of Fenchurch Street.'

'Oh. Acting for someone?'

'He spoke as if he had the business in his own hands, but there, I'm afraid, you'd have to ask him yourself.'

'Not communicative, are you? Well, when is this blessed solicitor to be seen?'

It was victory. Before Morrison left he had fixed up a meeting for the following Sunday.

Morrison chuckled with pleasure as he drove back to Town. If through his efforts Bristow was enabled to carry out his plan, the £500 and probably the job would materialise. In fact, if the thing went big, Morrison felt his future was assured.

But his satisfaction was lukewarm compared to Bristow's when that evening he was told the news. He was overwhelmed.

'My word!' he cried. 'What a chance! We'll never get a better! We must pull this off, Morrison, at all costs!'

On Sunday afternoon they drove down in Bristow's small Standard. In the back seat were two young men, friends of Bristow's.

'Salmon and Nickleby—Morrison,' said Bristow introducing them. 'We shall want a witness to the agreement if we get a bite, and these two can't be separated.'

All the way down the prospective witness and his friend kept up an interminable discussion about racing. Morrison, who scarcely knew which end of a horse went first, was bored beyond words, particularly as the chatter prevented him from discussing the coming interview. Fortunately for his peace of mind, Bristow left them in the car when they reached 'St Austell'.

The allies found Stott sitting under his tree with his book and whisky and cigars. Again he did not move at their approach, but contented himself with offering them drinks and smokes.

'Delightful place you have here, Mr Stott,' Bristow began conversationally, when they had settled down.

'Not too bad,' the owner admitted. 'But I don't expect you came down to tell me that. What's all this home cruising stuff Morrison was talking about?'

'Oh, that?' said Bristow as if a new idea had been suggested to him. 'It's a scheme for opening up big-ship cruising to the man in the street. We propose to hire or buy an Atlantic liner and put her on round the British Isles. We think we could fill her during the summer with people paying moderate fares.'

'That the sort of cruise you thought would suit me?' Stott said grimly, glaring at Morrison.

'Not as one of the herd, sir,' Morrison smiled. 'I suggested you should have a deck to yourself.'

'And what would a trifle like that cost?'

'That, sir, would be a matter of arrangement,' Bristow answered. 'We couldn't do it if you were an ordinary passenger. Morrison, I think, had in his mind that you might care to take some shares and some control of the undertaking.'

'I thought we'd veer in that direction,' said Stott unpleasantly, 'but I confess I didn't think we'd do it so quickly.'

'You must admit, sir, we haven't asked you for anything. We don't anticipate any difficulty in getting our capital subscribed.'

'The British public? Going on the "mostly fools" tack?'

'No, sir. We've had the figures of the scheme worked out by experts, and they tell us it would be very profitable.'

'Not a hope,' declared Stott. 'The price of these ships is prohibitive. Think it wouldn't have been done if it was any good?'

'I can only say,' Bristow returned, 'that the experts seem pretty sure of their figures.'

Stott made sceptical noises. 'Got out your prospectus?'

36

'It's drafted, but not yet printed.'

Stott drew delicately at his cigar. 'I'd like to see the figures,' he said at last.

It was now Bristow's turn to hesitate. 'I hope, sir, he went on more deprecatingly, 'that you won't think me discourteous if I say that the vital figures are confidential. When I tell you that we've got ideas for running the affair cheaply and that these are our capital, you'll appreciate the point. I should be delighted to put everything before you if we first had your guarantee of secrecy.'

'Damn it all, what do you take me for?'

'I'm sorry, sir, but I know you won't misunderstand me. Now I took the liberty of bringing down a draft agreement for your consideration. This pledges you to secrecy, whether you have anything to do with us or not, and if you sign I'll put all the figures before you.'

'Damn your impertinence!'

'It really isn't that, sir. This agreement does more than record your promise of secrecy. It also lays down terms on which, if you chose, we might collaborate.'

Stott chuckled grimly. 'You're more than impertinent: you're refreshing. If cheek pulls people through, you ought to succeed.'

Bristow grinned. 'I hope so, sir. The terms suggested here are tentative, and if you were interested we should be prepared to modify them to meet your wishes. The agreement covers two cases. First, if you're not interested. It goes without saying that in this case you're committed to nothing except secrecy. Second, if you should care to put up all or part of the capital, thus yourself owning or having part control of the business. In this case I suggest that you pay me fifty per cent of your nett income.'

For some time Stott did not answer. Then silently he stretched out his hand for the agreement and began slowly to read it.

Morrison, though for him comparatively little was at stake, felt almost painfully eager, and he could see that, in spite of his efforts to hide it, Bristow was equally affected. The episode recalled vividly one of the thrills of his youth, when through clear water he had watched fish swim up to and begin investigating his bait. Would Stott nibble? And if he did, would Bristow hook him? Bristow had done well so far, but Stott was obviously the more wily.

Presently Stott looked up. 'This gives you the right to proceed against me for damages if you can prove that I gave any of your ideas away.'

'You can't object to that, sir,' Bristow submitted. 'It's a purely formal requirement, because there's no fear of your giving us away.'

Stott grinned ruefully. 'You're a solicitor, aren't you? I congratulate you. It's a good bait. You've succeeded by not trying for too much. I'll sign.'

Bristow manfully repressed any sign of jubilation as he rose to his feet. 'I don't think you'll be sorry, sir, and I'm certain we shall not. Just a moment, if you please.'

Stott looked almost alarmed. 'What's it now?' he demanded.

'Agreement valueless without a witness. I've got one waiting.'

Stott looked after him with rueful admiration as Bristow disappeared towards the gate. 'Your friend deserves to succeed,' he said in a somewhat subdued tone. 'I'll be interested to learn his scheme.'

The ceremony of signing in duplicate was put through

quickly and Salmon and Nickleby were despatched to call on friends at Eton. Then Bristow got down to business. He first stressed the desire of the man in the street for the big-ship cruises he could not at present afford. Next he pointed out that this was not because of owners' profiteering, but because of the high running costs of great ships. Then he put forward his scheme, claiming that interest and depreciation on his ship should come to less than 15 per cent of that of a new vessel, while running expenses should be little more than 60 per cent. Finally, he gave estimates of passenger fares and probable profits.

It was obvious that Stott was impressed. As Bristow proceeded, the mocking condescension gradually faded from his manner and a growing interest took its place. He heard the statement without interruption, then sat in silence, evidently thinking deeply.

'I admit that sounds plausible enough at first hearing,' he said at length, 'and yet I cannot help feeling there's a flaw somewhere. What practical men have gone into it?'

Bristow moved uneasily. 'I think, sir, 'he answered 'that I must tell you the, exact truth. I'm afraid you'll be displeased, but here it is. No one knows anything of this except our three selves. I admit that my talk about others was only to try and get you interested. No practical authority has gone into it, and the experts I spoke of were Morrison and myself.'

Stott looked at him for some moments, then broke into a laugh. 'I hand it to you, Bristow,' he declared.

'I will say you've played your cards well. I was doubtful of you before, but now I believe you. Is that all you have to tell me?'

Bristow looked relieved. 'That's all, sir, except about

Morrison. Morrison—and I'm sure he'd be the first to admit it—hadn't until now put anything material into this thing. I didn't think therefore that he was entitled to a share, but, now, since he's aroused your interest, I've changed my mind. I suggest each of us give him five per cent of the nett profits, off our shares: that will be ten per cent for him. I also propose, if the scheme goes ahead, to offer him the job of agent on board to deal with the transport of passengers between their homes and the ship, at a salary of five hundred, all found. Would you be agreeable to that if you came in?'

'If I came in, yes,' Stott returned, 'but you mustn't count on that.'

'No, sir. But if you did, the clause would then read: "The nett profits of the said undertaking shall be divided between the said three partners to this agreement in the estimated proportions that their ideas, money and help shall have contributed to its success, this being at present estimated as follows: to the said John Mottram Stott forty-five per cent, to the said Charles Bristow forty-five per cent and to the said Harry Morrison ten per cent." That all right, sir?'

'Yes—if I go in. I admit I'm interested, but I'd have to think the thing over and get real expert opinion on the various points before I could decide.'

'It's extraordinarily decent of you both,' Morrison exclaimed warmly. 'I don't expect to be worth all that money, but I'll do my best.'

He was overwhelmed with delight. This was more than in his wildest flights he had expected. Optimistic in his pleasure, he told himself that the scheme would be a success and began to estimate to what 10 per cent of the profits, added to his £500 a year, might amount.

He was also astonished and pleased at the change in

Stott's manner. If the man were really like this, working with him would be a pleasure and not a nightmare, as it had been up to the present.

But he was losing some of the conversation.

'I think we'd have no difficulty about the certificate,' Bristow was saying, 'for our purpose: cruising at half speed in sheltered waters in summer. But if the Board of Trade refused, we might try abroad. I somehow imagine they'd be more accommodating than here.'

Stott shook his head. 'I doubt it,' he said. 'And, of course, if there's a hitch there, the whole scheme fails.'

'I know, sir, but my difficulty has been that enquiries would give away the idea. Therefore before making them I wanted to have an option on the ship.'

'What ship had you in mind?'

'The *Hellenic*, forty-seven thousand tons. She's lying at Southampton waiting to be sold for breaking up.'

'Yes, that's correct. I've crossed to New York in her several times and I will say she's a comfortable ship. She'd be the very ship for this job, if we could get her.'

This phrase fell happily on Morrison's ears. For another hour they discussed the affair, then Stott brought the interview to an end. That was as far, he said, as they could go at present. He would think over what he had heard, consult various experts, and let them know his decision.

On their way back to Town both young men felt as if they were travelling on air.

4

Preliminary Skirmish

'He's as good as hooked,' Bristow declared when, after dinner that evening, he and Morrison resumed their discussion in the former's rooms.

Morrison agreed. 'What he wants, as I said before, is an interest. I believe he'd put up the whole of the money if he thought he'd have a say in the running of the thing: just for the interest of it.'

'Well, he understands that. I made it clear enough.'

'You know, Morrison pursued his own train of thought, 'we've touched him at the right moment. He's bored and wants something to do. Two or three hundred thousand is nothing to him. He'll put it up all right.'

The subject of Stott and his reactions to the proposal eventually became exhausted, Bristow turned to another point. 'We've been taking the cost of the ship at a hundred thousand, but we mayn't be right. I mentioned it because the *Berengaria* is supposed to have been sold for that. I wonder if we should make some tentative enquiries about the *Hellenic*?'

'I thought you'd done so.'

'No. I assumed the two ships would cost about the same.'

Morrison thought this was scarcely satisfactory. 'We should surely be able to say to Stott: she's to be had for so much? How should we find out?'

'Go to the Lilac Star people, I suppose. Their offices are in Cockspur Street.'

'What about after lunch tomorrow? I could get leave for an hour.'

Bristow agreed enthusiastically. Though neither realised it, what they both wanted was action, and for this they would have jumped at any excuse.

Their interview, however, did not work out exactly as they had planned. Bristow's professional card gave them immediate access to the secretary, a polite man named Amberley.

'We shall not keep you long, Mr Amberley,' Bristow assured him. 'We called to make some enquiries about the sale of the *Hellenic*. I'm acting for some parties who might wish to buy her, and I should like any details which are available as to cost and conditions of sale.'

'Well,' the secretary smiled, 'perhaps the point which will interest you most is that she's practically sold.'

Bristow's jaw dropped. 'Sold!' he ejaculated in evident dismay.

'Not exactly sold,' Amberley qualified. 'As a matter of fact, a company has got an option on her. They're not quite certain yet whether they will buy.'

'Oh,' said Bristow, with some relief, 'then the matter's not finally closed. I'm glad to hear that, for I shall probably be able to make an offer on behalf of my clients. I suppose,' he smiled deprecatingly, 'it would be indiscreet to enquire if it's for breaking-up that she's wanted?'

Amberley hesitated. 'I don't think so,' he said presently.

43

'As a matter of fact, it's for popular cruising: a new venture altogether.'

Bristow's eyes goggled. For a moment he did not speak, then his brows drew together and Morrison could see that he was thinking deeply. Presently he slapped his thigh and broke into a laugh.

'Don't tell me,' he said with every appearance of amusement, 'that it's Home Waters Cruising Limited?'

Amberley looked surprised. 'Why, that's just what it is. Do you know them?'

Bristow laughed again. 'Do I know them?' he repeated. 'Well I should think so! Why, it's for Home Waters Cruising Limited that I'm acting! I'm their secretary.' He turned to Morrison. 'That's Malthus, or I'm a Dutchman. You can't get ahead of Mr Malthus. Our Chairman, Mr Amberley. He's stolen a march on me. A misunderstanding, of course. It was Mr Malthus, I suppose?'

The secretary seemed a little perplexed at this method of doing business, but evidently considered it was nothing to him and smiled politely. 'Yes, it was Mr Malthus. He called to see me himself. He said he hadn't all the money he wanted yet, but he expected to get the balance in a day or two.'

'That's correct,' Bristow declared. 'We have promises for practically the whole sum.' He grinned realistically at Morrison. 'Now, isn't that like him! To call here without telling me—*me*, the secretary—and fix up an option and then go off and get influenza without saying a word about it! I suppose you know something about chairmen, too, Mr Amberley?' Bristow did not wink, but he looked facetious.

The secretary shook his head lugubriously, suggesting melancholy experiences of an unpleasant side of life.

'And I don't even know the figure you finally agreed on,'

went on Bristow. 'Perhaps you could tell me that? It would help me at our meeting tomorrow.'

'A hundred and twenty-five thousand,' Amberley returned promptly. 'The option lasts for a month, but I was expecting a firm reply this week.'

'You'll have it,' Bristow assured him, 'and unless I'm greatly mistaken you'll have the money also. And I'—once again he smiled knowingly—'shall have something polite but pointed to say to my esteemed Chairman.'

'As a brother secretary, I wish you luck with it,' Amberley said gloomily. 'Then we shall see you again, Mr Bristow, if the deal goes through?'

'You certainly will, Mr Amberley.'

Morrison was seething with wrath and indignation against their fellow traveller in the Calais express. But when they reached the street he found that his feelings were lukewarm compared to Bristow's. The solicitor's manner remained quiet, but there was a look of cold implacable hate in his eye that startled Morrison. With his pale face gone almost white, his lips in a thin line, the strong outline of his set jaw and that almost ferocious gleam in his eye, he looked capable of anything. Certainly at that moment Morrison would not have cared to cross him.

'You were right, Morrison,' he said quietly, as they began to cross Trafalgar Square. 'That swine must have heard the whole thing. It's lucky you noticed his name.'

Morrison was astonished at his coolness. 'I thought you dealt with it magnificently,' he said with truth, 'and without any preparation, too.'

'It mayn't be any use,' Bristow answered in a small, cold voice, 'If Stott won't act at once we're sunk.'

'What could he do? Malthus has an option, you see.'

Bristow glanced round and his voice rose as if in spite of himself. 'I don't know what he could do, but if there's any way of putting that dirty thief where he belongs, I'll not rest till I find it.'

'What had you in mind in the office? You must have had some scheme to talk like that?'

'Only to gain time, I'm afraid. But I'll see Stott at once. You're stuck in your beastly office, I suppose?'

Morrison shook his head regretfully. 'I'm afraid so.'

Then I'll ring him up and go down as soon as I can get my car.' With a curt nod, Bristow disappeared into a telephone booth.

In spite of his interest, it was not till later that Morrison heard what took place.

Having fixed up his interview, Bristow drove to 'St Austell'. The day was showery and Stott received him in his library instead of under the great elm. He did not trouble with greetings, but got at once to business. 'What's all this?' he asked shortly. 'A trick to hurry up the purchase?'

'I wish it was,' Bristow returned. 'No, I'm sorry to say it's the genuine article. We're going to be done, or I am, if you're not coming in,' and he told his story.

Upon Stott the tale had an electric effect. Whether or not he had already intended to buy, Bristow did not know, but if not, the hint of opposition brought him to a decision. 'I'm damned if I'm going to sit down and be cheated by a blasted racing crook,' he exclaimed roughly. 'You say we have a couple of days?'

'I don't know that, but I think it's likely from what Amberley said.'

'Time enough to put a spoke in this Malthus' wheel, I fancy. Take a cigar and let me think.'

46

For thirty-seven minutes by the electric clock on the mantelpiece they sat in silence, broken only on two occasions when Stott barked out short staccato questions. Then he leant forward, tapped Bristow on the arm and said: 'See, with a bit of luck we'll get him. You go back and have some paper printed with the proper heading—like this.' He took a sheet and wrote rapidly. '"Home Waters Cruising Limited", here across the top. Then in small letters here on the left side, "Directors", Malthus' name first with "Chairman" after it, then six other names, invented names except for my own. Put my own second. Put them in a column, you know. Add someone imaginary as treasurer and yourself as secretary. On the other side put "Temporary Offices", and give Malthus' address and telephone number. That all necessary to make it look right?'

Bristow controlled his satisfaction at this turn of events. 'I think so,' he replied. 'If I spot anything missing, I'll add it.'

'Make a decent job of it. Quiet but business-like, you know. When can you have it ready?'

'A day or two, I should think.'

'I shall want it at ten o'clock on Wednesday morning in your office.'

Bristow nodded. 'I'll see to it.'

'You'll need to or we'll be disappointed. Have you a printer that does your firm's work?'

'Yes, of course.'

'Very well, get on to him at once. See the boss himself; don't be put off with any Tom, Dick or Harry in the office. Put up any blessed yarn you fancy. Tell him money's no object and to work his darned box of tricks all night if necessary. Get it done without fail.'

In spite of his satisfaction at having so completely hooked

Stott, Bristow found it hard to control his temper. Since he left school, he had not been treated as anyone's message boy, and he didn't like it. However, this was not the moment to stand on his dignity.

He nodded coolly and stood up.

'Ten o'clock in my office the morning after next?' he said. 'Right. I'll expect you.'

'I'll be there,' Stott promised, 'and with any luck friend Malthus will get what he's asked for.'

No difficulties about time were raised by the printers, and when Bristow reached his office on the Wednesday a packet of 1,000 sheets of tastefully printed letter paper was waiting for him. He had only wanted one, but thought that a smaller order might be suspicious. He was pleased with his effort, which looked entirely convincing.

At ten exactly Stott was shown in.

'Got the paper?' he asked, without further introduction. 'H'm, that looks all right. Now, see,' he went on, before Bristow could speak, 'can you type?'

'Slowly. But I can get a girl in.'

'Don't bother about any girl. Type this yourself,' and he handed over the draft of a letter. It read:

'October 3rd, 1937.

'Messrs The Lilac Star
Steamship Co., Ltd.
Cockspur Street, S.W.1.
          'Purchase of s.s. "Hellenic"
'DEAR SIRS,—With reference to the negotiations which have passed between us, culminating in the granting to us of an option on the purchase of the s.s. *Hellenic*, I am instructed to inform you that at a board meeting

48

held today, it was decided to complete the purchase immediately. We are enclosing our cheque for £125,000 (one hundred and twenty-five thousand pounds sterling) herewith, and would be obliged if you would kindly make arrangements to hand over the ship as early as convenient, as there is little time to carry out the alterations we require, before putting her into commission.

'Yours faithfully,

'*Secretary*'

Stott was in a much better humour than a couple of days earlier. 'Sign that, Mr Secretary,' he chuckled as he watched Bristow's face. Then he took a paper from his pocket. 'I've a good cheque to go with it,' he observed, handing it over.

Bristow metaphorically sat up and rubbed his eyes. It was a Lloyds cheque and it was filled in to read: 'Pay Messrs Lilac Star Steamship Company Limited One hundred and twenty-five thousand pounds sterling (£125,000),' and was signed, 'Home Waters Cruising Limited. J. Mottram Stott, director'.

'Countersign that as Secretary,' Stott added, 'and it'll look darned good.'

'How in Hades have you done it, Mr Stott?' Bristow demanded as he wrote his name.

Again Stott chuckled. 'Quite simple, he returned contentedly. 'I called at my bank yesterday and opened an account under the heading "Home Waters Cruising Limited" and paid a hundred and twenty-five thousand into it. It'll be paid out and the account closed today. I've fixed it with the manager.'

'It's as smart as anything I've ever seen,' Bristow declared as he put a sheet of the new paper in his typewriter. 'They'll suspect nothing.'

'Not if we're first in the field,' Stott returned a little grimly. 'However, that's a risk we can't avoid.'

'Could we not have gone yesterday?'

'No. Haste like that would have looked suspicious. Besides, we had to leave time for the supposed board.'

Having rehearsed what was to be said at the interview, they walked to the Cockspur Street offices and asked for Amberley. A glance at his face told them that they were in time.

'I'm back here sooner than I expected, Mr Amberley,' began Bristow. 'May I introduce Mr Stott, one of our directors?'

Amberley had been looking curiously at Stott, and when Bristow mentioned his name he made a little gesture of recognition.

'How do you do, Mr Stott?' he said, smiling. 'We've met before, though you've forgotten it. We crossed the Atlantic together in one of our ships, five—no, let me see—six years ago. It was the *Hellenic*, too, I remember.'

Stott, who Bristow now saw could be extremely pleasant when he chose, looked closely at Amberley, then smiled in his turn. 'Why, of course, Mr Amberley, I remember you well. But I don't think I tumbled to it that you were connected with the company.'

Amberley shook his head. 'I kept that dark,' he declared. 'Some excuse, too. I avoided complaints and suggestions and all sorts of embarrassments.'

'An emperor travelling incog. I hadn't thought of that. I'm glad we're going to prolong the *Hellenic*'s days. She's a fine ship.'

'She's always been a favourite: steady, you know; easy in a sea and no vibration.'

'Why are you selling her, if I may ask?' put in Bristow. 'Now that the price is fixed, I don't suppose it's a secret.'

'No secret at all, Mr Bristow. She's too slow and she burns too much oil. She does twenty-three knots, but that's no good when you're competing with over thirty.'

'But her hull's all right?'

'Oh, Lord, yes! If it wasn't, we daren't have run her across the Atlantic.'

Stott didn't seem pleased at the interruption, and Bristow quickly saw that he was a man who could never play second fiddle. He therefore remained silent and Stott went on:

'I've called with our Secretary, Mr Amberley, in the place of our Chairman, Mr Malthus, who's laid up with 'flu. We've come to tell you that the board has decided to take up our option on the *Hellenic*, and to hand over the purchase money. We had intended to defer the decision till our Chairman was again with us, but we want to carry out certain alterations before the cruising season begins, and there is so little time that every day makes a difference. So we got his approval over the telephone and went ahead.'

Amberley nodded gravely. 'That's very satisfactory news to us, Mr Stott. There's not a great demand for these big ships, and we'll be glad to have the *Hellenic* off our hands. Your hurry to get her will also please our board. As you can understand, harbour dues at Southampton are pretty considerable. I needn't say we'll facilitate you in every way possible.'

'Excellent,' Stott returned genially: 'it's pleasant when a transaction pleases both parties. I think you have the formal letter, Bristow?'

Bristow opened his attaché case. 'Yes, perhaps I may hand it over, Mr Amberley, with the cheque?'

'About that cheque,' Stott went on, 'I wonder if it would be asking you too much to come with us to the bank and satisfy yourself'—he smiled to indicate that he was making a joke—'that we really are solvent? If so, we could perhaps complete the sale documents while we're here. As you can see from the cheque, Bristow and I are competent to sign for the board.'

This was a proposal to which Amberley was unlikely to object. They went to the bank, saw the manager, and put beyond question the transfer of the cash. Then they returned to the Lilac Star offices, and the documents completing the sale were duly signed, sealed and delivered.

'A bit of luck that,' Stott observed, when they once more regained the street. 'If Malthus and company had moved during these last two days, we'd have been sunk. And a tremendous bit of luck that Amberley knew me. If he hadn't, he might have held us up till he made enquiries.'

'That's true,' Bristow admitted slowly. He was not enthusiastic. In fact, he was feeling a good deal worried. 'But are you sure that we are all right?' he went on. 'I'm afraid I'm not quite happy about it myself.'

Stott looked at him curiously. 'What's the trouble?' he asked with a rather mocking expression.

'Well, just who does the *Hellenic* belong to? As I see it, she doesn't belong to you or me severally or jointly. She belongs to a company, Home Waters Cruising Limited, of which Malthus is Chairman.'

'She belongs to a company, Home Waters Cruising Limited, of which I'm a director and you're the Secretary.'

'And Malthus is the Chairman?' Bristow persisted.

Stott shook his head. 'Not at all,' he retorted. 'Malthus doesn't come into it.'

'I don't see how you make that out. Malthus' name—'

'See,' interrupted Stott, 'what names were on that deed of sale? The Company's, mine and yours. There was no mention of Malthus.'

'The Company's name was given, and on our paper Malthus is shown as Chairman.'

'Ah, quite. But that name on the letter paper was the only reference to Malthus that there was.'

Bristow was becoming irritable. 'I know that's so,' he returned with some warmth, 'but it *was* there.'

Stott winked. '"Was" is the right word,' he declared. 'Show me that deed of sale again.'

They went into Stott's club and Bristow opened his attaché case and handed over the folded document. Stott opened it out. As he did so a letter fluttered to the ground. Bristow grabbed it and gave an exclamation.

'Yes'—Stott grinned—'our Company's one letter to the Lilac Star people got accidentally folded in the deed while Amberley was looking elsewhere. So he has no reference of any kind to Malthus. And as for the Company's title, it was your title which Malthus stole.' He dropped the letter into the fire and watched it slowly discolour and disintegrate. 'And now the letter's gone,' he went on, 'and your job is to see that its nine hundred and ninety-nine brothers follow it.'

'I tell you, Morrison,' Bristow said afterwards when he was recounting the story, 'I had to hand it to him. I just can't remember a brainier bit of work. No wonder Stott can pay about a quarter of a million without turning a hair.'

'He's living up to his reputation.'

'Lucky for us! I tell you, our fortune's made now we have him with us.'

Morrison was not so delighted as Bristow expected. To Morrison the whole thing didn't seem straight, and though he was not rabid on the subject, he disliked questionable dealings. However, he reminded himself that they were not stealing anything from Malthus, but only preventing him from stealing their idea from them.

'There'll be hell to pay when Malthus finds it out,' he observed.

Bristow smiled happily. 'Won't there? I only hope I'll be there when it happens.'

Morrison's prophecy was soon fulfilled, though he saw nothing of the trouble personally, only hearing of it from Bristow when everything was over.

It happened that on the very next day Malthus had called on Amberley to say that he had got his money and was ready to complete his purchase. The fat was then properly in the fire. A storm of No. 12 on the Beaufort Scale took place in the office, at the end of which Malthus flung furiously out, while Amberley collapsed limp and helpless in his secretarial chair.

Malthus then approached Stott. By this time he had cooled down and had evidently taken legal advice. He was outwardly friendly, said that Stott had been prompt in his action, and proposed an amalgamation, his people putting up half the money. Stott apparently was equally polite, though clear as crystal that nothing was doing. Malthus then lost his temper and became abusive, threatening Stott with proceedings involving all sorts of penalties. Stott in effect said, 'Go ahead,' and the interview terminated with heat and promptitude.

Further negotiations then took place through the principals' respective solicitors. Stott's position was that if an action for obtaining money, to wit the ship, under false pretences was brought, he would prosecute Malthus for stealing his idea. The position eventually was tacitly accepted as stalemate by Malthus, though Stott claimed to have won the match. Malthus replied to this that Stott might have won the first round, but that his turn would quickly come. Malthus, indeed, was very outspoken. Bristow was able to find no less than five distinct witnesses who had heard him swear that if he couldn't get legal redress, he would take the law into his own hands. He would do Stott in, even if he choked him with his bare hands and swung for it.

So far as Morrison was concerned, things then began to move. Bristow appeared with a revised agreement which guaranteed him his 10 per cent of the net profits of the scheme, as well as his £500 a year all found. Further, Morrison was to resign as soon as possible from the Agency, his new salary starting on the date the old one ceased. His work would be general assistance with the transport side of the venture and he would carry on in a suite of offices which Stott had rented.

With intense eagerness, Morrison looked forward to this new phase of his life.

5

Stott Springs a Surprise

Morrison found the days during which he worked his notice as irksome as any he had ever experienced. Faced with a revolution in his life, the common round and the daily task assumed monstrous proportions of distaste. His mind, full of coming excitements and delights, refused to concentrate on mere mundane matters, such as the services between Harwich and Flushing or the amount of free luggage allowed on French railways. He longed to fling out of the office, shouting to the world that his term of servitude was over.

The news that the *Hellenic* had been sold, not for breaking up but for summer cruising, revived public interest in the great ship. The papers were full of stories of her career: how at one time in her second year of life she had held the Blue Riband of the Atlantic; how she had stood by a foundering Greek tanker in a blizzard, and by the exercise of superhuman skill and courage, together with a liberal use of oil, had rescued her entire crew; how she had carried through the gales of the dreaded Western Ocean kings and potentates, film stars and millionaires, not to mention hundreds of thousands of smaller fry, all without the loss of a single life. She had been a popular ship, holding an established place in the public regard, as had the old *Mauretania* before her. Sentimentalists rejoiced that her approaching dissolution was postponed and amateur strategists wrote letters to the papers advising that she be kept available for the transport of troops in time of war.

For the first three days after leaving the Agency, Morrison found little to do, but on the fourth there came a summons to a conference in the new offices. He was early at the rendezvous. It was soon evident that the meeting was to be of importance. Stott was there, barking out questions and directions. Bristow, arranging papers, was obviously trying to hide both his annoyance and his excitement, and not entirely succeeding in either. Four other men were present, two middle-aged and two elderly. One of the elder was a short, stout fellow with a broad smile and a hearty manner. His eyes were small like a pig's and twinkled with such shrewdness that Morrison felt he was a man to be watched. This was Meaker, Stott's solicitor. The other older man was tall and well built, with good features, a firm mouth, and the air of one who expects to be first in whatever society he may find himself. Royal Navy Reserve, Morrison speculated, and soon he found he was correct. The man was Captain Gladstone, and he was going to take command of the *Hellenic*. Both younger men were pleasant-looking and seemed decent and quietly efficient. One was Gillow, Stott's advertising manager, the other Whitaker, a private secretary, brought apparently to act as secretary to the meeting.

Morrison was briefly introduced as the man who was going to manage transport to and from the ship, and all having taken their places round the table, the proceedings opened.

Stott, Morrison quickly saw, was a good chairman. He wasted no time with preliminaries, but came plump to business with his first phrase. His remarks were delivered in a quiet but forceful tone and with greater courtesy than Morrison had somehow expected.

'We have met,' he began, 'at the offset of an undertaking which we hope may be profitable to all of us, and our first business is to make sure that all of us are in sympathy with the policy to be adopted. This is obviously necessary for everyone who signs any hard and fast agreement to become associated with it. I need scarcely add the converse. Anyone who is not satisfied with our proposals should avoid service with us.' As Stott ended he looked gravely and questioningly at Captain Gladstone, Bristow and Morrison, as if he doubted their right to be there.

The words and gesture caused Morrison some surprise as well as a slight feeling of misgiving. There surely could be no question either as to policy or the desire of all present to carry it out? Wasn't that the very purpose for which they were assembled? He glanced at Bristow and saw the same doubt reflected in his expression.

'As you know,' went on Stott, 'the idea of buying a big ship which would otherwise be broken up, and using her for cruising round the British Isles, is due entirely to Bristow, and with Morrison's help he put his case very admirably before me. I thought there was something in it, though not as much as he suggested. I therefore agreed to think over the proposal and give a decision later. That decision, if favourable, would involve an agreement to bear the entire cost of the enterprise, and therefore to own it, as I should not be interested in anything less than control. I signed an agreement with Bristow as to his share in the profits, should the affair materialise, and the remuneration of the other four has been mutually agreed on—that is, provided they still wish to act.

'As I expected, the reports of the experts to whom I submitted the scheme were favourable, but not nearly so favourable as were Bristow's figures. I considered the matter carefully; and had almost decided not to touch it, when a further idea occurred to me, and one which I thought would ensure its success. Here I intended to make new enquiries and get out fresh figures, but an unfortunate incident of which you are all aware forced my hand, and I had to buy before my investigations were complete. However, they have now been finished, and I may say that the result is wholly satisfactory. I am now convinced that, as modified, the venture is likely to prove highly profitable. I may also point out that the *Hellenic* is now my property and that I have a right to use her as I think fit. Further, I think we all know that no other ship of similar type is likely to be on the market for some years.'

Stott spoke rather grimly and both words and tone added to Morrison's surprise and apprehension. However, before he could analyse his impressions, Stott resumed:

'This new idea will involve certain departures from the original plans. Bristow intended the cruise for the man in the street: the man who could pay a moderate fare for perhaps a week, or two. I have changed that. The appeal will now be to the wealthy and they will pay through the nose for their cabins. The *Hellenic* was built to carry four thousand passengers, but I am restricting her to eighteen hundred, all first class, so that there may be ample room for everyone to be comfortable. Every cabin will now have a bathroom, and at least half will have private sitting-rooms also. That is my first alteration. I may say also that I do not expect her ever to be quite full up.

'The second alteration is that instead of running for the six summer months, she will cruise during the entire year. This will practically double our profits. In winter she will give up calls to outlying islands or exposed portions of the coast and confine herself to the Irish Sea, the Channel and other sheltered areas. She may, moreover, anchor in these areas for long spells, still further lowering her running costs.'

Morrison was now listening with stupefaction. Had it not been for Stott's quiet, business-like manner, he would have supposed the man had gone off his head. His statement sounded completely mad. Would anyone who could afford to go round the world be bothered to steam round the British coast, even if he had a private bath and sitting-room? The small people who might have done it would now be debarred by the cost. And would anyone who could stay at home cruise in the Irish Sea in winter? Maddest of all, would anyone who could get ashore remain on a ship *anchored* off the coast, in cold weather certainly, and perhaps in wind or rain or fog as well? It was inexplicable.

A glance at his companions showed that their thoughts were travelling in the same direction as his own, all except Whitaker's, who simply looked amused. But Bristow and Gillow were obviously as puzzled as he was, and Gladstone's lips had gone into a thin line which suggested that if he disapproved the explanation, he would make the fact clear beyond possibility of error. It was Gladstone who spoke first.

'I don't think, sir,' he said politely but with firmness, 'that you can stop there. I think you must tell us the reason of these changes.'

Stott nodded. 'I am about to do so. It's for that purpose that we are met. I propose, or rather I am arranging, that the *Hellenic* will be a floating casino: a gambling ship.'

All four of his hearers stared at him, but before any of them could speak, Stott continued.

'I have already entered into a provisional agreement with the Casino authorities at Monte Plage. The ship will be altered to provide the required gaming-rooms, and the Casino will supply the necessary manager and croupiers, as well as giving general help. The gambling will be carried out with scrupulous care—in fact, as impeccably as at Monte Plage itself. It's a sport that English people have long wanted to have at home, and now they're going to get it.'

For some moments there was silence and then the reactions of the little audience became vocal. In spite of his own participation, Morrison was interested in their variety.

Bristow's face was glowing. 'Magnificent!' he cried enthusiastically. 'A stroke of genius! That's the finishing touch that was needed to turn the thing into an absolute gold mine! Congratulations, Mr Stott!'

Stott seemed pleased. 'Then you're with me, Bristow?' he enquired, rather unnecessarily, Morrison thought.

'With you? Can you ask it?' His face changed suddenly. 'But what about the law, sir? I'm afraid they'd stop us.'

'Meaker has got round that for us,' Stott answered. 'We'll come to it in turn.'

'Then I'm with you up to the hilt.'

'Good,' Stott returned. 'And you, Gillow?'

'To the hilt also, sir,' the advertising manager protested, though with less enthusiasm.

'Good,' Stott repeated. 'And what about you, Captain? Or,' he went on after a glance at Gladstone's face, 'perhaps you don't care to express an opinion? It won't affect your side of the affair, you know.'

The Captain was frowning and his mouth had become an even narrower line. 'It won't affect the navigation, I agree, Mr Stott,' he answered in a low but rather sharp voice, 'but I'll take the liberty of answering your question all the same. To be candid, I don't like your idea and I'll have nothing to do with it. Further, I think you owe me an apology for assuming that I would captain your gambling hell, and I'll wait to hear it before wishing you "Good morning".'

Morrison held his breath, expecting an outburst. But Stott merely smiled sardonically. 'You have it, Captain,' he answered in a slightly mocking tone, with a wide gesture as if to make the apology inclusive. 'You have it now. If you don't like my idea, I can assure you the loss is mine.

Gladstone got up. 'Then the matter is satisfactorily closed between us. Good morning, Mr Stott. I'm—I'm'—he hesitated, then his good manners triumphed—'sorry that our association has ended in this way.' He bowed to the company and disappeared.

Stott smiled at the closed door. 'A good man, but crotchety. We're well rid of him. Ring up the second on the list, Whitaker. Captain Hardwick, isn't it?'

'Yes, sir.' The Secretary made a note.

Stott turned to Morrison. 'Now, Morrison, we've had two opinions in this matter. What's yours? Do you wish to stay or leave us?'

For a moment Morrison hesitated. He made no pretence

to stricter morals than other people, yet he didn't like the idea that he would be helping to carry on a gambling hell. What would he feel like, he thought, if he learnt that his livelihood had brought someone else to suicide?

Then he told himself that such ideas were morbid. If there were suicides, it would not be his fault. Besides, not only had he no other job, but nowhere else could he get another like this. He mustn't be a sentimental fool.

The others had noticed his doubt, and now he hastened to assure Stott of his loyalty. He thought Stott's expression slightly mocking as he nodded, while Bristow's glare, which had been fixed on him in surprise and indignation, relaxed. Morrison saw he had had a narrow escape. A little more delay and he might have antagonised both, men and perhaps permanently damaged his prospects.

'A nuisance about Gladstone,' Stott observed, passing from the subject. 'We'll be held up now till we can get Hardwick, unless,' he added with scorn, 'his old maid's conscience or his damned stuck-up pride prevents his—er—*acceptance*'—he stressed the word—'of the job. But you, Morrison, can begin work. You'll have to check your results with the new captain, but, still, you can do a good deal yourself.'

'I'd be glad to get busy, sir.'

'Very well. I'll take you first, and then you can get away. Your job will be to arrange transport between the passengers' homes and the ship. I'll tell you briefly what I have in mind, though it won't work as I'm stating it. You'll have to devise modifications to make it work. You follow?'

'I follow, sir.'

'Good. Then I want the ship during the summer—it'll be the summer before we can put her on—to cruise to all the best bits of coast from the scenic or general interest points of view: and you'll have to find out what those are. If possible, I'd like to include the Orkneys and Shetlands, the Hebrides and the west coast of Ireland. *But* I want also a frequent connection to and from London, a daily connection, if possible. It would be ideal, for instance, if there was a good train leaving London about ten in the morning which would reach the ship that day, and a train back from the ship arriving in Town about six in the evening.'

'You think day travel best, do you, sir? What about travelling by sleeper and saving two days?'

'I'm open to consider any properly worked out suggestions. This, again, would be ideal: and again perhaps impracticable. Suppose the ship is going south. Your tender leaves her some time in the morning and catches, for argument's sake, a good train at Holyhead. It then hurries to Fishguard and meets the contingent which has left London in the morning. It puts them on board. It follows the ship and the next morning puts a party ashore to get the London train at Penzance, steams on to Plymouth and takes aboard those who have come from London that day. You see the idea?'

'I see it, sir. I think it's splendid. But it would scarcely work for the Orkneys or the Hebrides.'

'I agree. But that's where you come in. Your first job will be to make a scheme for the whole coast. You will first make a list of convenient ports with good rail connections, then you'd better go and see them all, so as to be sure that they're suitable from the transhipment point of view. You follow me?'

'Yes, sir. Clearly.'

'You will get your expenses from Whitaker. Note that, Whitaker. Then make a provisional time-table for all ports at which the *Hellenic* might happen to call.'

'Am I limited to one tender?'

'No, you're not limited to anything, though naturally I want to keep expenses down. But I want to run practically in all weathers. Therefore your tender must be a good size. There you'll have to consult the Captain. Don't forget it may be too big for some of the smaller ports. Remember also that the *Hellenic* will come to the most convenient places to meet the tender, and can fill up time by making circuits.'

'Yes, sir, I think I've got all that clear. I'll get on with it at once.'

'Then when that's done you may consider stores. They'll have to go out by the tender, and enough time will have to be allowed for transferring them to the ship.'

'What about coaling?'

'She uses oil fuel and you'll have to arrange times for fuelling. The oil tanker and the tender might lie alongside at the same time, one forward and one aft. Or, if the weather permitted, at opposite sides. Something of that kind: think it out. You'll have to discuss that also with the Captain. Any other questions?'

'I don't think so, sir.'

'Good. Then there's the point Bristow raised, which may affect your arrangements. In order to avoid a gaming prosecution under the British law, we shall have to adopt certain precautions. Tell them, Meaker, will you?'

'Eh? Yes.' The solicitor woke up to life. 'Formalities, you know.' He nodded, twinkling his little eyes. 'Can't risk being run in, eh? There are only three; all very simple. First, the ship must be foreign owned. Next, she must keep outside British territorial waters: means more than three miles from the coast. Third, if she should want to come into a British port, the gaming rooms must be sealed before she enters the three-mile limit, and kept sealed till she leaves it again. That clear, eh?'

Morrison nodded, but before he could speak Stott chimed in. 'Naturally I don't want the nuisance of sealing the rooms unnecessarily, so she must be kept as much as possible out of ports. That's why you must use a tender and have stores and oil transferred at sea. Any questions about that?'

'No, sir; it seems quite clear.'

Stott nodded. Then we needn't keep you, Morrison. Get ahead with your enquiries, and if you get up against any snags, let me know.'

Morrison would have liked to hear what was still to be discussed, but after so pointed a dismissal he dared not remain. He was disappointed at being left out of the inner counsels, but he felt he could later get any information he wanted from Bristow.

There now began one of the most delightful periods of his life. He was his own master, free from the routine of the office and able to plan without let or hindrance his comings and goings. His new job was at the same time his fascinating hobby. He enjoyed the planning and the travelling and the continual interviews with interesting people. In fact, he was as happy as the day was long.

The second applicant on Stott's list, Captain Hardwick, had jumped at the chance of taking over the *Hellenic*, and had been duly appointed Master. Unlike Gladstone, he had no scruples about commanding a gambling ship. 'I don't do it myself,' he said; 'can't afford it. And my officers won't do it, either. I'll see to that. But the passengers can bankrupt themselves to their hearts' content for all I care.'

Morrison met him to discuss his report, and liked what

he saw of him. In appearance, Hardwick was not unlike Gladstone: the same tall figure and strong face, and with the same air of personality and command.

But this man was younger and more approachable. He had been recently promoted captain of one of the smaller P. & O. ships, and as his prospects with his own company were good, Morrison wondered why he had applied for the *Hellenic*. However, he had done so, and Morrison was glad he had got her, believing he would prove a pleasant man to work with. His first job had been to take the *Hellenic* round to the Clyde, where her alterations were already in progress.

Bristow, Morrison found, was growing slightly aloof. He was putting in a vast amount of legal work, principally with Meaker. Usually he was too busy to see Morrison when the latter called, and when they did meet he would only discuss details of Morrison's job. Morrison was disappointed at this want of confidence. However, he reminded himself that the venture was Bristow's and Stott's, and that he was lucky to be in it even on these terms.

To his own immense satisfaction, he had solved the problem of transport to and from the ship when she was too far from London to be reached by rail. Stott had vetoed a longer journey than six hours—five in the train and one on a tender, which ruled out everywhere outside England. Morrison had suggested flying boats. Flying boats, he pointed out, could reach in three or four hours the furthest point to which the *Hellenic* would ever penetrate. The morning outward plane could make the return journey in the afternoon. Moreover, such a service would be popular. It would be considered up to date and incidentally would be the best advertisement that could be devised.

Captain Hardwick had next added his quota. He believed that he could design a floating pier which could be lowered from the *Hellenic*, and to which the flying boat could come alongside. This would enable passengers to walk direct from plane to ship, without using a launch.

Only on the question of cost was the flying boat idea doubtful. 'It couldn't be done with Bristow's original scheme,' Stott declared, 'but I think it could with mine. We'll get out figures and see.'

After a report from his experts, he approved the suggestion. Indeed, he went further, deciding that the boats should be used irrespective of the position of the ship. Every morning, Sundays included, one or more would start from the nearest possible point to London, visit the ship wherever she lay, leave in the afternoon and arrive back at the starting point before dinner time.

After these thrilling experiences there came to Morrison a period of monotony. He and all concerned settled down to work. Time began to slip by. Weeks drew out into months, while the launching of the scheme drew nearer. By January Morrison's plans and time-tables were complete, and arrangements had been made for the hire and staffing of the flying boats. The bogus French company had been formed and had 'bought' the *Hellenic*. Details of her French registration and certificate had been fixed up. The alterations to the ship were well in hand and she would shortly be ready for service. A large number of the officers and crew had been engaged, and more were being selected daily. Then towards the middle of March the first advertisement appeared.

This took the form of a short news paragraph saying that an enterprising French company were proposing to provide the British public with a double attraction: a chance of luxurious cruising to the beauty spots of their own islands, and an up-to-date and well-run casino, where those who wished might indulge in harmless gaming.

The paragraph appeared in all the principal papers and was followed by a flood of letters to the editor from persons all over the country. (Each received from two to five guineas for allowing his or her name and address to be attached to Gillow's effort.) Most of the letters were complimentary, congratulating the French firm on its determination to confer this double benefit on the British, and arguing that if we in this country had not groaned under the most grandmotherly legislation known to history, we would long since have had our own casinos. A few—enough to dispel the suspicion of inspiration—took a rabid view of the evils of gambling, and asked what the Churches were doing to allow such a blatant misuse of the sea.

In reply to these letters, several other people wrote from genuine conviction, with the nett result that by the time the correspondence ceased, interest in the venture was both general and keen. This was kept alive by judiciously worded advertisements until at last, a month before the time, Tuesday, May 24th, was named as the opening date.

It had been Stott's intention to issue invitations to a thousand of the great of the land to visit the ship for lunch and a short cruise on the day before the opening. But so many of those tentatively approached indicated a regretful inability to be present that he abandoned the idea. From his subsequent moodiness, Morrison saw that he was hard hit, and thought that for the first time the possibility of failure had seriously entered the the man's mind.

However, this doubt was speedily relieved by the avalanche

of bookings which now began to pour in. It was soon evident that not only would the ship be full up on her first night, but that many applications would have to be refused. Stott again became jubilant and everywhere optimism reigned.

As each booking was registered, it became Morrison's duty to arrange the journey from the passenger's home to the ship. On this first occasion, when a greater number would be embarked than on any subsequent occasion, it was decided that the ship herself should berth at Southampton. Morrison had arranged with the Southern Railway to run three Pullman specials from Waterloo in the forenoon, the ship being timed to sail just after tea.

But if this day, May 24th, was to be the red-letter day of the scheme as a whole, Morrison's came some fortnight earlier. He had been told on that day to close his temporary office in London and, with his staff of two, to move to his permanent establishment on the ship. To heighten the illusion of the French company, the *Hellenic* had been worked down from the Clyde and was now lying at Havre. Morrison, who had never been on a really big ship, was looking forward with intense eagerness to the experience.

Excitement prevented him from sleeping on the Southampton boat and he was on deck long before they drew in between the moles at Havre. There she was at anchor in the Avant-Port! She looked absolutely huge, dwarfing all the other shipping! And what grace she showed! What elegance! What lovely lines! His heart swelled, as if she were his own private possession. He noticed also that her name had been altered. She was now the *Hellénique*. A happy touch, that! Here was ocular demonstration of the reality of her new nationality. Whimsically, he wondered how it would square with the sea superstition. Did the mere alteration from the English to the

French form of the word constitute a technical change of name? He noted it as a point for use on board, should he ever run out of conversation.

As they passed across the harbour, he was joined by his clerk, Anderson, and secretary, Miss Pym, both apparently as excited as he was himself. At the wharf a launch, smart as a man-of-war's, was waiting, and soon the three travellers were bobbing across the harbour over the tiny waves raised by a fresh breeze. The sun was bright and the dancing foam of the little white caps shone dazzlingly, a brilliance that Morrison took as a good omen for the venture.

The size of the ship overwhelmed him. He knew that a 47,000-ton liner must be big, but he had had no conception of how enormous a vessel of this tonnage really was. From her landing ladder she seemed really to tower above him like the proverbial cliff. Surely it must be all of 100 feet up to that projection, a little forward of overhead, which he recognised as the starboard cab of the navigating bridge?

A minute more and he had climbed the ladder and passed in through her side port. At last a dream had been realised and he was on board.

6

Under Way

The side port opened into a fair-sized vestibule, attractively decorated as if to offer a welcome to arriving guests. An alert-looking steward was hovering in the background. Morrison hailed him.

'I'm Mr Morrison, your transport officer,' he explained, 'and these are my assistants, Miss Pym and Mr Anderson. Can you show us to our quarters?'

'Certainly, sir. Come this way.'

They went up three decks in a lift, and, after walking along some 100 yards of spacious alleyway, came to an alcove in which was a door labelled 'Transport Officer'. It led into a small but well-furnished office divided into two parts by a counter. It was a replica on a tiny scale of the Boscombe Agency's headquarters, and Morrison felt that when he had filled his racks with shore excursion leaflets and hung some beauty spot pictures on the walls, he would feel completely at home. Somehow he had not expected the telephone, but when he remembered that he was now about to live in the equivalent of a small town, it did not seem so out of place.

A door led from the office to his private cabin. With this latter he was enchanted. Though it was perhaps 50 feet from daylight—indeed he imagined it must be pretty near the centre of the ship—it was well lit and ventilated. It was much roomier than he had anticipated and was furnished as a bed-sitting-room, with a couple of armchairs, an electric fire, a folding wash-basin and plenty of shelves. Here also was a telephone, and he presently learned that every cabin had one.

He unpacked at once. Placing his clothes in the wardrobe and his books on the shelves gave him a feeling of propriatary satisfaction. It had been decided that he was to wear uniform, and he now put this on. It was the first time he had worn uniform, and he was young enough to find a real excitement in his unwonted appearance, as revealed in consecutive areas by an adroit use of his tiny mirror. He practised carrying his cap under his left arm, lest such a feat should later become necessary.

Someone had told him that it was etiquette to report his arrival to the Captain, and he presently left his cabin and adventured himself into the maze of alleyways and companions which filled the interior of this amazing vessel. He had no idea of his whereabouts, but he felt that his general direction should be upwards. When therefore he came to an ascending flight of steps, he took it. This plan succeeded so well that eventually he found himself in a lounge from which there was actually a view of the sea. A moment later, with a feeling of triumph, he stepped on deck.

Registering his position carefully for the return journey, he pursued his explorations. The stretch of deck was wide and long and from it he could see the waterfront of Havre laid out like a painted back curtain. Men were giving the railings a finishing coat of white, and he asked one to direct him to the Captain's cabin. Just as he reached it, Hardwick stepped out. He was a fine figure of a man at all times, but in his spotless, well-pressed uniform Morrison thought him really imposing.

'Morning, Morrison,' Hardwick said curtly and yet genially, with a quick glance at the new clothes. 'Got on board?'

'I was just coming to report to you, sir,' Morrison answered, trying not to look self-conscious. 'I'm afraid I'm ignorant of sea procedure, but I was told I should do so.' Captain Hardwick in uniform on the deck of his ship somehow seemed less approachable than had the tweed-clad man with whom he had discussed transport.

The Captain gave a short-lived smile as if to indicate that there was goodwill behind his attention to business. 'That's all right,' he answered, 'but if you keep Mr Grant informed of your whereabouts it will be enough. And a word in your ear, Morrison. Make friends with Grant. You'll find him a good fellow, and if you two pull together things will run more smoothly. Above all, things on the ship must run smoothly.'

Morrison wondered if this was helpful advice or a threat. He decided to assume the former.

'Thank you for the hint, sir,' he answered. 'I'll see to it.'

Grant, he knew, was the purser, and later he made his acquaintance. Having spent some hours in learning his way about the ship and arranging his office, he dropped into the lounge for tea. Grant was there and Morrison took the next chair.

'Luxury for me, tea like this in the afternoon,' he remarked when he had introduced himself. 'I didn't see it when I was working for the Boscombe people.'

'Yes, we're going to be well done,' returned the purser, a big Yorkshireman with a pleasant manner. 'I didn't know you were with Boscombe's. How did you come to join this show?'

Morrison told him.

'Then you're in it from the start? I hope it's given you a pull?'

Morrison smiled. 'It's got me my job and I think that's good enough. Of course, also, I've got in to a certain extent with Bristow and Stott, which'—he thought it better to avoid any appearance of bragging—'I'm hoping may be more helpful in the future than it has been up till now.'

'You're lucky,' Grant assured him. 'I got wind of it through one of the engineers.'

Morrison smiled. 'You were on an Orient liner, weren't you? Perhaps it's impertinent, but I should have thought your old job was better than this? It was certain to go on, while this may crash any time.'

Grant seemed pleased at his interest. 'I thought of that,' he replied, 'but I was fed up with the Australian service. Not that it isn't good and all that. But I wanted a change and I thought this might be an interesting ship to serve in.'

'It'll be all of that,' Morrison agreed, 'when the gambling gets going.'

'I expect you're right. Seen the rooms?'

'No, but I'd like to.'

'Come on, then.'

The gaming-rooms were at the bottom of the ship, immediately forward of the boilers. They occupied the former Nos. 3 and 4 holds, a huge space. Three large lifts had been installed which descended into a central hall, from which opened the eight rooms. Four of these were large and four smaller. In the centres of the larger were roulette tables, while the smaller accommodated other games. Round all of them were easy chairs and sofas, each room having its separate bar. The decoration was modern and effective, the atmosphere fresh, and the arrangement of the hidden lighting was so admirable that the place was as brilliant as day, yet with neither glare nor shadow.

Next morning Morrison's work began again, a huge mail coming aboard shortly after breakfast. A plane had been engaged to carry the ship's letters to and from the London office, and Morrison's contribution was no small part of the whole. However, he worked quickly, and with the help of Anderson and Miss Pym he had reasonable time for games and to make the acquaintance of his shipmates.

Then another major event took place in his life. In the small hours of May 24th a soft murmuring began in the lower parts of the ship. It was a pleasant companionable sound and it told Morrison that the engines were moving. When he came up early in the morning they were out of sight of land.

Every minute that he could spare from his work that day Morrison spent on deck. Presently the English coast came in sight and grew gradually clearer. That highish ground to port was the Isle of Wight, the lower line to starboard being the mainland near Hayling Island. Soon he could recognise landmarks: the Foreland, Brading Harbour and Ryde on the island and Southsea and Portsmouth opposite. Breakfast was served as they passed the mouth of Portsmouth Harbour, and when he regained the deck they had just left Calshot. He watched entranced as they moved up Southampton Water, past Lee-on-the-Solent and the Hamble, Netley and Hythe. By ten o'clock they had berthed in the New Dock at Southampton.

Stott and Bristow were waiting for them and came aboard when the gangway was lowered. Stott had very nearly swallowed Morrison's bait. He had not reserved a whole deck to himself, but he had done the next best thing. His large and elaborate suite opened on to a quite considerable area of deck, screened off, not with rails, but with solid partitions, so that he could enjoy the sea and air in privacy. Bristow's accommodation did not run to anything so sumptuous, but he didn't do so badly with a bedroom, private sitting-room, office and bathroom.

Stott seemed rather worried as he came on board. He nodded absently to Morrison and went off at once to see the Captain. But Bristow was in an expansive mood.

'Hullo, old man!' he greeted Morrison. 'How goes it? What do you think of the ship?'

He seemed to have lost his aloof air and was as friendly as at that first interview in the Calais express. He was jubilant about the success of the scheme. The ship carried 1,800 passengers and nearly 3,000 had applied for accommodation. Most of the latter were coming later—in fact, the ship was booked to capacity for the first three months.

'Infinitely better than we could have hoped,' he declared enthusiastically. 'Why, we're already fingering the gold, and if this goes on we'll have our hands right into it. But I have a message for Grant. See you later.' He hurried off importantly.

Presently the first train arrived. Morrison examined curiously the people whom he was to serve as they began streaming across the wharf and up the gangways. They were too far away to exhibit great detail, but even at that distance he was struck by their commonplace air. They looked exactly like all the first-class passengers he had ever seen. When they began actually to enter the ship he went below to his office. Should any of them want his help, he must be available.

Several did. People who had lost rugs and handbags on the journey, or who wanted to return earlier or stay later than they had said. He did what he could to satisfy them, while gradually the ship began to hum uneasily and take on an air of unrest contrasting disagreeably with its peaceful atmosphere during the previous fortnight. He was kept busy all the afternoon, and when during a lull he slipped on deck it was to find that they were already half-way down Southampton Water.

At nine o'clock on that first night when they were well out in the Channel, the gaming-rooms were thrown open and at once were filled. They remained full till, by what was stated to be the rules of the ship, they closed down at 1.00 a.m. Play was cautious: no big sums changed hands and the gains to the bank, so Bristow told Morrison later, were not large. But they were an earnest of what was to follow. Next day the shore service began, the first flying boat leaving the ship after breakfast when they were passing Plymouth and returning in the evening when they were off Penzance. The boats operated to and from the Southampton base, which had proved the most convenient. No one used the service on that second day nor for some days to come, but it ran regularly as advertised. Then gradually passengers began to leave, their places usually being filled on the same day.

Morrison soon settled down in his job, with which he was entirely satisfied. The work was congenial, his quarters comfortable, his fellow officers friendly, his leisure filled with pleasant amusements and, above all, his income greater than a few months earlier he could have imagined in his wildest dreams. His salary was paid on the nail, and his expenses were so trifling that he was able to save almost the whole of it.

People ashore, however, did not seem so pleased. On the sailing of the ship a new and much more intense newspaper warfare arose. All sorts of people wrote condemning the venture as immoral, and calling on the authorities to find some way of stopping it. It was, they said, a disgrace to Britain to have such a vessel about her coast, and they urged that if, as was said, the authorities had no power to take action, the law should immediately be amended.

All this was magnificent grist to Gillow's mill. He and his myrmidons joined battle with a flood of letters taking the opposite view. More members of the public then aired their opinions, increasing the advertising value of the campaign by several per cent. In the end the correspondence died down inconclusively. The Government made no sign and took no action: at least, so thought Stott and his friends.

Contrary to Stott's previously expressed opinion, it was found that a good many people came on board for the cruising alone, never entering the gaming-rooms. The ship's itinerary and the shore excursions therefore assumed greater importance and everything was done to make these items as interesting as possible. The first excursion took place on the third day out—to Glengariff and Killarney, and nearly every day after that some trip ashore was provided. The gaming-rooms were not opened in the morning till ten o'clock, which allowed the boats to put excursionists ashore, and the ship to get out to sea with the rooms closed, and they were shut again from five till nine at night, enabling her to go inshore again to pick up.

The detailed arrangements for these shore excursions involved a lot of work. Previous to the sailing of the ship, Morrison had done this, having fixed up some dozen of which the date of running alone had to be given to an agent ashore. But now a difficulty arose. It was found that Morrison could not be spared from his duties on board to visit the locales of the necessary new trips.

Under these circumstances, it was arranged that Bristow should do the work. Morrison was annoyed for two reasons. First, he thought he was the man to go, and that his assistant Anderson should carry on in his place. Secondly, if someone else were to do it, he did not think Bristow was the right person. It was not a lawyer's job.

However, Bristow went, and as it turned out, he did the work well. Even Morrison had to admit that his arrangements were good, and no unpleasant hitches followed.

Time passed and slowly the weeks grew into months. The venture was proving more and more successful, and already Morrison was beginning to wonder when the first instalment of his 10 per cent on the net profits would materialise. So far no untoward incident had taken place. No one, so far as was known, had lost his all in the gaming-rooms, and there had been no suicides aboard, a possibility which had given Stott some anxiety.

When considerably over a year had passed, an event took place which vitally affected the fortunes, not only of Morrison, but of many others on board. The affair began with the application of three separate parties for accommodation. They were all small, and Morrison heard of them in the usual way, through a notification from the purser's department that they had booked for certain dates.

The first party consisted of a Major Wyndham Stott, Mrs

Stott, Miss Margot Stott and a Mr Percy Luff. Major and Miss Stott were coming aboard in ten days' time, the other two following some days later. They lived near Basingstoke and wished for transport arrangements to and from their house.

There was nothing unusual in this except that the names were underlined in red. The purser's people had a system of underlining in various colours, indicating confidentially the status of their clients. Red meant important people, to be given special attention.

Morrison dealt with the case in his routine way. The ship's itinerary showed that about midday on the date in question they would be off Kirkwall in the Orkneys, which was perhaps the prelude to the most interesting part of their cruise. He arranged for a Daimler service car to be at the house near Basingstoke to run the pair to Southampton, and for the best seats on that morning's flying boat to be reserved for them.

The second and third parties contained only two members each. One consisted of a Mr and Mrs Forrester from London. They were coming aboard on the same day as Stott and his daughter, and Morrison automatically allotted to them adjoining seats in the plane.

The names of the third party, which was due about a week after the others, caused Morrison to sit up and take notice. They were Mr Alex N. Malthus and Mr Clarence Mason. Apart from the initials, Morrison saw at once that this was *the* Malthus, because Mason, he had afterwards learnt, had been one of the directors of the abortive company.

It happened that, just as he was entering the names on his records, Stott looked into his office on other business.

'Did you hear who were coming, sir?' Morrison asked when this had been discussed.

'You mean Malthus and Mason? Yes, Grant told me. It doesn't affect us. They can't do anything.'

'I expect they'll try and catch us out in a breach of the gaming laws.'

'They can try till they're black in the face. We're not breaking them.'

Stott was in an exceptionally expansive humour and discussed the matter more readily than Morrison expected. Then, as he was leaving, Morrison remembered the Stott family and a possible reason for the red underlining occurred to him.

'I see that a Major Wyndham Stott and his family are coming aboard. I wondered, sir, if they were connections of yours, and if so, whether you'd like any special arrangements made for them?'

'As a matter of fact they are—the only relatives I've got. Major Stott is my nephew and incidentally my heir—though we don't get on. So if I get knocked out, you'll have him to deal with. Margot Stott is his daughter by his first wife. Mrs Stott is his second wife and Luff is her son. Wyndham's a born gambler and I expect when he gets my money he'll not keep it long. No, I don't want anything special done: just carry on as usual.'

Morrison dropped the subject, but he was by no means convinced about the special treatment, and when later that day he met the purser, he asked his advice.

'That's right,' Grant agreed. 'They'll have to have everything possible done for them. I've already given them better cabins than they've paid for. The Old Boy's saying that we're to make no difference is all my eye.'

In staff references a subtle terminological distinction was drawn between Stott and Captain Hardwick. The former was the Old Boy, the latter the Old Man.

'He said they didn't get on,' Morrison repeated.

'Don't you worry about that,' Grant advised. 'If there are complaints, they'll get to him all right, whether they get on or whether they don't.'

They were off the Land's End when this conversation took place, and from there they worked along the south and east coasts, stopping at what Morrison considered comparatively dull places till they reached Scotland. There they had a couple of days in the Edinburgh district, and, after calling at Aberdeen and Cromarty, reached next day the aphelion of their orbit, the bleak and barren Shetlands. Here a number of loch excursions in the ship's launches were organised which gave general satisfaction.

On the way back to the Orkneys they came in for their first real gale. There had been many gales, of course, but Captain Hardwick had, up till now, always managed to have the ship in some sheltered anchorage before the sea rose. On this occasion he appeared to have been caught napping. Even the *Hellénique's* 47,000 tons was unable to keep her on an even keel, and she was rolling heavily. Several of the passengers had discreetly retired to their cabins and the rest exhibited a tendency to stay put. It was the most severe motion Morrison had yet experienced and he was not himself feeling too happy.

He emerged from the port door of the music-room and, clawing his way round the structure, met the full force of the wind to starboard. Clinging to the deck-house handrail, he gazed with something approaching awe at the sea. It was a full gale, so he had heard the Third Officer say, and he hoped he would never witness anything worse. The waves were like hillocks, great greeny-grey masses of water, coming up irregularly out of the west and seething with acres of boiling foam. The wind felt solid. It pressed him against the deck-house, and it tore great lumps of the tossing whiteness off the waves and threw them against the ship. The decks, even at 60 or 70 feet from the water, were streaming, and he felt the quivering shock as waves hit the side. Dragging himself forward, he could see the entire fo'c'sle blotted out as by a white sheet, as the *Hellénique* put her nose down into a wave and, as it seemed to Morrison, charged and burst it.

For nearly an hour he stood enjoying the spectacle. As he was clawing his way back to the music-room he came on Grant.

'Pretty stormy,' Morrison shouted as he stopped.

'A gale all right,' Grant returned. 'Pity we've got it. A lot of the passengers are ill already and they won't forget it when they go ashore.'

'"The ship which avoids the storm",' Morrison grinned, as he quoted one of Gillow's masterpieces.

'We've done it up to the present,' Grant pointed out. 'Pity we've broken our record.'

To be caught in a gale once in eighteen months was not such a bad record, Morrison thought, as he cautiously clawed his way back to his office and began trying to work at a desk which heaved itself about in the most disconcerting and distracting way imaginable.

7

Enter Margot

By nightfall the gale had blown itself out and next day the weather was again delightful. The sun shone brightly, the atmosphere was clear and the islands showed up in colourful detail. A mild westerly breeze was blowing, raising tiny wavelets which sparkled like diamonds in the sun. It was warm and fresh on deck, as if summer was coming instead of being practically over: a perfect day for the journey of the Stotts and Forresters.

The flying boats carried eighteen persons, and as twenty-nine travellers were arriving that morning, two of them were in operation. They reported their progress by wireless and when the time came, Captain Hardwick stopped the ship and completed his preparations for receiving them. The boarding ladder on the side port was dropped, while two derricks swung out and lowered into the sea the Captain's patent floating wharf. Guy ropes held this out at right angles to the ship, its inner end being clamped to the ladder.

This operation was scarcely completed when the drone of an aircraft was heard and one of the flying boats appeared.

It circled over the ship and came down, taking the water skilfully. Then it taxied towards the ship, manoeuvred up to the end of the floating wharf, and made fast. Waiting officers threw open the doors and the passengers began to emerge. As they did so, the second flying boat appeared in the distance.

Morrison stood by the rail on the promenade deck watching the operation, with Grant beside him.

'That'll be the nephew and his daughter,' Grant said suddenly, 'and those other two the Forresters.'

A stocky man with a head slightly large in proportion to his body, a clipped moustache and an alert air, had just climbed down on the wharf and was being followed by a young woman in a red felt hat, a fur coat and brown brogues. The Fourth Officer was superintending the embarkation, and the man spoke to him, the girl smiling at him pleasantly. Following them was a rather short, stoutish man in tweeds, who helped out a plain but kindly looking woman with greying hair.

The identity of the first pair was put beyond doubt a little later. As Morrison was leaving his office for lunch they passed. The man looked at the notice above the door and stopped.

'I'm Major Stott,' he explained. 'Are you the officer responsible for our journey here?'

Morrison, wondering what mistake he had made, admitted that the arrangements had been his.

'Then all I want to say is that we've never been so well done in our lives. Have we, Margot?'

'No, indeed,' the girl returned. 'It was a delightful journey and I enjoyed every minute of it.'

This was a different greeting from what Morrison had

somehow expected, presumably from his knowledge of old Stott. He could not imagine the uncle commenting on anything done for him otherwise than to find fault. As he murmured his thanks, he took more careful stock of the newcomers.

The Major at close quarters was just a little disappointing. He somehow failed to substantiate the suggestion of alertness and precision given by his more distant view. He had, indeed, a slightly gone-to-seed appearance. His features were good, his expression pleasant and kindly, and he was well dressed and groomed. But Morrison thought he had a faint air both of weakness and of obstinacy. He looked straight, though a trifle dissatisfied and unhappy.

Margot Stott also looked a little worried. As he glanced at her, he thought he had seldom seen a more attractive face. Indeed, once he had looked at her, he found it difficult to turn his eyes elsewhere. She was of medium height and slight build, with an excellent carriage and small, shapely hands and feet. Her colouring was dark, and though not in any sense beautiful, her features were regular and well-formed. But it was not the details of her appearance, but the general impression he received from her, that affected Morrison. She seemed to radiate goodness in all its forms. Her clear, dancing eyes and delicate complexion—natural, he felt sure—showed health and intelligence and vitality. Her firm little chin indicated strength, and her every movement competence and capability. On her kindliness as well as complete straightness he would have banked his future. And yet over it all was this unhappy suggestion of anxiety.

The fleeting interview was over and father and daughter had disappeared down the alleyway before Morrison remembered what he was supposed to be doing, and got on with it.

He was aware that in his job it would be unwise to allow the vision of any female passenger, no matter how charming, to fill his mind. He knew also that even if this were not so, he could not hope for any social intercourse, let alone friendship, with a girl who moved in so different a sphere from his own. Conversation with her, if he had any, would inevitably be confined to business, and even this was unlikely, as he did not see what business there was which could possibly require discussion between them. Policy, in fact, as well as peace of mind postulated immediate forgetfulness of the meeting.

Morrison's own common sense, indeed, accepted this view, but, as it happened, a small incident made it harder for him to carry it out than might otherwise have been the case.

As he was returning along A Deck from Captain Hardwick's cabin, where he had been on business, he met Miss Stott walking in the opposite direction. She looked at him doubtfully for a moment, then stopped and smiled.

'You're the transport officer, aren't you? I don't know your name?'

Morrison's heart beat a trifle faster. 'Morrison. Miss Stott,' he answered, trying to speak naturally. 'Harry Morrison.'

She smiled again. 'Well, Mr Morrison,' she went on, 'I want some help and I think—though I'm not sure—that you're the person I should apply to.'

'I hope I am,' Morrison declared. 'At all events, if I can't handle it myself, I can at least put you in touch with the proper officer.'

'Thanks,' she returned. 'That's very kind. I've done such a stupid thing. I've forgotten an attaché case. It's not important in a way except that all my books are in it, and I was hoping to get some time to read while on board.'

Morrison thought rapidly. 'Who is there at your home who knows about it?' he asked.

'I think either Redpath, the butler, or his wife could find it. They've been left in charge of the house, but the other servants have gone on holidays.'

'Well, if you'll instruct your butler to find the case and hand it over, I'll arrange for a car to call for it tomorrow morning. It would then come on tomorrow's plane and you'd have it about midday.'

'Oh, splendid!' She was obviously pleased. 'But how could I instruct him? I suppose a wireless cablegram?'

'Easier to telephone, wouldn't it? There's a continuous wireless telephone service in operation between ship and shore. You'd simply ring up your butler in the ordinary way. You can do it at any time from your cabin.'

'You don't say so! Rather marvellous that, really! I'll certainly do it, and if you'll be kind enough to arrange for the case to be brought down, I'd be so grateful.'

Morrison gave the proper assurances, expecting that once business was over she would pass on. But she didn't. She stood beside him at the rail looking at the bare contours of the islands between which the ship was slowly passing.

'You know, I love this sort of scenery,' she went on. 'Wild, bare mountain and moorland; particularly with outcropping rocks.'

'I do, too,' Morrison agreed, 'but most people prefer trees with their mountains.'

'We shall have better scenery further on?'

'Oh, lord, yes. The Gairlock and Skye, for example. You know the Cuillins, perhaps?'

'No, but I'm told they're wonderful. Why do we all crowd off to the Riviera and the Italian lakes and places like that, and miss our own scenery at home?'

'One reason perhaps,' Morrison returned, 'is that before this ship began to run it wasn't so easy to see it. At some of the places a steamer calls, but, to others there's no regular service.'

'I'm looking forward to it all so much.'

'I don't think you'll be disappointed. There are lots of charming places down the west coast and across in Northern Ireland. You've come aboard at the best point in the whole trip.'

She chatted for a few minutes, then said she must go and telephone. As Morrison watched her tripping off along the deck he realised that, though policy and peace of mind might urge forgetfulness of her image, this no longer lay within the realms of practical politics.

Half an hour later she rang him up to say that she had spoken to her butler, who would have the case ready for the messenger.

To ensure that his arrangements should function without a hitch, Morrison made them with extreme care. But this was no longer because it was being done for his employer's grandniece, but solely for the sake of that young lady herself.

Next day he met the flying boat and was much eased in mind when he found that the case had come. Margot Stott was with some passengers on the promenade deck and he gave himself the pleasure of handing it to her in person.

She thanked him, not exactly with warmth, but with friendliness. She kept him for a moment chatting, but he thought it wise to pass on as soon as he could properly do so.

90

Certainly she was very attractive. Indeed, when at times he found his work was not progressing with its usual speed, he could not but be aware of the cause.

Four or five days later, as, before dinner, he was passing through the music-room lounge, he heard his name called. It was Major Stott, who was drinking cocktails with some companions.

'Here's the officer who can arrange it for you,' he said to a tall, white-haired man with a rugged face standing next him. 'When we came aboard, my daughter forgot some books in our house near Basingstoke. She told Morrison about them that night and they were here on board before lunch next day. That was at Scapa Flow. Jolly good, I call it.'

'Can you do the same for me, Mr Morrison?' asked the rugged-faced man. His name was Carrothers and Morrison thought he was a stockbroker. 'I want a document from my office in Galashiels. Can you have it here before lunch tomorrow?'

Morrison smiled. 'Not so easy, Mr Carrothers, seeing that you don't live near Southampton. However, I dare say I can deflect one of our flying boats to the Forth and pick it up there. It'll cost you something. You don't mind?'

They discussed details and then Carrothers turned to the others. 'In spite of my friend's presence, I will admit that the transport to and from the ship is good,' he declared. 'I was told to be ready to start from my house at ten in the morning. At nine fifty-nine a Daimler drew up at the door with a uniformed chauffeur. I got in and was driven to the pier at Leith. A launch was waiting and just as we got into open water a flying boat came down beside us. I climbed on board and we were on the *Hellénique* about half-past twelve. That was at the Orkneys. Quite good, I call it, too.'

'Yes, those flying boats are an idea,' agreed a small, dried-up man with the face of a lawyer.

'There's no doubt the cruise is well run,' said a third man, the Mr Forrester who had travelled to the ship with the Stotts. 'But you people'—he looked at Morrison—'know how to charge. And yet even with the high charges I wonder it pays. It does pay, I suppose?'

'Oh, come now, Forester, you mustn't ask him for secret history,' Stott protested, evidently anxious to help Morrison out. 'Not fair. Eh, Morrison?'

Morrison grinned. 'I can't tell you about our finances, Mr Forrester,' he explained, 'for quite a good reason: I don't know about them myself. All I know is that my salary's been paid all right up to now, and I hope it'll go on.'

'The main thing from your point of view, no doubt,' Carrothers put in. 'And quite right, too.'

Morrison smilingly agreed.

'It ought to pay all right if you're not too lavish in your expenses,' Forrester went on. 'It's certainly a good idea. Whose was it, by the way? I mean, the idea?'

Rather an inquisitive man, this Forrester, Morrison thought. He had booked from London and was evidently in some business, but Morrison did not know what. He was mildly popular on board. He had played at the tables in moderation and had taken a number of the shore excursions. He had shown himself friendly to Morrison and had stopped on different occasions to chat, but sooner or later he had always begun to ask questions. Indeed, in some subtle way he gave the impression that he was on board for some deeper motive than mere pleasure.

It occurred to Morrison that perhaps he represented a group of people who thought of running a rival ship. Probably not a gambling ship—there would not be room for a second—but a cheap cruising ship, as Bristow had originally intended.

Morrison had wondered whether, if so, he might himself take a hand? His notes would be worth a substantial sum to anyone considering such a venture. Why should he not have a try for the money?

Obviously, if a rival to the *Hellénique* were proposed, he could have nothing to say to it. But there would be no rivalry in a scheme for poor man's cruising. On the other hand, if the idea of another ship was being mooted for either purpose, should Stott not be informed?

Altogether it had seemed to him that either for his own benefit or Stott's he should find out what Forrester was after.

When, therefore, the man asked whose idea the cruise was, he answered him fully.

'The result at all events is certainly good,' Forrester approved. 'And very ingenious also how you people have got round the anti-gambling laws. I shouldn't have thought it was possible, but you seem to have done it.'

'Counsel's opinion, I understand, that was,' Morrison said, smiling. 'Some barristers were asked how it could be done and this is the result.'

'A nasty one for you, Willcox,' Carrothers chuckled, glancing at the small dried-up man. 'Mr Willcox is a barrister,' he explained to Morrison.

Morrison felt the temper of the group. 'No names were mentioned,' he said gravely, but with a twinkle in his eyes. 'I feel sure I've given nothing away, Mr Willcox.'

'Let them go on,' Willcox answered, 'and with luck we'll make the cost of the trip out of them for slander.'

That same evening Morrison had an experience which moved him intensely: indeed, he was rather shocked when he realised to what extent.

After dinner he went out on the deck for some air. The night was surprisingly warm and balmy for the time of year and most of the passengers were somewhere in the open. There was a dance forward and the strains of the band came to him, agreeably softened by distance. Dancing by the ship's officers was for some reason frowned on, and he therefore kept away from the festivities, sinking into a chair beside the rail overlooking the after well deck. There he sat, enjoying the luxury and the peace and dreaming in a rather somnolent way of Margot Stott.

Presently a woman passed him, stopped, and after a moment came back. He had not glanced at her, but now he did so.

'Miss Stott!' he exclaimed, springing up. 'Are you enjoying the night as I am?'

She moved over beside him and stood at the rail looking out at the reflection of the moon across the tiny wavelets.

'Yes, isn't it gorgeous! I should be dancing, but I've had enough of it for the moment. I'd infinitely rather look at that sea.'

'Won't you sit down?' he begged, drawing over another chair. 'There's no draught in the shelter of this boat.'

'I must go back soon,' she returned, 'but I'd like to sit here for a little. It's so extraordinarily peaceful. And *lovely*. I'd no idea there was scenery like what we've been seeing in the British Isles. I'm afraid I said that before, but it really is marvellous.'

They chatted in a desultory way about the cruise and its itinerary, and every moment Morrison felt himself coming more and more under the girl's spell. Then she suddenly surprised him by asking the same question as Forrester had earlier. 'Whose idea was the cruise? It certainly seems to have been an astonishing success.'

Morrison told her. She listened, apparently enthralled.

'Then the gambling part was my great-uncle's?' she said when he had done. 'Neither you nor Mr Bristow had thought of it?'

'No. Bristow's idea was simply to throw large-ship cruising open to the man of small means. He never contemplated either the gambling or doing the thing in such an expensive way. Take the flying boats, for example. They simply lap up money. Though they were my idea, it was only in response to Mr Stott's wish for comfort and convenience regardless of cost. Bristow's idea had been a third-class sleeper and a local tender from the nearest port.'

'And you think Mr Bristow's plan would have paid?'

'I'm sure it would. You see this ship was built to carry four thousand passengers and we would have carried at least three: at very nearly the same cost as we're now carrying eighteen hundred. We didn't contemplate a private bathroom for every cabin, you see.'

She was silent for some seconds, then gave a little sigh. 'Oh, dear,' she said earnestly. How much better all that would have been! What a pity Mr Bristow's idea was not carried out!'

Morrison was startled. 'You mean,' he asked anxiously, 'you don't approve of the gambling?'

She shook her head decidedly. 'No, nor the luxury. I feel it's all wrong. Don't you think so yourself, Mr Morrison?'

Morrison hesitated. 'Well, I confess I was brought up to consider gambling an evil,' he said slowly, 'but I don't know how far that was just the feeling of the time. The rooms are very well run, of course.'

She turned in her chair and looked at him. 'I believe you're hiding what you really think because my father and my uncle are mixed up in it. You needn't really. I know enough about it. I've seen—' She broke off and shrugged lightly. 'Oh, well, we needn't talk about it. But tell me more of Mr Bristow's original idea. That would have been really good. It would have given health and pleasure to a lot of people who couldn't afford this.'

He enlarged on the plan, to her evident approval. They chatted on for a few minutes, then she changed the subject.

'You know my stepmother and her son are coming on Thursday?' Both words and tone were correct, and yet something in her manner suggested a feeling of regret.

'I know,' he answered. 'You see, I have to arrange seats for them in the plane.'

'Of course.' She paused. Then continued: 'They'll enjoy all this; the dancing and, indeed, the gaming, too.'

The suggestion was now unmistakable. Undoubtedly there was bitterness in her mind. Morrison hesitated, hoping to avoid offence. 'You and they don't see eye to eye on these matters?' he presently essayed.

'We don't really,' she returned; 'but it isn't that.' Then, as if she had been about to say too much, she added with a smile: 'I'm afraid I'm jealous. I like to have my father to myself.'

'Naturally.' Morrison was glad of something safe to say. 'Have they been married long, he and your stepmother?'

'Five years. These two couldn't come with us because Percy had 'flu; quite a bad attack really.'

'Hard luck.'

She answered, 'Yes, wasn't it?' in an unsympathetic voice. 'Father wondered if he ought to wait for the others, but I persuaded him not to.' She glanced round. 'Oh, dear, there's Mr Redfern looking for me. I promised him this dance and I forgot all about him. I must run.'

Morrison found he had a good deal to think of that night. He has never met anyone whose presence moved him as did Margot Stott's. On many occasions he had had what he called 'affairs' with social acquaintances, waitresses, girl clerks, and so on. But all these had proved slight and passing entanglements, from which no consequences, good or evil, had resulted. This time he hoped—or feared—things were different. Not only did he feel drawn to this young woman as never to any before, but on this occasion a strange and unexpected element entered into his desire—that he should not only obtain, but deserve, her good opinion.

It looked as if she did not pull too well with her step-mother: not perhaps surprising if one considered her age. Margot he judged to be about five-and-twenty, and if her mother had been dead any considerable time, as was probable, she and her father would have become excellent friends. From their manner to one another it was obvious that they were so still. It was natural that Margot would resent losing her privileged position.

But it was not natural that so sweet-tempered a girl should feel bitterness from such a cause. If Margot did not like her stepmother, it must be because she was an unpleasant woman. And if Margot was unsympathetic towards Percy Luff, it must be because he was an unpleasant young man. Morrison's heart warmed still further to her, and he began to imagine her as unhappy in her home and needing sympathy and comfort, and to long for the intense joy of giving her both.

He continued all that night to halt between two opinions, at one time filled with delight that he had made this marvellous acquaintanceship, at another apprehensive that all he could possibly get out of it would be disappointment and pain.

All the same, the idea of avoiding her to save that pain never for one moment entered his head. He felt that no matter what the consequences might be, he would take what the gods seemed to be offering.

The next morning there took place another event which was to leave its mark on Morrison's life. In itself it was entirely trifling, but later it became a source of worry and fear.

It occurred in connection with a hobby of the owner's. John Stott was interested in archaeology and particularly in the prehistoric or very early architecture of the British Isles. For years he had been amassing notes from which he intended one day to write his *magnum opus*. From this point of view, the cruise had been a godsend to him, as he had been able to visit and sketch and photograph a large number of coastal ruins which would otherwise have been more difficult to reach. Usually he did the work himself, but if engaged elsewhere or not in the humour for the excursion, he was not above sending a deputy in his place. This was usually Bristow, but on occasion Morrison, who also was a fair amateur photographer, had been pressed into the service. Morrison had no particular objection to these researches—in fact, he rather enjoyed the work.

On that next morning, Stott called him to his suite, and, opening an Ordnance map of the Ullapool district, pointed to a couple of dots in an apparently inaccessible place on the northern shores of Loch Broom.

'Interesting old ruin there,' he explained. 'Believed to belong to early Viking times. A man told me about it and advised me to see it. But I can't get ashore today. I wish you'd go and get the usual stuff.'

Now, that day Morrison was busy and didn't want to take the time off. However, he thought he could manage by letting Anderson do part of his work in addition to his own, and himself clearing up the remainder in the evening. Morrison disliked working after dinner, but it was often necessary, and when the need arose, he did it without grousing as part of his job.

He carried out his plan, explaining the matter to Anderson and getting an early boat ashore. Then with a copy of the map, he set off to find the ruin.

It proved a difficult job. There was no path to the place and the ground was rough and stony. Once he came to a stream, the bank of which he had to follow for nearly a mile before he could get across. Twice he reached peat bogs, dangerous-looking places with water shining between the coarse grasses and mossy patches of too vivid green. To get round these involved long detours, and nearly three hours had passed before, hot and tired and irritable, he reached his goal.

The ruin, when he did find it, was disappointing in the extreme. Only a few rough stones remained of what presumably had been an outer wall. With a bad grace, he photographed it from various angles, made a rough sketch with dimensions, took the orientation with a pocket compass, and finally sat down to eat his sandwiches.

He had further trouble on the return journey. In trying

to avoid the bogs, he went too much towards the east, missed his way, and had a long, wearing tramp over difficult ground before regaining the road. There he found that a boat had just gone and he had to wait over an hour for the next. This, as he remembered all the work waiting to be done, still further exasperated him. Altogether it was in an unusually disgruntled frame of mind that eventually he reached the ship.

Stott was not in his cabin, and he left the roll of films with a note on his desk. The one alleviation in these photographic excursions was that Stott liked to do his own developing. Then Morrison went to his quarters, had a bath and some dinner, and settled down to his day's work.

He found what had to be done tedious, but not difficult, and he tackled it with system and efficiency. He was congratulating himself that he would be finished by eleven when his telephone rang. Stott wanted to see him about the photographs.

Mentally consigning Stott and all his works to an uncongenial sphere, he went at once to his suite.

Stott was seated at his desk holding a strip of wet film. 'Look here,' he greeted him in an indignant and complaining tone. 'These photographs are no good. They only show the top of the blessed thing. There's sure to be a lot below the ground. Why didn't you dig away all this grass and stuff?'

For a moment Morrison saw red. Then with an effort he controlled himself. 'I thought I hadn't done too badly, sir,' he returned, 'getting there at all. It's a terrible way over very rough ground with a river to be crossed and stretches of bogland. There's no road or path, you understand. It took me three hours to make it.'

'Not much good your making it, as you call it, if in the

end you don't get what you went out for,' Stott returned unpleasantly. 'Couldn't you have got a man with a spade for half an hour, if you weren't up to the job yourself?'

'No, sir, I couldn't,' Morrison answered firmly, 'The place is a wilderness. I saw no one about and there were no houses anywhere near. If you want excavation done, it'll require proper arrangements to be made beforehand.'

Stott looked at him, then shrugged contemptuously. 'Oh, well, if you couldn't, you couldn't. But my experience in these matters is that where there's a will, there's a way. That'll do. I'll have to do with them.'

He turned away discontentedly. Morrison was fuming, but something either in his character or training prevented him from the reply which came to his lips. Without a word, he turned and left the office.

As it happened, in the alleyway he met Bristow. The latter stared at him.

'Hullo!' he exclaimed. 'What's happened? Had a spot of trouble?'

Morrison glanced round. He could see no one. 'It's that dirty skunk, Stott,' he declared savagely, and he went on to describe the owner's reception of his day's efforts.

His previous repression made him more outspoken than he might otherwise have been. He left no doubt in Bristow's mind as to his feelings towards Stott. And yet he didn't really convey the truth. He had no actual hatred towards the man. His ill feeling was only grouse. Bristow, however, was sympathetic, as he also had suffered in the same way. He agreed that Stott was the 'dirtiest and the meanest bloke unhung'.

The whole thing was a trifle and Morrison would quickly have forgotten it, had it not been that, looking round again, he saw a figure shuffling away. It was Pointer, a steward whom he believed he had made an enemy of when he had reprimanded him for not mischief. Instantly Morrison realised that his outburst had been overheard.

'There's that blighter Pointer,' he said in a lower tone. 'He's a bad egg and I bet he's heard all I said.'

Bristow shrugged. 'What matter if he did?' he returned. 'You said nothing to harm anyone.'

All the same, as Morrison thought over the encounter, he realised that he had spoken unwisely. The look in Pointer's face made him feel sorry he had let himself go. He was not exactly uneasy, but he wished he had been more careful.

8

Prelude to Adventure

Next day the ship lay off the Gairloch, a party going ashore for a drive through the fine scenery of the surrounding mountains. Morrison stayed aboard with the idea of clearing off arrears of work, though actually thoughts of Margot Stott filled his mind to such an extent that the arrears grew greater instead of less.

That she was unhappy in her home life he was now convinced, and while all his sympathy went out to her, he found in the belief the dawn of a wonderful hope. If it were true, she would naturally look more favourably on matrimony: the wrench of leaving home would be less. But if she wished to marry, was there any reason why he might not be the lucky man? His present social position was admittedly beneath hers, but he was not going to remain a transport officer for ever. He had been brought up in circumstances like her own and had been properly educated. Though he had not actually taken his degree, he had at least been to a good school and to Cambridge, and he could hold his own with people of her world. Of course, he hadn't a millionaire for a great-uncle, but Wyndham Stott didn't seem more than comfortably off, and when his own 10 per cent of the cruise net profits materialised, he would be fairly well-to-do himself.

He wished desperately that he could see more of her. She was invariably friendly, and they were on intimate enough terms considering the number of times they had met, but she was so much taken up with her father and the other passengers that only at odd moments could he get a glimpse of her.

Then that very afternoon something happened which completely altered the terms on which they had previously been, and left them with a new sympathy and regard.

As he was dreaming over his desk at about the time at which thoughts of a cup of tea begin to enter the mind, his telephone bell rang. His surprise and pleasure were great when he heard Margot's voice, though not as great as when he received her message.

'Are you very busy, Mr Morrison?' she asked.

He explained with fervour that he was only working on routine matters and was quite free for anything she might desire.

'Then I'd be greatly obliged if you could meet me in the library in ten minutes.'

His heart was beating a good deal more rapidly as he replaced the receiver. The rendezvous was suggestive. The library was in a corner of what had been the tourist smoking-room and at this hour it was closed. On such a lovely day the place would be deserted.

When a few moments later he set off to keep the appointment, he felt as nervous as if he were about to be interviewed for a new job. Fervently he hoped he would not fail her in carrying out whatever she wanted him to do.

The saloon was empty when he entered, as he expected it would be. It was an unattractive place, low and small and with drab decorations and plain fittings. In a few seconds she joined him, and he instantly realised that she was in some serious trouble.

'Miss Stott!' he greeted her. 'I see there's something wrong. Can I do anything?'

She smiled deprecatingly. 'I feel dreadfully ashamed, Mr Morrison, for troubling you like this. But I'm rather worried and I don't know anyone else on board that I would care to ask for help.'

Morrison's heart leaped, but he controlled himself. 'It would be an honour to help you,' he said quietly. 'What has happened?'

She made a little gesture of distress. 'I hate to say it,' she answered, 'but it's my father. It seems like criticising him, and he's the best father in the world. But just occasionally he—he takes a little too much whisky. And when that happens, his gambling becomes reckless. Then when the— when it has passed, he's so sorry and upset.'

She hesitated, as if finding her confession too painful to continue. Morrison thought he should fill the gap, and he tried to speak sincerely and yet without emotion.

'I can appreciate all that,' he declared. 'I've known cases where the best and most lovable people have become temporarily changed just by taking a little more than they intended to. And, of course, there's nothing it affects so quickly as the judgment.'

She glanced at him gratefully. 'I thought you'd understand. Now, the trouble is that he's taken—a little—too much this afternoon. I don't mean for a moment that he's at all—well, drunk. But as you put it, his judgment has been affected and he's gambling wildly. He's losing more than we can afford. And when he—recovers, he'll be so sorry and wish so much he hadn't.'

If Morrison had any doubt of it before, he had none now. He loved this girl, loved her to distraction. He would do anything for her and be thankful for the chance. But, he told himself grimly, this was not the moment to think of it. Crushing down his feelings, he asked: 'What do you usually do under such circumstances?'

'He'll often do what I ask him. But this afternoon I've been down to the rooms twice and he just won't attend to me. I can't do anything with him. Besides, my running after him worries him.'

Morrison at last saw what was coming. 'And you wish me to try if I can do anything?' he asked, his heart slowly sinking. If this indeed were what she wanted, almost inevitably he would fail her.

She nodded, looking anxiously into his face. 'I thought perhaps your uniform would help you: give you some sort of authority, you know. He might listen to you when he won't to me.'

Morrison hated it, but only one answer was possible. 'I'll do my level best,' he declared. 'Shall I try and bring him to you here, or just ask him to go on deck?'

'If you could get him away from the rooms, I think I could manage him. Perhaps you'd better bring him here.'

Morrison, however, remembered that very shortly the library steward would be opening up the shelves and people would be coming in and out.

'I don't think this place would do after all,' he said. 'The library will be opening soon. But I'll tell you: come along to my office. No one will want me at this time and I'll close it for half an hour. Then I'll try and get Major Stott to go there.'

'That is good of you,' she said gratefully. 'Of course, you'll explain to him that I've asked you to do this. He may be annoyed at the moment, but he'll thank you for it later.'

Morrison turned aside. 'You may trust me to do everything I can,' he assured her earnestly.

'I do trust you, and I'm more grateful than I can say.'

Though it gave him a thrill of sheer delight to be attempting something unpleasant for Margot, Morrison shrank from what he knew would be a horrible ordeal. In the first place, no officer in uniform was allowed in the gaming rooms on pain of instant dismissal. He thought his excuse for breaking the rule would be accepted by the Captain, but old Stott would have the final decision, and he might resent the interference with his nephew. Then, it would be impossible to speak to the Major in private, and a public discussion of the matter would be out of the question. His quest, indeed, seemed hopeless; then, just as he reached the rooms, he saw what he might do.

The door attendant made as if to stop him, but he whispered: 'Message from the Captain for Major Stott,' and passed in before the other could recall his wits.

Except from the door, he had never before seen gaming in progress. He now found himself in one of the large rooms devoted to roulette, and every chair round the big table was occupied. Behind the chairs stood a ring of observers. Both sexes and all ages were represented. The armchairs and settees round the walls were deserted, but a few people stood vaguely about, as if too unsettled to sit down.

He had read many descriptions of the play at Monte Carlo, and he heard with an odd little thrill, delivered in a colourless monotone the words he had so often see in print: '*Messieurs et mesdames, faites les jeux.*' Fascinated, he watched the coloured counters being placed on the various spaces, some deliberately as if weighty consideration and judgment had gone to the selection, some hesitatingly as if fear and doubt were uppermost in the player's mind, and others in the hurry of last moment decision. Then, like the knell of fate came the croupier's, '*Le jeu est fait: rien ne va plus!*' followed by the whirl of the wheel with its dancing ball, the equally fateful number with '*Impair, manque, rouge*' following, and the quick skilful movements of the rake pushing out and drawing in—but mostly drawing in—counters.

Morrison, waiting for the turn to end, glanced from the table to the faces of those playing. Here he saw something else of which he had read, though till now he had never quite believed it. No one showed the feverish excitement naturally to be expected. Practically everyone looked bored. Only three—two terrible old women and a small, sallow man—watched with real eagerness. One of the women was successful, and he thought he had never seen cupidity stamped so plainly on human features as when she stretched out her wrinkled, claw-like hand to draw in her chips.

He had no trouble in finding Stott. He was in this room seated almost directly facing the croupier, and with his back to the door and Morrison. When the turn was over Morrison advanced, and taking his courage in both hands, spoke to Stott.

'I beg your pardon, Major Stott,' he said as officially as he could, 'but Captain Hardwick sends his compliments and would be grateful if you could see him in his cabin. Some telegram he wishes to discuss with you.'

Stott leant back. He had obviously had drink and was red-eyed and quarrelsome-looking, though by no means incapable. He stared truculently.

'He does, does he?' he returned in a loud voice. 'Well, I'll go when I'm ready.'

Morrison took a fresh hold on himself. 'Sorry, sir,' he declared, 'but I daren't take back such a message. He's waiting to see you now.'

'Well, he can wait. What the hell do I care?'

Several players glanced up with annoyed expressions and Morrison felt he would presently have their opposition. He smiled pleasantly and went on as firmly as he could: 'I'm sorry, sir, but he's the captain. We've all got to humour him while we're aboard. Perhaps you wouldn't mind coming for just a moment?'

Stott began a fresh outburst, but it was quickly quelled by the other players. There were cries of 'Hush!' and 'Silence!' and someone said: 'Steady on, old man. Go and see the lord almighty and we'll keep your place.'

For a moment Stott seemed undecided, then he got up. 'All right, curse the lot of you. Here, you'—to Morrison— 'lead the way and be damned to you!'

As they entered one of the lifts Morrison felt that the preliminary skirmish had been won. But the main action, now in sight, was a more serious affair.

He stopped the lift at D Deck and led the way to his cabin. 'One moment here, sir, if you please,' he said as he ushered Stott in. 'Perhaps you'd kindly sit down just for a second?'

'What's all this?' Stott answered suspiciously. 'If you try on any monkey-tricks with me, the Lord help you,' All the same he sat down and waited. Morrison took his place opposite and tried to stiffen his resolution with thoughts of Margot.

'I have to tell you, sir,' he began slowly, 'that what I said to you just now was not true. The Captain does not want to see you, but someone else does. I mentioned the Captain instead of that person in order not to disgrace you.'

Stott's eyes goggled. 'Do you happen to know what you're saying and who you're speaking to?' he asked with dangerous quietness.

'I'll put it to you, sir, as I see it, and leave it at that. You can do what you like: get me sacked if you like. But what do you think of it when your daughter had to come to me, a complete stranger, and a young man at that, to try and stop her father from throwing away his money at the tables because he had taken too much drink to listen to her or to know what he was doing?'

For a moment Morrison thought his visitor was getting apoplexy. Stott's face grew crimson, the veins swelled on his forehead and his eyes bulged from their sockets. Once or twice he gasped as if unable to speak. Then very slowly his expression changed. He leant forward and put his hands over his eyes. For a little there was silence in the cabin. Then at last he spoke—in a different voice.

'Is this true,' he asked, 'that my daughter did really come to you with that request?'

'Absolutely, sir. I was simply trying to do what she asked me.'

'Where is she?'

Morrison pointed. 'She's next door in my office. Will you see her, sir, if I ask her to come in?'

Stott nodded. Morrison passed into the office and spoke as unemotionally as he could.

'Major Stott's in there, Miss Stott. He'd like to see you.' He held the door, she passed through it, and he closed it behind her. Then, feeling slightly sick, he went on deck.

What took place in his cabin he never heard. When he went back half an hour later it was empty. But apparently the interview turned out satisfactorily: indeed, he was practically told so by both participants. Just before dinner he met Margot on the promenade deck and she stopped him.

'I just can't say how grateful I am—we both are,' she said earnestly. 'I don't want ever to refer to it again, but I'll not forget your kindness. Thank you. Good night.' She had vanished before he could reply.

There was a good deal in the words, and there was even more in the glance which went with them. Warmth began flooding into Morrison's heart. His misgivings began to disappear. The world grew suddenly brighter and happier.

These feelings were strengthened later that night by an interview with Major Stott, as short and decisive as the other. Morrison was on his way to the boat-deck for a breather before bed, when he ran into the man coming down the companion-way. Stott stopped, glanced round, saw they were alone, and said in a low voice:

'I should like you to understand, Morrison, that I'm not resentful for what you did this afternoon. In fact, I'm very grateful. You handled what must have been an unpleasant job tactfully.'

'That's very generous of you, sir,' Morrison answered, and he really meant it. 'Thank you very much.'

'We needn't speak of it again, but I'll not forget it, the Major answered, almost in his daughter's words, then nodded and passed on.

Morrison soon found that though the incident was buried,

it was not forgotten. Next day he passed Margot seated with some friends on deck and she greeted him with unusual friendliness. 'Come and tell us what's going to happen to us tomorrow,' she called, and when he went over she introduced him as she would a complete equal, 'Mr Morrison's been so kind to me, she went on, telling the story of the forgotten books.

'Tomorrow's the star turn of the trip,' he assured them. 'We'll be off the Cuillins between Skye and Rum. Gorgeous views both sides.'

'I thought it was always foggy there?' asked a Miss Maudsley, who sat next Margot.

'I'll see that it's clear for you tomorrow,' he returned gravely. 'But I recommend the shore excursion. A bit tiring, but well worth while.'

'We should have been ashore at Portree today, only that we've got people coming aboard.'

'They'll be here in half an hour,' he explained, passing on.

He was on deck when the planes arrived and he witnessed the Stott reunion. Elmina Stott—he knew her name from his registers—was a tall, hard-faced woman of perhaps five-and-forty, with a domineering manner and ultra-fashionable clothes. In her somewhat perfunctory greeting to Wyndham there was a hint of contempt, while her cool nod to Margot suggested absolute dislike. Her son, Percy Luff, was a weedy-looking youth of some two- or three-and-twenty, with a vague air of dissipation, a vacant expression and a loud laugh. Morrison at once ruled him outside the pale because of the offensive way he spoke to a steward who was carrying his suitcase. Morrison had no opportunity to register further impressions, as the party drifted below to inspect their cabins.

Their coming proved an unexpected blessing to Morrison. Margot seemed less occupied and was to be seen at more frequent intervals as he went about the ship, ostensibly on business, but really in the hope of meeting her. She was friendly at all these encounters and did not seem to want to hurry away. He was careful to avoid personal matters and at first they kept to generalities. But on the Sunday on which they were off Barra and Eriskay, she asked him directly about himself, and their talk became more intimate.

'You told me how you came into this ship,' she said, after a pause, 'and that you had been with the Boscombe travel people before. I've wondered whether you're pleased or sorry you made the change?'

'Pleased,' he returned decidedly. 'Oh, yes, definitely. I like travelling of any sort, you see. And I like being on a big boat. Then, the work's pleasant and the pay's good. And'— he hesitated for the fraction of a second, then decided to risk it—'if I had stayed with the Boscombe people I shouldn't have met you.'

'An important matter,' she laughed, and once again he breathed freely. 'Had you always wanted to go to Boscombe's?'

'No.' He felt that with this opening he might be excused if he told her the history of his life. 'As a matter of fact, I was intended for the diplomatic service. My father was a merchant. He was the head of a big firm with branches at Calcutta and several of the towns of India. I went to Haileybury and then on to Cambridge. Then my father died suddenly and it was found that though he had been so well off, he had left very little money. He had, as a matter of fact, been speculating. My mother—there were then just the two of us—had enough to live on, but her money ceased when she died two years later. Though I had a little, it was not enough to continue at Cambridge, so I chucked it and began looking for a job. My love of travel and my rather slight knowledge of languages got me my place at Boscombe's, the first agency I tried. And that's'—he smiled—'the whole of my eventful life.'

'I'm glad you told me,' she said. 'It was good of you. But I guessed you'd been at Cambridge.'

'You didn't? How?'

'I don't know. There's something about Cambridge men. It's unmistakable.'

As she spoke, her friend Miss Maudsley passed. She called her over. 'I'm getting more information from my travel oracle,' she explained. 'Come and listen.'

'I can tell you all about every place,' Morrison played up.

Miss Maudsley cocked a supercilious eye. 'True stories?' she demanded.

'Oh, well, you can't have everything,' Morrison protested. 'You can have the truth or the story, whichever you like. No reasonable being would ask for both.'

'Tell us about Staffa and Fingal's Cave,' Margot suggested. 'I'm anxious to see those.'

He enlarged on the subject, finally coming to geology. 'Columnar basalt,' he explained. 'A great bed of it is believed to cross the sea basin to Northern Ireland. If the weather's kind to us, we'll see this end of it on Tuesday, and in a week more, the other end at the Giant's Causeway near Portrush. That bed is the actual causeway, where the giants crossed in old times.'

'Can you promise us any giants?' asked Miss Maudsley.

'I should be glad to arrange it,' he returned; 'only, unfortunately, it's not my department. Giants are done by the Chief Officer.'

'I believe that's only an excuse,' drawled the young woman.

'Well, I'll tell him about it,' Morrison declared; 'but, of course, I can't guarantee what he'll do.'

'At all events, I hope you'll come in the boat with us and show us what to look at.'

Crushing down his exultation, he promised, and presently Miss Maudsley passed on.

'Another place I want to see is Portrush,' continued Margot. 'I've always heard it's a wonderful place.'

'It's all of that,' he assured her, delighted that she had remained behind. 'But it wants good weather to enjoy it properly.'

'Do you know all the places in the world?' she mocked. 'Personal reminiscences of everywhere?'

'There were no personal reminiscences of Staffa. I've never been in Fingal's Cave. Every time we've called it's been too rough to see it.'

'You are'—she looked appraisingly over him—'a complete fraud.'

'Oh, no, I assure you,' he protested. 'That's just business. It sounds more impressive if you hold forth on places. And not a bit of a fraud. All the information was dead right.'

'How do you do it?'

'Pity to kill so fine an illusion, but before we started cruising I filled up my office with the best set of reference books I could find. Easy when you know the way, isn't it?'

'I still think you're a complete fraud.'

'Well, I call that mean, after my telling you how it was done. But I'm not a fraud about the Giant's Causeway. That I have not only read about, but seen. And after all your offensive remarks, you owe it to me to let me prove my statements by showing you round it.'

'I'd love that. But I'm afraid it's not going to be possible. They're all mad to cut the Causeway and play golf instead. The Portrush Links, you know.'

'I'll tell you about that, Miss Stott. On the first visit to Portrush the experienced traveller goes to see the Causeway, Dunluce, and perhaps Carrick-a-Rede, and on the second he plays golf. Don't make the mistake of putting it the wrong way round.'

'I know. I do feel that way myself, but what can I do?'

'I'll tell you what you can do. Let those who will play golf, and you come with me.'

'I'd love it,' she repeated. 'We'll settle it between this and then.'

Though neither of them knew it, their tentative arrangement was to prove the most momentous either had ever made. From the moment of speaking these few sentences, their entire history became changed and tragedy crept into their up-to-then peaceful lives.

Two days later, on the Saturday, while the ship still cruised to the south of Skye and there were excursions to Mallaig and Loch Alsh, Malthus and Mason came aboard. Morrison recognised Malthus the instant he stepped out of the flying boat, but he never supposed that Malthus would remember him. However, meeting on the deck after lunch Malthus looked at him and stopped.

'I've seen you before,' he observed. 'Where was it?'

'In the Paris–Calais boat-train,' Morrison answered pleasantly. 'About two years ago, Mr Malthus. I was travelling with Bristow.'

For a moment Malthus looked slightly taken aback; then

he grinned. 'I remember. I also remember thinking how unwise it was of you two to talk secrets in public.'

'So we found it, sir,' Morrison assured him drily.

'Then you should thank me for a useful lesson. Well'—his manner changed—'that's past and forgotten. You seem to have done well with the idea!'

'I've nothing to complain about,' and Morrison repeated the remark about his salary which he kept for such emergencies.

Just then Mason strolled up and Malthus introduced Morrison. 'This is one of the young men I told you about who travelled to Calais a couple of years ago. I don't think I heard your name? Ah, Morrison. This is Mr Mason, one of our would-be directors.'

Mason was a small clean-shaven man with sharp eyes. 'How do?' he said carelessly. 'That belongs to ancient history which we've forgotten.'

'I've told him so,' Malthus returned; 'and to prove it we're going to call on Stott and offer to smoke the pipe of peace.'

They were specious, almost friendly, and yet Morrison didn't take to either. There was that altogether too wide-awake expression about their eyes which made it hard to bank too heavily on their good faith. He made a civil reply and passed on.

9

At the White Rocks

Ten days later, in faultless weather, the *Hellénique* passed up the coast of County Antrim in Northern Ireland. She had worked gradually south round the Mull of Kintyre, past Sanda and Pladda and into the Firth of Clyde for Arran and Bute. She had just now called at Larne to set ashore a party who were to drive by the famous Coast Road to Glengariff and Ballycastle.

Keeping well—but not too well—outside the three-mile limit, the great ship left the Maidens Rocks with their lighthouse astern, while faint on the horizon showed Kintyre and Wigtown on starboard bow and quarter respectively. To port every detail of the coast could be seen in the clear air: Garron Point, the Glengariff Gap and the great cliff of Fair Head. After circling Rathlin Island, she put into Ballycastle Bay to pick up the shore party, then, turning west, she passed as it grew dusk Benbane Head and Pleaskin Head beside the Giant's Causeway. Till 1.00 a.m., while the gaming-rooms remained open, she cruised at dead slow out at sea; then anyone who was awake would have heard the engines increase their speed for a little time, then slow and stop. Some of those with outside cabins might have distinguished the subsequent roar of the chain from the hawse-holes as the anchor was dropped. Finally, silence reigned on board.

When Morrison came on deck next morning he found they were lying in the Skerries Roads off Portrush, with the town to the south, the Skerries Islands to the north, the promontory of Ramore Head to the west and Dunluce and the Causeway Heads to the east. In the clear morning sunshine, he thought it as charming a prospect as any he had seen. The hard, cold blue of the water reflected the more delicate azure of the sky and contrasted with the rich yellow of the sand, which ran up into dunes of paler tint, crowned with the greyish green of bents and grasses. Sea and sand appeared almost incredibly clean. Even the rocks, showing a huge variety of browns and greys, looked as if they had recently been washed—as, indeed, in that country of frequent rain, they had. Even the further headlands, faint as if viewed through blue gauze, were beyond all question spotless. Everything, indeed, that Nature had done was perfect: it was only when he came to view the works of man, as exhibited in the houses of Portrush, that his critical faculty revived.

Morrison was on fire with eagerness as he stood on the boat-deck looking round him. It was not the beauty of the view which had excited him, but something much more personal. The great excursion had been arranged! Margot, alone, was going with him to visit the Causeway!

He could scarcely believe in his good fortune. And yet perfection was not absolutely perfect. He was not to enjoy the drive with her from Portrush. He was to go in the forenoon and she to follow later.

119

In this disappointment, he had simply been hoist with his own petard. He had devised an elaborate scheme to ensure his being sent for lunch to the Causeway. His plan had worked so far as he himself was concerned, but her contribution had broken down.

'I think,' he had told old Stott, 'that we should do a new excursion in these parts: the Causeway in the morning, lunch there, and along the coast in the afternoon. If you agree, I'll slip out to the hotel and see if they could do the lunch.'

Stott readily agreed, and Morrison rang up the hotel manager, making an appointment for the morning. Then at the last moment Margot announced that she had been forced to accompany her family to lunch with some friends who were staying at Portrush. She was sorry, but she would take a taxi out immediately after lunch.

Morrison at once rang up the hotel manager, only to find that he would not be available after one o'clock. After all he had said to old Stott, Morrison felt he must see the man, so the drive with Margot had gone west.

Portrush being a popular port of call, a good many more people than usual went ashore. Some, on excursion bent, were bound for the Causeway, the Salmon Leap at Coleraine or other points of local interest, but by far the majority plumped for golf on the famous links. Bristow belonged to this party. He went ashore in the same boat as Morrison, his clubs beside him.

'Golf for you?' asked Morrison. 'Ever been round these links?'

'No,' Bristow answered, dabbling his hand into the tiny passing wavelets. 'I've never had the nerve. I'm not much of a golfer, you know. I intended to go round when I was here six weeks ago settling up for this call, but the links were too crowded. This time, with the season over and the place half empty, I'm going to try my hand.'

'Photography, too?' went on Morrison, glancing at the camera slung over the other's shoulder.

Bristow made a grimace. 'Victimised again,' he complained. 'Old Stott has heard of some bally ruin on that hill behind the town and wants the usual. How did you escape this time?'

'Been sent to the Causeway to get information for further trips.'

'Good Lord I should have thought we'd fixed up all the trips in the British Isles. Well, here are two men from the Club to meet me,' he continued, as they stepped ashore at the temporary boat-slip near the Ladies' Bathing Place. 'Cheerio, and don't die of overwork.'

Once more Morrison had that little feeling of surprise that he did not take more to Bristow, who could be, as on this occasion, exceedingly pleasant. But there was something in him which he found vaguely repellent. Whether the man had too keen an eye to the main chance, or whether in his composition lurked some hidden streak of selfishness, he didn't know. All he was sure of was that he felt towards him as the poet to Dr Fell.

Morrison duly drove out to the Causeway, discussed his business with the manager and, passing on to the dining-room, began his lunch.

In these last ten days he believed that he and Margot had drawn much nearer to one another. She now greeted him as an old friend, and it no longer happened that when they met she was just on the way elsewhere. He thought she was actually growing to like him, and he gloried in the belief.

121

He had no plans for the future. He was still in that state when he could see no further than the moment. To be with Margot: just to bask in her presence: that was what he longed for. If this were to lead to problems in the future, well, the future could look after itself. He would take what joy he could get, while it was to be had.

This afternoon, he felt, was going to be the greatest of his life. At worst, it would be joy unmixed: at best he might—or was he mad to think so?—he might propose, and—she might accept! His lunch was a good lunch, but he was too eager and excited to eat.

Then suddenly the bottom fell out of his entire world.

A summons to the telephone: Margot's voice. A crescendo of joy swept up in him, followed immediately by a dashing, ghastly, hideous disappointment. She was extremely sorry, but she was being carried off to visit friends at Castlerock, and she couldn't therefore come to the Causeway. Again she was so sorry, and she hoped they would have their excursion elsewhere on another day.

The sun still shone, but there was no longer brightness and warmth in its beams; just a cold, pitiless glare. The landscape was still there, but a dead landscape; hard and austere and repellent. The later accessories of his excellent lunch lay before him, but now the thought of food made him ill. The world was a great void—loathsome, damnable. For the moment he wished he was dead.

Like a man in a dream, he paid his bill and wandered out into the hateful void. Once again he had no plans. The remainder of this ghastly day had somehow to be put in. How should he do it?

At first he neither knew nor cared. Then gradually an urge for physical movement grew up in him. It was some eight miles to Portrush. He might as well walk back. It would pass the time and, though this he thought unlikely, the exercise might possibly relieve his feelings.

He took the Portrush road, tramping along like an automaton with head down and shoulders hunched forward, paying scant attention to the scenery and nursing his dull load of disappointment. But gradually the extreme sombreness of his mood changed. After all, everything was not necessarily lost. He had no reason to suppose that this would be the last day either of his or Margot's life. In all human probability, he would see her again, and the Giant's Causeway was not the only beauty spot in the British Isles.

Passing through Bushmills, he began the long ascent to the White Rocks, taking as he walked a gradually increasing interest in his surroundings. The sun began to cheer up slightly, and the country grew less repellent. The sea, indeed, was looking almost attractive, clear and fresh and vividly blue. Far out on the horizon he could see the great bulk of the *Hellénique*, creeping very slowly westward towards the open Atlantic. He pictured what was taking place on board: Anderson and Miss Pym doing his work in that office, the routine of the ship, and those maniacs down in the bilges, sitting round their tables at their infernal games. Bad and all as were his present circumstances, he was at least better off than they.

He tramped on, the road rising and getting closer to the sea, till it was skirting the edge of the cliffs. Presently he reached the summit and rounding a little bluff, saw lying before him the sandhills, the golf links, the splendid East Strand, with Portrush and Ramore Head beyond.

He had come to a straight stretch of the road some three or four hundred yards long, when he decided to get out on to one of the headlands for a better view of the cliffs. Accordingly, he climbed the low wall bounding the road, and made his way to where the grass ended and the cliff dropped sheer to the water below. It was a broken coast and at each side of him were gullies, with further irregularly-shaped rock masses beyond. For a few moments he gazed in admiration, then turned back to the road.

He had just reached the wall, and was about to climb over, when he saw a man appear a couple of hundred yards nearer Portrush. The man entered upon the road from the sea side, and, after looking up and down, appeared to consult a map. Then he crossed the road and disappeared over its inland side. It seemed unlikely that he could have seen Morrison, hidden as he was by the wall.

Now there was nothing remarkable in all this. But what immediately aroused Morrison's interest was that the man was old Stott. On the prowl for ruins, he thought. A second lot, evidently, as Bristow had said his was on Ballywillan Hill at the back of the town.

The matter, of course, had nothing to do with Morrison, and he climbed back over the wall and resumed his walk towards Portrush. In a few seconds he came to the place where Stott had crossed, and he saw that on the sea side there was an easy ascent from the beach. Visible evidence of Stott's passage up it remained in the shape of three footprints across a patch of sandy earth.

On the other side of the road was a curiously shaped basin or dell full of stunted trees and shrubs. Trees in the open on that windswept coast were practically non-existent and the occasional ones which had survived were small and distorted, with their few branches turned inland, like hunched-up old men cowering before the blast. To look at those trees was almost to see the wind, and their appearance made Morrison think what a magnificent sight a winter gale in such a place must be.

The wooded basin was an exception to the rule. Here was shelter—of a kind. The surrounding lip broke the fury of the wind. The trees had seized on the protection, and though they were all stunted and miserable, they were at least putting up a fight for life. At the back of the hollow Morrison could see high ground, bleak and deserted.

It was into this thicket that Stott had gone. Presumably the ruin was in the hollow. Though admittedly the ancients chose hills rather than hollows for their buildings, the circumstances here were special. No doubt early man selected the place for the same reason as had the present-day trees. Giving it an interested glance, Morrison was about to pass on when a sudden sound brought him up with a jerk.

A choking shout or cry came from the spinney, a hoarse scream cut off quickly and dying away in a rather hideous gurgle.

For a moment Morrison stood as if turned to stone. It was obviously his duty to investigate, but he was no hero and always shrank from taking unweighed responsibilities. However, he did not delay long. Screwing up his courage, he stepped off the road and hurried into the little wood.

'Anyone there?' he shouted. There was no answer. He repeated the call.

The coppice was surprisingly thick. Between the trees were masses of close-growing bushes which made passage difficult and a view impossible. But he pushed ahead, calling out at intervals. He worked through to the opposite side of the saucer, then turning, came more slowly back.

About half-way to the road, almost in the centre of the

little wood, he happened to notice on his left a freshly broken twig. He turned past it, devoutly wishing he were out of the horrible place. Then, after walking a few yards, he once again became rigid.

On the grass of a tiny clearing between clumps of poor-looking pines lay a man, and though Morrison could not see his features, he knew instantly that it was old Stott. He had fallen forward in a heap with his back bent and his head down near his knees. His arms were twisted beneath him, and he looked as if he had not gone down instantaneously, but had made some kind of struggle. His hat lay close by. Morrison was sure he was dead. Though he had only once before seen a corpse, there was that about Stott that left no doubt whatever.

Gingerly he stepped nearer, and then saw what he had missed in that first quick glance. The back of Stott's head was dented between the bald top and the light fringe of grey hair. Though the skin was not broken and there was no blood, there was a definite hollow beneath which the skull must be shattered.

Morrison shivered. Even in that first moment of shock he realised that this could be no accident. There was nothing in the spinney to produce an injury of that kind. No fall could do it, no branch pushed aside and slapping back into position. No, only human agency could have brought about such a result.

With a shrinking horror growing in his mind, Morrison realised that he was in the presence of murder. Murder! And only just committed. It seemed fantastic, incredible. Five minutes before, Stott had been alive and well: and now—he would never move or speak or take photographs again.

And there was more than that in it. Murder involved

murderer, and that murderer must be close by. He must almost certainly be in the spinney. Perhaps, Morrison felt, he was at that moment watching him. Perhaps he was creeping up behind him, ready with whatever he had killed Stott, to make a second blow.

Morrison realised that he was in very real danger. He knew too much. The murderer would see that his presence meant that within a few minutes the Portrush police would be on the scene, whereas only for him the body might not have been found for days: not until the scent was cold.

Fearfully, Morrison glanced behind him. He could see nothing untoward, but the shrubs were thick and horribly close. Anyone could approach unseen, and a single blow might make his head like Stott's.

It was clear that for his own sake he must get out of the wood as quickly and silently as he could. For poor Stott's sake also. He could do nothing for him, except to help to avenge him. And the quicker he brought the police, the greater their chance of doing it.

His heart was thumping like a mill as he retraced his steps, darting quick glances round in search of an enemy. But he saw no one, and had almost reached the road when another idea struck him, and for the third time he stopped dead in his tracks.

He had been hurrying to the police partly to do his obvious duty, and partly also to escape a threatened danger. Now he wondered if he was no about to incur an infinitely more hideous peril. Would the police believe his story?

There were, indeed, some disquietingly good reasons why they should not. For one thing he was believed to hate Stott. On various occasions Stott had been extremely offensive to him in the presence of others, and hatred would not be unnatural. Indeed, he had been overheard expressing something very like it. Only recently he had been abusing the man to Bristow, when that reptile Pointer, the steward, had overheard, Morrison imagined with what secret joy Pointer would tell that story at the inquest, and he could not but see how badly it would look. And Bristow would have to admit its truth. He certainly had been foolish.

His story would also sound anything but convincing. What an extraordinary coincidence it was, it would be said, that he should just be passing the spinney at the precise moment that Stott screamed! The coincidence had happened, but who would believe it? The story, moreover, was suspicious. It would be precisely what a guilty man would tell. He would realise that, having been beside the body, he might have left some trace of his presence: a footprint, some small object dropped. The story would explain this innocently, hence its adoption.

Another point. Could anything be made out of his friendship for Margot? The proposed lunch and excursion to the Causeway would come out, and he was sure his talks with her aboard the *Hellénique* had been witnessed. Could it be assumed that old Stott had heard about the affair and had warned him off? Of course there would be no proof of this, yet the police might assume something of the kind to strengthen their case.

The more Morrison thought over his situation, the more uneasy he grew. Would he be wise to report what he had seen? Would it not be safer to walk on to Portrush and go aboard the ship as if nothing had happened? If he did so, no one could disprove his statement. If he slipped out of the spinney unobserved, no one could know that he had ever been in it.

Then suddenly he felt the first beginnings of real panic. Suppose he returned to the ship and it was discovered that he had left a trace of his presence? If so, he could scarcely escape conviction. That he had lied about the affair would prejudice any jury. No, better to go at once to the police than risk that.

But the original objection to that course remained. Morrison waited in a fever of indecision. One thing, however, was certain. Whatever he did subsequently, he must get out of this damned wood immediately. The murderer couldn't be far away. As he stood thinking, he felt like a man being stalked by a tiger.

Suddenly he knew that he could not tell the police. It would be too dangerous. Circumstances had woven a net round him, and he could not prove his innocence.

Then the possible footprint?

He set his jaw. There was only one thing to be done. He must retrace his steps and examine every foot of the way he had walked. Only so could he have an easy mind.

It took all of his not very obtrusive courage to do it. As he walked, he kept glancing to right and left, as if behind some of these closely pressing shrubs a sandbag might be raised in waiting. All sorts of strange sounds leapt to his excited ears, little rustlings and cracklings, suggesting stealthy movements relentlessly following him up.

He did not, however, find any footprints—his own or any other person's. Most of the ground was covered with a poor grass, but there were many patches of sandy earth where such should show. Fearfully, he hoped his search was adequate.

At length for the second time he reached the body. No, there were no traces here either. And yet, what was that?

Just as he was about to turn away he saw a definite footprint.

Its discovery gave him a shock. If he had missed this at first glance, might he not have missed others? He fervently hoped not, but he felt he simply *could not* go over his route again.

The print showed a smooth sole, and as he wore rubber soles with a pattern, it could not be his. He need therefore do nothing about it. He was just turning away when his eyes caught an irregularity in the centre, and he stooped to examine it.

Some pieces of thread stuck out of the smooth earth. He felt he should let them alone and get away, and yet some urge came over him and he seized them and pulled. There was a slight resistance, and they came away, drawing after them a button.

Morrison gasped as he examined that button. It was one of those round ones covered with plaited leather which are often worn on tweed sports coats. And like a flash he remembered where he had seen just such another: hanging by a loose thread. It was on the sleeve of Percy Luff's coat!

10

Morrison and the D.I.

Morrison had been dismayed when he found the body of Stott, but now as he stood dangling the little leather-covered ball he was filled with absolute horror. Percy Luff! Margot's step-brother guilty of murder! It couldn't be!

Yet if this button had really come from the man's coat-sleeve, what other conclusion was possible? Had Luff been there for an innocent purpose, Morrison would have seen him. He, Morrison, must have reached the body within three or four minutes of the murder, and he had called 'Anyone there?' close to the place quite two minutes earlier, when he passed it on his way across the basin. It was inconceivable that Luff could have been out of earshot. And he had not answered. Why not? Could there be any explanation but the one?

And yet might there not be another? Might Luff not have come on the scene while the tragedy was actually in progress, have seen the murderer and have given instant chase? If so, might he not have been too far off or too much engaged to hear Morrison's call, even two minutes after the crime?

Morrison tried to comfort himself with this view, but with poor success. Horror at what might come to concern Margot remained his chief emotion.

The discovery, however, solved his most pressing problem. If there were any chance of Luff being guilty, the police must be told nothing. As Morrison had already seen, the sooner they got on the job, the greater the likelihood that success would crown their efforts. In this case they must not succeed. There must be no chance of Margot's step-brother being brought to justice.

It followed that the button must be removed. But Morrison could not bring himself to destroy it. If by any evil chance his own visit to the hollow were discovered, self-defence might require its production. He therefore slipped it into his pocket, intending to hide it in some safe place on the ship.

He looked sharply round to see that no other traces remained near the body. Then he returned to the road and, after prospecting carefully, managed to slip across it, as he believed, completely unobserved. He avoided treading on the sandy patch where Stott had left his footprints, working gradually down to the shore. There he continued on for the two remaining miles to Portrush, walking above high-water level, where the sand was running and would leave no clear footprints.

His horror grew as he thought of the motive Luff might have had for the deed, or which at least might be imputed to him. He was in the direct line of succession. Wyndham Stott was to get John's money, and Elmina would see that her son was not overlooked. Luff had been gambling heavily since he came on board, and might very well be near the end of his resources, and for current needs Wyndham would be more squeezable than John. Further, old Stott had on

132

occasion a very rough tongue. He might well have spoken offensively to Luff, and equally well this might have been overheard. A strong case for motive could certainly be made, and more than ever therefore that finding of the button must be kept secret.

How could he, Morrison wondered, meet the people on the ship that evening and not give himself away? And how should he account for his afternoon if he were asked to do so? *When* he was asked to do so, he corrected himself, for he most certainly would be.

The truth, he thought, would be his only hope: the truth, that is, with the one significant omission. Probably he had been seen during his walk: very well, admit the walk. Now he was sorry he had not trodden on the sandy patch after leaving the road. If the matter were investigated early, the absence of his footprints might be commented on. Then he thought that no such early investigation would take place. Many hours must elapse before the discovery of the body.

By the time he reached the temporary boat-slip, he had himself well in hand, and he did not think his manner could arouse suspicion. There were few people returning in the boat, for it was early. The *Hellénique*, indeed, had just come inshore. As good luck would have it, he sat beside Carrothers, the Galashiels stockbroker, whom he knew but slightly, and who therefore couldn't so well judge abnormality in his manner. Once on board he escaped to his cabin and fortified himself with a double whisky before resuming his ordinary routine.

He found it easier to get along than he had anticipated. The complete normality of everyone else helped him, and the fact that his absence had left a good deal of work to

133

be done made it natural that he should spend the evening in his office.

All the same, he had some difficult moments. The first was his meeting with Margot. He would like to have postponed this until old Stott was missed, as in the resultant general excitement his own would be less noticeable. But he thought that politeness required it to take place as early as possible.

He therefore kept a look out for approaching boats. Soon Margot appeared, he was thankful to see, without her father.

'Frightfully sorry you couldn't make it,' he greeted her. 'I'm hoping for better luck next time.'

'Yes,' she answered, and her manner indicated that she really meant it, 'I was sorry, too. But I couldn't help myself. I just had to meet those people at Castlerock.'

One other person Morrison watched for, though he knew he would be wiser to go back to his office and stay there. But he felt that he must see if that button was still on Luff's sleeve. While not certain, it was likely that Luff had worn that coat that day.

The second boat after Margot's brought the young man, and a glance showed Morrison that he was wearing the coat. It was easy to get behind him as he walked down the alleyway. Then once again Morrison felt a little sick. The button was missing.

There was, of course, no actual proof that his find had come off this particular sleeve, but Morrison found the doubt too slight to afford him much comfort. Luff, and Margot's peace of mind, were in danger.

He delayed going down for dinner till late and was glad to find on arrival that all at his table had gone except one man. This luckily was a short-sighted, self-centred individual, and Morrison was sure he would not notice any agitation in his manner.

He was just finishing dinner when one of the Captain's boys approached him. 'Captain Hardwick's compliments, sir, and he would like to see you in his cabin.'

It was beginning!

Hardwick was seated at his desk, and Bristow and Grant, the purser, were on a settee facing him.

'Sit down, Mr Morrison,' Hardwick said shortly, pointing to a chair. 'Mr Stott has not come aboard and apparently has sent no message. I want to know if he said anything to you about his movements.'

Morrison shook his head. 'No, sir,' he answered in what he hoped was a normal voice. 'Nothing at all.'

'And you don't know his plans?'

'No, sir. I didn't even know he was going ashore.'

Hardwick nodded. 'All right, thank you. That's all.'

It was now getting on towards nine o'clock and the ship was still at anchor. Unless a move was soon made, either the law would be broken or the devotees of roulette would remain shut out of their paradise. As Morrison returned to his office, he would have given a month's salary to know what was being said in the Captain's cabin.

A decision had evidently been quickly reached, however, for he had not been working for more than a few seconds when the murmur of the engines came slow and muffled through the ship.

Next morning Morrison was early on deck, greeting as many of the ship's company as he could find and noting their demeanour. None showed the slightest excitement, and it was evident that the death of Stott was still unknown. Now, so amazingly do circumstances alter cases, he did something which, twenty-four hours earlier, would have been utterly inconceivable—he avoided Margot. Passing down the promenade deck he saw her appear round the end of a deck-house, and instantly had business in the vacant cabin of some complete stranger.

About nine he was summoned again to Captain Hardwick's cabin, just as the first shore boats were getting off. They were lying in Lough Swilly and there were excursions to Derry and certain districts of Co. Donegal. This time the Captain was alone.

'We've had no news from Mr Stott,' he began. 'I left a quartermaster ashore on the landing-stage at Portrush to wait for him. I've just rang him up and he tells me he was there all night, but saw no one.'

Captain Hardwick absently kneaded the lobe of his left ear between his finger and thumb, a habit he had when puzzled.

'It is so unlike Mr Stott not to advise me of his whereabouts that I have decided to inform the police. But I don't want to do it by telephone. I want you to go and see the chief officer at Portrush, or wherever he lives, and impress on him that the affair must be handled with discretion. You will realise that Mr Stott would be annoyed if there was unnecessary publicity, apart from the damage it would do the ship.'

Morrison received the commission with mixed feelings. The idea of discussing the affair with the police gave him cold shivers. It would be so fatally easy to make a slip; to know just a little too much. If the police were to say after the interview, 'How could he have told that?' it might be the end for him.

On the other hand, it might give him what he wanted

more than anything else in the world; first-hand information as to what was being done and how much the police had learnt. It simply meant that he must keep his wits about him, and school himself to appear only moderately interested.

'I understand, sir,' he returned; 'but the police will certainly ask me what was known of his movements aboard, and I'm not in a position to tell them.'

Captain Hardwick passed over a couple of typed sheets. 'I appreciate that,' he returned. 'I've got the available information here, with all the photographs of Mr Stott that we could find. You may explain that I've not made a general enquiry. I've only questioned a few people to whom he might have spoken—like yourself. If Mr Stott has not turned up by the time you reach Portrush, I want you to discuss that point—the making of enquiries aboard. Legally, I can do it, and I don't know who else can. I don't want the job, as it's outside my line and it requires an expert. And don't forget to mention that this is a French ship.'

Morrison thought over that last remark as the launch took him and some forty other travellers ashore to the wharf at Buncrana. Could British police function aboard a French ship? Would French police interest themselves about a tragedy in Northern Ireland? It looked as if some interesting legal questions might soon arise. But, whatever was done, he feared there would be no chance of the enquiry falling between two stools. Some authority would be out to bring the murderer to justice.

He took a bus into Derry, arriving in time to catch the midday train to Portrush. Again the weather was good, and in spite of his perturbation he could not but admire the views as they ran along the bank of the River Foyle.

Then, when they turned inland, over the flat lands of the Eglinton Intakes, he took out the papers Captain Hardwick had given him.

They contained but little helpful information. It appeared that Stott had gone ashore on the previous morning, taking his camera. He had then hired a local boat and been rowed over to the biggest of the Skerries, the islands lying a couple of miles out to sea. He had spent some time wandering about, returning to the Northern Counties Hotel about one o'clock. There he had lunched with Carrothers and one or two other passengers, not by arrangement, but through meeting them accidentally in the lounge. He had told them of his excursion, saying he had been looking for a ruin of which he had been told, but which he had not found. He was going, he explained, in search of another ruin in the afternoon, and they wished him better luck.

After lunch they separated, Carrothers and his friends going for a drive. This was corroborated by the Wyndham Stott party, who had also lunched in the hotel. When they left, John Stott was sitting in the lounge, reading the paper. He nodded and exchanged a few remarks as they passed. All who saw him agreed that his manner and appearance were completely normal. He was last seen by the Second Officer, who had leave ashore, walking past the Ladies' Bathing Place in the direction of the East Strand.

This information was obtained in the first instance from Wyndham Stott, who was the first person Hardwick approached. He had put the Captain on to Carrothers, whom he had seen with John at lunch.

It seemed, then, to Morrison that his idea had been correct: that Stott had gone ashore to photograph some ruin in the wooded saucer. If so, someone else had known where he

138

was going. Luff had known and had denied it, unless the evidence of the button was wholly misleading. And if Luff were not the murderer, then someone else had known it also. Whom, he wondered, had old Stott told?

Then Morrison saw that to reason in this way was madness. All he knew was that old Stott had not returned to the ship on the previous night and that Captain Hardwick had sent him to report to the police. To fill his mind with the pros and cons of the case meant a terrible danger of saying too much in the coming interview.

At Portrush he began by seeing the quartermaster who had been left to look out for Stott, only to learn the not surprising fact that no further trace of the man had been seen. He must therefore carry on his mission. He thought lovingly of a double whisky before adventuring himself in the lions' den, but he realised that if by chance he became suspected, the fact that he had done so might increase that suspicion. Rallying his courage, he therefore went to the police station, or barracks, as it is called in Ireland.

'I want to see the chief officer, please,' he said, handing over his card to the saturnine-looking constable who came forward.

'The D.I.'s here this morning by chance,' the man returned gloomily. 'Would it be him or the sergeant you were wanting?'

This was a poser to Morrison, who had no idea what a D.I. was. 'Whichever is the superior officer,' he explained.

The constable looked scandalised. Then a crafty look appeared in his eyes. 'You would be English maybe?' he asked, and when Morrison admitted it, his expression relaxed as if he were granting him a fool's pardon. 'Then it'll be the D.I.,' he concluded. 'That's the District Inspector from Ballymoney. He's over the whole area. The sergeant's only over Portrush.'

'Then the D.I., if you please.'

The man hesitated as if he were considering asking Morrison his business, then, thinking better of it, he vanished through an internal door. There was a muttering of voices, ending with the words, 'Show him in.'

'He'll see you now,' announced the constable, reappearing.

A large, good-humoured looking officer with three chevrons on his sleeve followed the constable from the room. He glanced shrewdly at Morrison and wished him an agreeable good morning. Morrison passed in and the door closed behind him.

He found himself in a small but efficient-looking office facing a tall man with a dark, intelligent face and a strong jaw. He was dressed in tweeds which had seen better days, and his cap, reposing on a side table beside a bag of golf clubs, was also well worn. Yet at his first word Morrison realised he was a man of education and breeding. Instinctively also he felt he was efficient and tenacious, and anything but a fool. His panic, which he thought he had overcome, surged back, but with all his strength of mind he pulled himself together.

The D.I. half rose in his seat as he waved his visitor to a chair. 'Mr Harry Morrison,' he read from the card, then swung round with a faint smile. 'And what can I do for you, Mr Morrison?'

'I'm transport officer in the *Hellénique*, as you see from my card,' Morrison answered, 'and I've been sent by her Captain to report that one of the passengers came ashore yesterday morning here at Portrush and has not returned to the ship. It was a Mr John Stott,' and he went on to describe the man's position on board, passing over the photographs and statements. 'In one sense,' he continued, considering his words carefully, 'Captain Hardwick has no reason to fear that anything may have happened to him. It is merely the fact that he didn't come aboard and didn't send a message, and that such a thing never occurred before. Mr Stott has changed his arrangements previously, but he always let us know.'

'But if the Captain has reported the matter to us, he must think it serious. What exactly does he want us to do?'

'He wanted really to get your advice. If, from what I have told you, you think enquiries should be made, then he would be grateful if you would make them. On the other hand, if you advise waiting a little longer, he will be satisfied to do so. But he hoped in any case that as far as possible you would avoid publicity.'

The D.I. looked at him doubtfully. 'We can't make enquiries as to the whereabouts of a missing man without some publicity,' he pointed out.

'Of course, Captain Hardwick realises that. It was only to ask you to keep the affair as quiet as was reasonably possible.'

The other nodded. 'Well, wait till I read these statements. Smoke if you want to.'

Hoping it would steady his nerves, Morrison lit a cigarette, while he stole glimpses of the dark, powerful face with its intent expression. The D.I. read everything through twice, then he fixed his eyes on Morrison's. 'Now I'd like to know what's not in these statements, he said shortly. 'What's your own idea as to what has happened, and what's the Captain's?'

Morrison gaped, then answered: 'I don't know. I have no idea myself and Captain Hardwick expressed no opinion.'

'What I want to get at its whether he has any reason to suspect foul play?'

Again Morrison hesitated. It would be unwise to be too glib. 'As far as I know, he has none. I personally imagine that Mr Stott stayed ashore deliberately and sent us a message which miscarried. But, of course, I've no evidence for that.'

'What sort of a man was this Stott? Might he have got drunk?'

'I've never known him to take too much, but, again, I can't say.'

'I'm to take it then that, for all you or the Captain know to the contrary, he might be lying drunk somewhere, or have had a fall when he was looking for his ruin? If it was Dunluce he went to photograph and he fell down the cliff, he might well be dead. We'll have a look round and make a few enquiries.'

'Thank you: that was what Captain Hardwick hoped you'd do.'

'We'll do what we can. But if there should be more in it than meets the eye, I imagine the solution would lie on board. Someone would then have to make more enquiries.'

'That's another point I was to discuss with you. Captain Hardwick wasn't very sure about procedure. You see, the ship is a French ship registered in Havre and licensed by the French Marine Department. He didn't know who would have the right to ask questions on board.'

The D.I. stroked his chin. 'I'm sure I don't either,' he returned, 'at least offhand. A new question to me altogether. The Captain, I take it, would have power to ask any questions he liked.'

'Yes, he said so. But he also said such an enquiry was out of his line and should be held by an expert.'

The D.I remained silent for some moments, evidently thinking deeply. 'Is there any reason for trying to keep this disappearance secret on board?' he then asked. 'I doubt if you'll be able to in any case. These things get out, you know.'

'I know they do,' Morrison agreed. 'I expect it's known already. The Captain's idea was merely not to make a fuss too early, which would have annoyed Mr Stott if he was all right.'

'Well, I suggest that if you hear nothing today, your Captain should post a notice saying Mr Stott has not advised him of his whereabouts and asking anyone who may have known his plans to communicate with him.'

'I'll tell him; and thank you for the hint.'

'Very good. Then we'll look into it at this end. How can we communicate with you?'

'You can telephone at any time. We have continuous wireless connection with the shore.'

'That's great. Then why, if I may ask the question, didn't you ring us up in the first instance?'

'Three reasons. The Captain thought he might have heard from Mr Stott by midday, and that till then he needn't trouble you. Secondly, we couldn't telephone the photographs. And, thirdly, generally speaking, he thought an interview would be more satisfactory than the phone.'

'I agree with him there.' The D.I. got up, again transfixing Morrison with his keen, shrewd glance. During this quiet conversation Morrison's panic had largely subsided, but that look brought it back. However, the fact that he was also getting up helped him to hide it, and he did not think the other noticed anything amiss.

'Thank you very much,' he said, he believed quite

143

normally. 'It's very good of you. I'll tell Captain Hardwick what you have said.'

A moment later he was once more in the open air, and certain that so far he was entirely unsuspected.

11

Fat in the Fire

Seated in the train on his way back to Derry, a new idea flashed into Morrison's mind.

Malthus and Mason!

A great relief surged through him as he realised that here in all probability was the explanation of the affair, and that Luff might not be guilty after all. If so, Margot had nothing to fear from the discovery of the truth; indeed, rather the contrary, as legatees in a murder mystery can seldom entirely escape suspicion.

What had Malthus and Mason come aboard for? Was it merely to gamble or have an unusual cruise, or was it for a more sinister purpose? Had their enmity against Stott been a running sore which could only be healed through action? If so, the affair was explained. If not, their presence on board at just this time was more than a strange coincidence.

Morrison could not understand why he had not thought of all this before. Then he saw that his mind had been too much filled, first, with his own peril and, second, with Luff's—or rather Margot's, for he didn't care two hoots

145

what happened to Luff. He had been obsessed with the button, as if there were not millions of buttons of that type in the world. It was a warning to him against jumping to conclusions.

He wondered if the idea had occurred to Hardwick? It now seemed so obvious that it was impossible to doubt it. Hardwick had had no personal emotions to cloud his judgment.

But suppose Hardwick had not thought of it? Would it be his duty to suggest it?

Then Morrison saw that he was forgetting—and it gave him a shock that he could have done so—that Hardwick didn't know that Stott was dead. Only himself and the murderer knew that. To have mentioned his idea would have been to have signed his own death warrant. His oversight brought out a cold sweat of fear.

When he reached the ship he found that news of the disappearance had leaked out. He had not left the deck before he was buttonholed by the inquisitive Mr Forrester.

'What's all this mystery about old man Stott?' he began, carefully blocking Morrison's path. He winked and Morrison became aware that a joke was about to be perpetrated. 'We hear he's run away with a barmaid.'

'That's news to me,' Morrison returned solemnly, 'and I'm interested to hear it. Have you heard who the barmaid is?'

'I hoped you could tell me that.'

'No. I've been ashore all day and I've not heard anything. What else is being said?'

Forester grew serious. 'That he went ashore yesterday afternoon and hasn't turned up since, and that foul play is feared.'

Morrison shook his head. 'That's news to me also,' he

146

declared. 'It's true he went ashore yesterday afternoon and hadn't returned when I left this morning, but the foul-play touch seems a rather gratuitous addition. I've not heard it mentioned.'

'Then what's your own theory?'

Morrison shrugged. 'Goodness only knows,' he answered as lightly as he could. 'Met a friend probably, and stayed over with him. Felt unwell and went to an hotel. Got drunk possibly. I don't know. Whatever he did, his message to the ship went adrift.

'You won't talk?' Forrester returned. 'Oh well, I could hardly expect you to.'

'I won't put out tales that I believe to be false, if that's what you mean,' Morrison retorted, robbing the words of offence with a smile, 'though I grant you they would be more interesting.'

Forrester made a pretence of sighing. 'Oh, well, if you won't, you won't. Had an interesting day?'

'So so. Local transport business, you know.'

Morrison was pleased with himself as he nodded and passed on. He had been afraid of the inevitable discussions which the affair would cause, and now, after sustaining the first, he felt reassured. He had borne himself better than he could have hoped. No one could possibly have suspected that he knew more than he pretended.

Captain Hardwick made no comment when he heard the D.I.'s advice, but later on Morrison saw the suggested notice posted in the ship. It increased the gossip and he was stopped on several occasions by curious passengers. This general belief that he knew something of the affair would have startled him had it not been that he found everyone in uniform was being similarly pestered.

The first real test of his self-control came when he met Margot on the promenade deck after dinner. She was alone and stopped.

'I'm so sorry,' he began, 'that you should have this annoyance and worry. I'm afraid it won't improve your holiday.'

'My holiday!' she returned sadly. 'This has been no holiday for me. I hated coming, and except for meeting new friends and so on, I've hated being on board. I begged my father to go an ordinary cruise to the Mediterranean, but he couldn't resist the tables. Then he suggested coming alone, but I wouldn't agree to that. I thought I could at least be a brake on him—with what success you know. Then this news about Uncle John! No, it hasn't been a holiday for me.'

Morrison had never heard her speaking so bitterly. She was usually so cheerful, giving the impression that she hadn't a care in the world. Now she seemed really upset. A warm flood of feeling towards her rose in his heart.

'I didn't know,' he said hesitatingly. 'I'd give anything to be able to help.'

She glanced at him gratefully. 'You have helped me already,' she returned, 'and it's a shame for me to grouse. I suppose there are thousands of girls in England who would give their ears to be able to do a trip like this. Tell me about Uncle John. What do you think has happened to him?'

This was the hardest question Morrison had yet had to answer. He could lie without difficulty to the police and to his fellow travellers. He could even lie on occasion to his Captain. But to Margot he felt he couldn't lie. And yet it had to be done. Not that he couldn't trust her with his secret. He would without hesitation trust her with his life. But if after all Luff should prove to be guilty, to tell her would probably make her feel an accessory after the fact, if, indeed, she would not actually become one. Apart from himself altogether, he could not risk that.

Therefore he replied as coolly as he was able. 'Not necessarily anything very dreadful, I feel sure,' he declared. 'I imagine he has acted in some quite normal way, gone home with a friend or something of that sort. I presume he sent a message to the Captain, and the whole trouble has arisen because that message has miscarried.'

'That's a comforting thought. It's not that I'm fond of Uncle John. I dislike him intensely; indeed, at times I almost hate him. So does Father, except that I think he hates him all the time. But, all the same, it would be dreadful if anything had happened to him.'

'There's no reason to suppose anything of the sort. We may hear something from him at any moment.'

'And that in spite of seeing the police about it? Captain Hardwick told Father you were going.'

'Oh, yes,' Morrison admitted. 'That was Captain Hardwick's obvious duty. If anything *had* happened and he had taken no steps, he would have been held to blame. But that doesn't say that he believes anything is wrong.'

'That's comforting again. I thought his informing the police was a sign that he feared the worst.'

'Not a bit of it: just an obvious routine precaution.'

'Well, I wish we could hear. The talk through the ship is horrible.'

She seemed in no hurry to move, and they stood together watching the rugged shores of Lough Swilly passing along on either hand. The Lough is a very deep gash into the land, an estuary, only that no large river flows into it, and the *Hellénique* was moving at nearly full speed to get outside the three-mile limit before 9 p.m. The evening was calm and peaceful, but beginning to get slightly chilly, even in the shelter of the music-room.

'If anything *has* happened to Uncle John,' Margot went on presently, 'what will they do? I mean, will there be enquiries on board and all that?'

'I really can't tell you,' he answered with truth. 'One thing that might become important is that this is a French ship.'

'Oh, but she isn't,' she retorted. 'The entire crew is English. There's nothing French about her except her name.'

'No, she's French through and through—legally. She belongs to a French company and carries a French certificate and sails under the French flag.'

'She belongs to Uncle John.'

'No doubt that's the actual fact, but he holds her through a French company—his own representatives, of course, but still French.'

'Well, suppose she is technically. What difference will it make?'

'Just that if she were English, English police could come aboard and make enquiries. As it is, I question if they can. I really don't know what the position is.'

As Margot was about to reply, Major Stott appeared round the corner of the music-room. She called him over.

'Mr Morrison has raised an interesting point, Daddy. We were talking about Uncle John and Mr Morrison's visit to the police today. He says that this is a French ship, and that if—if enquiries should have to be made, that might make a lot of difficulty. Tell him, Mr Morrison.'

Morrison did so as far as he was able. Wyndham Stott seemed interested. 'I knew she was technically French,' he observed, 'but I thought that was only to get over the legal difficulty of the gaming.'

'That's true, sir,' Morrison agreed; 'but all the other results of being a French ship follow.'

Wyndham nodded, as he drew slowly at his cigar. Then as if by an afterthought, he produced his case. 'Have one?' he invited. 'I don't know if you like cigars, but they're very mild.'

Morrison didn't particularly want it, but he thought it politic to accept. There was silence for a few seconds, then Wyndham changed the subject. 'Fine old ship this,' he declared, 'and unexpected to find her ending her life in this way. I knew her well in her best days. I went to the States in her on her second trip, and I've crossed in her, I suppose'— he paused—'five times altogether.'

'You know the States well, sir?'

Wyndham knew the States, and talked interestingly of his travels. When a little later Morrison parted from them, he was well pleased with this interview also. It had been a much more trying one for him than that with Forrester, and he had carried it off equally well. No other encounter would be as difficult, unless actual suspicion arose and he were interrogated by the police. And every hour that passed made that less likely.

His troubles for the evening, however, were not yet over. He had scarcely parted from the Stotts when he met Bristow.

'I was looking for you,' the latter said with some eagerness. 'Come to my cabin.'

Bristow's sitting-room was large and its furnishing was the last word in luxury and 'art'. Morrison sank back in a well-padded armchair and helped himself to the whisky to which the other pointed.

'What happened about the police?' Bristow asked, pouring out a larger allowance of the spirit than Morrison had yet seen him take. 'I didn't know you were back till I saw you just now.'

'Nothing very much happened,' Morrison returned, going on to give a more or less detailed report. 'The officer in charge—a D.I. they call him—looks no fool,' he ended up. 'If anyone can clear the thing up, I bet he's the man.'

'I've heard they're good, these Northern Ireland police,' Bristow commented. 'He didn't throw out any hints?'

'None, except for recommending the notice the Old Man has put up.'

'Then he thinks it's serious.'

'I imagined so. But he was a cautious gentleman: he wasn't giving anything away.'

'Hardwick thinks it's serious.'

'I imagined that, too, else he would scarcely have put up the notice.'

Bristow moved uneasily in his chair. 'What do you think yourself, Morrison? After all, you've known Stott longer than any of us. Would he have gone off like that and not let any of us know—unless he couldn't help himself?'

If Morrison had not been so afraid of saying the wrong thing, he would have seized this opportunity to get some of his own back. 'I've known him longer than you,' he admitted, but you've seen much more of him than I. I should have thought he'd have let us know. What's your own view?'

'It's because I feel certain of it that I am so uneasy, I feel absolutely convinced that if he hasn't phoned out, it's because he can't; in other words, because he's ill or dead.' Bristow seemed quite concerned.

'I agree with you,' Morrison admitted. 'But, you know, I

couldn't rise to any particular sorrow if he were. I don't like and never did like the man, and I don't see what matter it would make if he were dead.'

Bristow looked shocked, 'No matter?' he exclaimed. 'What are you thinking about, Morrison? You're surely not forgetting that he's carrying this entire outfit on his shoulders. Only for Stott your job and mine might go phut. Don't you know that?'

'But the outfit's paying, even if it hasn't paid well enough for me to get my ten per cent. For the matter of that, it's not paying you your forty-five either. You've been grousing enough about it, too.'

Bristow made a gesture of impatience. 'Yes, I know,' he said irritably. 'I agree it's paying for the moment, but if we got a bad spell Stott would carry it. If Stott has pegged out, and we get a bad spell, we'll go down: there's no margin nor reserve to carry us on. No, if anything's happened to Stott, it may be a damned serious thing for us.'

Morrison had not thought of this. He didn't, as a matter of fact, believe there was much in it, for Stott's money would go to Wyndham, and of all people Wyndham was less likely than any other to close the venture down. Moreover, the exchange of ownership might well be to the good. With Wyndham in charge, everyone would probably have a better time. He would be straight for one thing, and Morrison had grave doubts of old Stott's probity. Bristow, however, did not agree.

'Wyndham would mean well,' he admitted. 'He's decent enough in his way, and I dare say straight. But he's no business man. If he began trying to manage this thing he'd let it down. I agree old Stott's a swine, but, all the same, I'd rather work with him. He'll make the thing pay or carry it.'

'I imagine Wyndham wouldn't try to manage it,' Morrison suggested. 'He'd probably hand it over to you, or perhaps to you and Hardwick. He'd be too busy amusing himself at the tables.'

Bristow grunted, 'Another thing he might do would be to close the thing down. That daughter of his hates his playing, and if she had any say in things she'd make him do it. Morality stunt, you know.'

At this Morrison saw red. For calling Margot 'that daughter of his', and suggesting that her action under any conceivable circumstance could be otherwise than perfect, he could for the moment have killed Bristow. He did not answer while he struggled to get himself in hand. Then his fury passed, and he was able to reply normally.

He was interested to see how friendly and confidential the fear of disaster had made Bristow. He was now speaking as to an equal, with the same attractive and deferential manner which he had shown in the Calais express when the venture was only his unattained and apparently unobtainable dream. His superiority had vanished. He seemed indeed anxious to lean on Morrison, and received his optimistic replies with apparent satisfaction.

Next day they felt the slow, easy sweep of an Atlantic swell, their nearest land westwards being Labrador.

Early they were cruising along the rugged weatherbeaten coast of Donegal, past Melmore Head and Horn Head, round the grim-looking island of Tory, and down past Bloody Foreland, Gola, Owey and Aran. That day the shore excursion was from Burton Port to Killybegs, through Glenties and Ardara. Morrison had heard it was not a very interesting drive, and for once he watched the party start without wishing to join it. He enjoyed the open sea and the easy roll of the ship, and was glad to be on board.

Then when they had passed Rathlin O'Birne Island and were off the terrific cliffs of Slieve League there was news. John Stott's body had been found.

Morrison heard it from Bristow. He happened to be on deck after tea and noticed him leave the Captain's cabin. Bristow saw him and came over. He looked a good deal upset.

'Stott's dead,' he said shortly. 'Murdered!'

Morrison had no need to simulate distress. The news horrified him. He had never imagined that the body would be found so quickly and instantly he realised his own danger. His trail was far too fresh. Whatever had led the D.I. and his followers to that sinister saucer might well have told them that he had been on the scene at the time of the crime.

'Good God!' he muttered. 'Murdered!' He strove to keep calm. 'Then you and the Captain were right.'

Bristow nodded gloomily. 'I was afraid of it from the first.'

'Where was he found?' Morrison went on presently.

'I don't know. Hardwick didn't show me the message.'

'No details?'

'No: just that the body had been found and that foul play was evident.'

'Evident, not suspected?'

'No. They seemed sure of it.'

Panic was rising in waves in Morrison's mind, but he fought it down. 'Good God!' he said again; then after a few minutes he added: What do you think they'll do?'

'Do? What about?'

'I mean about an enquiry. There's bound to be one, I presume?'

Bristow looked at him in surprise. 'Bound to be an enquiry?' he repeated. 'Of course there's bound to be an enquiry. What in Hades do you mean?'

'Well, how can they hold it?' and Morrison put the point about the *Helénique's* French ownership.

'Oh, that?' Bristow answered. 'I don't know how they'll do it, but you may take it from me it'll be done. And if your description of this D.I. is correct, it'll be a pretty searching one at that.'

'I don't see how they'll manage it, all the same. Apparently the Captain's the only person who has the power to hold it, and he doesn't want to.'

Bristow seemed a good deal upset. 'It may make a lot of difference to us,' he said slowly, after a pause, 'how and where it's held. I can tell you I don't feel too happy about it. I've said a lot against Stott that I shouldn't have. And, for the matter of that, so have you.'

'I know,' Morrison returned, 'and I wish I hadn't. But I don't see that it really matters.'

'Oh, don't you? Can you account for all your time ashore? Because I can't.'

Morrison did an admirable imitation of a man staring in surprise.

'Bless my soul, Bristow,' he exclaimed, 'what do you mean? You're surely not suggesting that we could be suspected?'

Bristow made a gesture of impatience. 'Of course I'm suggesting it,' he retorted irritably. 'Can't you see it for yourself?'

Morrison tried to look baffled. 'Well, I can't,' he replied. 'Why should we? You've only just pointed out yourself that we stand to lose by his death.'

'I know I have, and it's true. But look at it from the police point of view. Our possible loss is hypothetical, but our grousing at the man was actual and concrete. A lot of people will tell the police that they heard us cursing him.'

Morrison could not help feeling relief at the thought that Bristow was as nervous as he himself, though he probably had less reason for it.

'How much of your time ashore can you not account for?' he asked.

Bristow looked at him curiously. 'An hour at least,' he returned 'I was with that golfing crowd all day except when I went off by myself to get those blessed photographs.'

Morrison was on the point of asking where he had taken the photographs, then he saw just in time that this again was the sort of remark that he should avoid.

The location of the photographs could only be of importance if one knew that of the murder. If Bristow said he was in the opposite direction to that of the crime, it would be so easy to reply: 'Then you're all right.' And a remark of that kind, once made, could be neither withdrawn nor explained.

Then he saw that to ignore the point might seem equally suspicious. 'I wish we knew where they found Stott,' he therefore went on, 'I was at the Causeway till getting on to three, and then I walked back to Portrush. It's a couple of hours' walk or more, and I got the boat that left at five. So I think I'm fairly all right. Where did you take your photos?'

'On that sloping hill at the back of the town—Ballywillan it's called, I believe. But I might have gone anywhere if I had hurried.'

'But you took the photographs? How many?'

'Five, as a matter of fact. But what has that to do with it?'

'Simply that if you were taking photos at Ballywillan you couldn't have been anywhere else. Won't the photos prove you were there?'

Bristow hesitated, then brightened up slightly. 'Confirmatory evidence of my statement, yes,' he admitted. 'It might or it might not be helpful. It depends, as you say, where Stott was found.'

Morrison was pleased with the conversation, which he thought he was carrying on very naturally. 'Can't you find that out?' he persisted. 'If we knew, it might relieve both our minds.'

'We'll hear it soon enough,' Bristow returned, relaxing into gloom.

Morrison thought that the propitious moment had at last arrived. 'Tell me,' he said in a lower tone, 'have you thought about Malthus and Mason?'

Bristow looked at him sharply. 'The first thing that occurred to me when I heard the news,' he returned. 'They were ashore, I know, for they came back in my boat.'

'You don't know how they spent the day?'

Bristow shook his head. 'I didn't see them. I'm sure they weren't on the links.'

'Do you think,' Morrison said hesitatingly, 'the police ought to be told about that business?'

'I do think so. But it's not our job. Hardwick will be running the thing and he knows all about it.'

'Does he?' Morrison's tone suggested doubt.

'Yes. I was present when he and Stott discussed it. That was when we knew those two were coming aboard. Stott wondered if they were out for trouble and warned Hardwick to be prepared.'

Morrison left the cabin with an anxious mind. Obviously

all he could do was to sit tight and say nothing, at least so far as the police were concerned. But about Margot he was not so sure. He felt he ought to express at least conventional regret at old Stott's fate, but he did not wish to go to her cabin. Finally he compromised by ringing her up.

She seemed but little affected by the news, and that more for the publicity it would bring than for the loss of her great-uncle. To avoid the condolences of the passengers she was for that evening keeping her room, but she would be glad to see him next morning if he would call round.

The message cheered him immensely, but it did not banish the increasingly heavy load of fear and foreboding he was beginning to carry.

That night there was a fresh notice on the board.

'I deeply regret to state that news has been received from Portrush that Mr John Stott has been found dead under circumstances pointing to foul play. An enquiry into his death has therefore become necessary, and I hereby invite anyone on board who may be able to throw any light on his movements or intentions ashore to report to me.

'H. J. HARDWICK,
'*Commander.*'

PART II

Through the Eyes of French

12

High Politics

One of the attributes of the great of the earth is that weighty consequences may follow from their lightest actions. This was exemplified in the case of the murder of John Stott.

It happened that some three weeks before that tragic event, the envoy of a powerful mid-European country was visiting the British Prime Minister. 'Conversations' had taken place between them, with satisfactory results to both. The Press in each country was loud in approval of the results of the negotiations and the meeting was coming to an end in a well-organised blaze of glory.

On the last evening there was a banquet to mark the happy consummation of the visit, and his natural enthusiasm for good work well done caused the foreign envoy to supplement the official toasts with a large number to various eminent personages in his immediate vicinity. The result was that, while remaining entirely sober and decorous, his appreciation of what was humorous was slightly broadened. It was as a joke, harmless and well meant, that when the talk touched on the *Hellénique*, he turned to the Prime Minister and remarked:

'We're grateful to you, over our way, for your efforts to stop the gambling. You've given us a classic phrase. When anyone wants rapid and drastic action he says: "Look slippy or the British will have cleaned up the *Hellénique* before you're through."' A few more toasts and he would have nudged the P.M. in the ribs, but, happily for diplomatic relations between the countries, the banquet came to an end before this climax was reached.

Though he took the sally as it was meant, as humour of the highest type, the Prime Minister was displeased. It was not the first time he had been twitted with his Government's failure to stop gambling in what was virtually, if not legally, Great Britain. Personally, he didn't care two hoots whether gaming went on or whether it didn't, while the Home Secretary, whose job the affair really was, held that the ship was a blessing in disguise: that it provided a useful safety valve for undesirable energy and kept money in the country which might otherwise have gone abroad.

But the Home Secretary had not developed this opinion until his efforts to stop the proceedings had failed. At first he had considered the venture an outrage—a positive insult to himself and his department. In a lordly manner, he had directed that action be taken against its instigators. And he had been coldly displeased when his advisers had advised that nothing could be done: that Stott and company had managed to outwit the majesty of the English Law.

Then there had come the popular outcry, the barrage of letters to the Press, the questions in Parliament, and his cold displeasure had given place, first, to impotent fury and, when that proved unavailing, to the cynical approval of the venture already mentioned. But though he successfully concealed it, his *amour propre* had been wounded, and he would have been glad to wreak his vengeance on the transgressors, had he only known how.

To a lesser degree, the Prime Minister shared his feelings, and it thus happened that on the day following the banquet he heard from his chief full details of the envoy's taunt.

'You'll have to do something, ffoulkes,' the P.M. ended up, in an exasperated tone. 'We can't have every Tom, Dick and Harry throwing the damned thing in our teeth.'

Whether the classification of the distinguished foreigner as a Tom, a Dick or a Harry would have led to a war had it become known was an interesting though immaterial point. The two Ministers were talking *in camera*.

'But it's been running for a year and more,' the Home Secretary pointed out aggrievedly, as if offering a complete justification.

'A year too long,' grunted the P.M. unsympathetically. 'See what you can do about it,' and with finality he changed the subject.

The matter thus once again became a personal one to the Home Secretary. Later that day he sent for the files of the case and re-read his expert's opinions. From these he only grew more firmly convinced than ever that Stott had indeed outwitted them. Nor could he see any possibility of getting beneath the man's defences.

But Sir Marmaduke ffoulkes had not reached his present altitude through admitting defeat. He had previously dropped the matter because a solution of its problem had not been apparent. Now it was different. His personal prestige was at stake. After what the foreign envoy and the P.M. had said, he could no longer afford to be beaten.

In his younger and less palmy days, the Home Secretary had been a barrister, and in court he had learnt that circuitous means often succeed where the direct method has failed. Now he recalled his training. If Stott could not be got at through his methods, might he not through some failure to carry them out?

To the Home Secretary it seemed the only possibility: worth trying at all events. Later that afternoon he moved the affair a step further on.

It happened that there was penal reform conference at the Home Office at which, representing Scotland Yard, was Sir Mortimer Ellison, one of the Assistant Commissioners. After the proceedings were over, the Home Secretary asked him to wait.

'This blessed *Hellénique* gambling business has cropped up again,' he told him. 'The P.M. has been getting his leg pulled about it, and he is not pleased.'

'We went into that, sir, as you know,' Sir Mortimer answered. 'We were advised we could do nothing.'

'I'm aware of that,' the Home Secretary returned a trifle drily. 'I agree; provided those people carry out their scheme to the letter.'

Sir Mortimer glanced at him keenly. 'You mean—' he was beginning when the other interrupted him.

'The thing has been running for over a year without any apparent interest from the authorities. It would only be natural if they were to grow a little careless. One slip, and we might get them.'

'You mean they might, for example, come into a British port with their gambling rooms open?'

'Scarcely that, I fancy. But they might come inside the three-mile limit.'

'I don't know that I quite follow you there,' Sir Mortimer returned. 'I take it your idea in raising the question is that I should arrange for the boat to be kept under observation?'

'Of course.'

'I should do that by putting one or more officers on board: as passengers. You meant that, sir, didn't you?'

'That would be your pigeon, but it's what I had in mind.'

'Well, the point that occurs to me is that none of my fellows would be in a position to say whether the ship was inside or outside the limit. That would require sea knowledge and charts and possibly instruments.'

The Home Secretary paused. 'I could send a navigator from the Navy to assist your man, if that would help,' he suggested. 'But I don't confine it to observing the three-mile limit. I rather thought of having a general watch kept in the hope that they may do something that will let us prosecute.'

Sir Mortimer Ellison agreed without enthusiasm. He had already given a good deal of thought to the problem, and he did not believe that the Home Secretary's suggestion would produce results. However, too lavish an application of cold water to the suggestions of one's superiors was untactful.

'There is one instance in which even a man without nautical knowledge might obtain conclusive evidence,' he therefore went on, 'and that is if, with the rooms open, they went between two pieces of land less than six miles apart. They're always coasting round islands. Suppose an island lay five miles from the mainland and they went between. We'd get them then all right.'

'I'm afraid they'd never do that.'

'Well, there's what you said about their becoming careless.

I suggest I put a man aboard her for a week or two. We could perhaps be guided about the naval officer by his reports.'

The suggestion was favourably received. Sir Mortimer was told to do what he could with his own men for a fortnight, when the question of further action would be considered. Pleased to have shelved the necessity for immediate decision, the two men parted amicably.

When, an hour later, Chief Inspector Joseph French was summoned to Sir Mortimer's room and given the job, he had little idea that for it he had to thank the expansiveness of a foreign diplomat who allowed himself to drink more toasts than were good for him.

'This will be a new experience for you, won't it, French?' the A.C. went on. 'You'll have to do an impersonation. Have you ever been anyone but yourself?'

'Never, sir,' French smiled.

'The trouble's on your own head. If you will ape a cheap notoriety and allow that friend of yours to write his wretched books, you can't expect to get off scot-free. Whom will you go as?'

French, still grinning, thought for a moment. 'John Forrester, sir,' he said at last, 'from near Tonbridge. A hop-grower.'

Sir Mortimer looked dubious. 'But do you know anything about hop-growing?' he asked doubtfully.

'I used to stay with hop-growers when I was a boy, sir.'

'And, trusting to the English love of being in the forefront of scientific progress, you assume methods have not altered since then. Well, I expect you're right there. But you don't look the part, you know.'

'No, sir?'

'No—definitely. And besides, the Tonbridge area is too small. Suppose you have someone on board from Tonbridge.'

'*Near* Tonbridge, sir. Too far away to be known by anyone in the town.'

The A.C. shrugged. 'Well, well, I see you've made up your mind. Do what you like. It's your funeral. What about taking your wife?'

French hesitated.

'Add to the hop-growing illusion,' the A.C. prompted.

'I'd love it, sir, but I'm afraid she wouldn't go.'

'Well, your daughter or sister, or, if you can do it without involving the Yard in a scandal, some woman friend. Are you normally henpecked?'

French laughed outright. 'An embarrassing question, sir,' he declared.

'It shouldn't be,' Sir Mortimer retorted. 'I suggest you take your wife and be very much married. That would dissipate any strong, silent, Scotland Yard stuff that might be put up.'

French grew serious. 'It would be expensive, sir, if we both went, and took excursions, and soon. Would that be all right?'

'And you'd want a spot of gambling, too, I suppose? Well, I don't want you to bankrupt the Home Office, but there's no reason why they shouldn't pay for their amusements.'

'I'll try and get my wife to go, sir,' French decided, and after some discussion as to what exactly he was to look for, the interview came to an end.

French felt as if he was walking on air as he returned to his room. He could scarcely preserve his accustomed professional dignity. For some time he had been working on unpleasant cases: tedious, wearisome, sordid, and without any intellectual interest. They had taken him either to slums, or to areas which were rapidly becoming slums: a world of grimy bricks and mortar, of smells and insects and unwashed humanity. He was sick of the work and of his less fortunate fellow citizens, and longed for a breath of clean, fresh air and the green of the country. For the blue of the sea he had not longed: it had seemed too utterly beyond his dreams. But there was always a chance of an application from some county force, and he had hoped for luck had one come in.

And now, suddenly and unexpectedly, he was to have the holiday which, of all holidays, he would most enjoy: a fortnight—and perhaps longer—on the super-luxury cruising liner, *Hellénique*. For fourteen days—or perhaps more—he would be at sea, surrounded by *clean* air and *clean* sunshine! He would have shore excursions to the best bits of the British Isles, a luxurious cabin, excellent food and, so far as he could see, little or nothing to do. He would see for himself the most talked-of ship in the world: a mystery ship about which all kinds of secrets were whispered and thrilling tales told. Even now, after all the A.C. had said, he could scarcely believe it!

His thoughts turned towards his wife. *What* a chance for Em! Often they had discussed cruising together, but somehow their plans had never materialised. Now, if Em would only go, they might have the time of their lives.

But when he had told Sir Mortimer that he did not think she would, he was giving his real opinion. While she was an intelligent and well-educated woman, she had a complex about what she called 'grand people'. He knew that but for this feeling she could hold her own in any ordinary company, but it made her awkward and tongue-tied, and allowed those with aggressive tendencies to assume a superiority which they did not possess. He wished he could get her to agree, as he thought the experience would break her fear.

He felt that if he were to ask her to share his glorious holiday, she would turn the scheme down. He therefore tried another approach. He did not refer to the plan till they were half-way through supper, then began by saying rather dolefully that Sir Mortimer Ellison had let him in for an awkward job, and had advised him to get her help with it. He enlarged on it to the point of verbosity. It was, of course, a lot to ask and he wouldn't press her if she disliked the idea, but as a matter of fact it was rather important, as his future might largely depend on how he handled the affair. And so on.

'What is it?' she asked suspiciously, when his prologue at length came to an end.

'It's that gambling ship, the *Hellénique*. It seems the P.M. himself has ordered an investigation. See if we can catch 'em out anywhere. The whole Yard's buzzing, but I've been given the chance.'

'And what are you to do?'

'Go as a passenger, for a fortnight. That's what the A.C. wants you for. If I go with my wife, I'm less of a suspect. See the idea?'

She did. 'Oh, Joe,' she exclaimed, 'I couldn't go there. Among all those grand people. I couldn't really.'

He registered effective disappointment. 'I hoped you would, Em. As I say, I know it's a lot to ask, but it's an honour to be chosen for this Prime Minister's job, and it would be a big thing if I could pull it off. Sure you wouldn't try it, at least for a day or two? If you didn't like it, you could go home.'

She hesitated, and he went on to describe the luxury of the cabins, and the fact that she could sit in hers as much as she liked. In the end, it was the private bathroom that did it. She had never had a bedroom with a private bathroom, and she couldn't resist the experience. Curiously, she had no objection to being Mrs Forrester, which he thought would have proved an insuperable difficulty.

Next day Mr Forrester called at the head office of the Boscombe Travel Agency to make enquiries about the *Hellénique* cruise. There he was supplied with the wrong folders by a slightly condescending young product of our higher education, who, when his error was pointed out, seemed to regard his client as an unreasonable purist who might be troublesome were he less negligible. A couple of days later Mr Forrester telephoned reserving accommodation from the following Wednesday.

That Wednesday was the day on which the *Hellénique* was cruising off the Orkneys, the day on which Wyndham Stott and Margot also went on board. As has already been mentioned, the two couples not only travelled by the same plane, but occupied adjoining seats. That they quickly became on friendly terms was due to Margot's good fellowship and kindly feeling.

French had travelled by air on various occasions, but it was his wife's first flight and she was scared stiff by the novelty. Valiantly she tried to hide her feelings, but Margot instantly saw through her pretences. Some travellers would have smiled and affected a pitying superiority: not so Margot. She felt that a few friendly, commonplace words would help her companion, and she was not slow to speak them. Mrs French instinctively recognised the kindly intention and responded to such an extent that before they reached the ship they were firm friends. And as their women-kind chatted, so did French and Wyndham Stott.

In spite of her fears, however, Mrs French enjoyed every minute of the trip, as indeed did they all. The weather was perfect, fine and sunny and warm. The air was steady and without pockets, and the plane moved smoothly along on an even keel without those sudden drops and rises which are so disconcerting to the inexperienced traveller. Visibility was first class, and the country beneath them showed clear and sharp like a magnificently executed relief map. A country it was, too, of extraordinary variety and interest. From their start over the rich, prosperous and well-wooded landscape of Hampshire, to their finish over the wild and bleak Orkney Islands, there was scarcely a dull mile. At last, in surroundings with a beauty all their own, they came in sight of the monster ship, circled slowly down and made a gentle landing close beside her.

Their cabin really did come up to Mrs French's rosiest anticipations. It was an outside one on B Deck, and, in addition to the well-sprung twin beds—not bunks, as she had half expected—there were a couple of luxurious armchairs placed in admirable daylight. Directly she saw these, her courage rose. If she didn't like the public rooms, she could be comfortable here with her knitting and books. About the bathroom she had no words to express an opinion.

'Come and let's have a stroll on deck,' said French.

He had made no sartorial concessions to the sea save to add rubber-soled shoes to rather dilapidated plus-fours and a sports jacket of Harris tweed. His wife had been horrified, suggesting a yachting outfit of blue and white. But she had taken his advice as to her own get-up and now was delighted to find most of the others on deck in a similar rig.

French was a good mixer, and he soon drew in beside another couple who were standing at the rail looking at the slowly passing coast. A chance remark to the other man, and lo! in five minutes they were deep in a discussion on cruising in the Western Mediterranean. The man's wife turned with a friendly smile to Mrs French, and thereby dealt the latter's inferiority complex a blow from which it never fully recovered. By lunchtime French was delighted to see that his Em was feeling at home and enjoying herself.

He himself was revelling in everything: the freedom, the freshness, the sea and air and sky and view, the comfort and the pleasant companionship. All the same, beneath all this superficial pleasure, he was feeling as worried as ever he had done in his life. This job that he had been given! He did not see how on earth he was to carry it out. It would not do to put his superiors to the expense of such a trip and do nothing to earn it.

His difficulty was that his search was for something ill-defined. He was to find out if these people were breaking the British law, and he believed it unlikely that they were, at least to the extent which would enable the gambling to be stopped.

With deep misgivings, he told himself that all he could do would be to keep his eyes and ears open. He had provided himself with charts of the coast, folded so that they could be placed in a novel and consulted without causing comment. He began by dotting in as best he could the ship's position, and he determined to keep this record up-to-date, marking on the points at which the gaming-rooms were opened and closed.

Next he laid himself out to meet and chat to everyone he could, including the ship's officers. He must know, he told himself, all the gossip of the ship; all those tales of mystery and imagination which are generated more particularly in the smoking-room, though by no means confined to that area. Not that these were usually of value. Still, it sometimes did happen that where there was smoke there was fire.

The matter of the supply of drink was also important. Inside the three-mile limit, British licensing laws ran, and a conviction under them might be valuable.

But he had to admit that in none of these directions did there seem any hope of obtaining what he wanted. Rather despondently, he moved about, trying to pick up the gossip of the ship.

During the next few days his gloomy anticipations proved only too well founded. The more he learnt about the conduct of the ship, the more eminently law-abiding it appeared to be. The opening and closing of the gaming-rooms was always carried out so well outside the three-mile limit that, even with his rough methods of fixing their position, there was never doubt that the law was being kept. With drinks it was the same, and, though all kinds of spicy tales were whispered, none were of any use for his purpose.

By the time the ship touched at Portrush, however, he had made a certain kind of progress. He had met practically everyone of importance on board, including Captain Hardwick and his officers. He had been over almost all the ship, engine-room, bridge, kitchens, fo'c'sle, pantries. He had made a reputation as a quiet, decent, harmless chap—though rather inquisitive—who was pleasant enough, if not very likely to set rivers on fire.

But towards the purpose for which the trip had been undertaken he had achieved absolutely nothing. He was greatly worried, and was beginning to believe he had been given an impossible task.

Only in one matter was he profoundly satisfied. His wife had been a success. Her innate good fellowship and unpretentiousness had been appreciated, and she was enjoying a mild popularity.

Then occurred the disappearance of John Stott.

French had talked to John as well as to the other Stotts, and had discovered their relationships. He had also met Morrison on various occasions, and he shrewdly suspected his feelings towards Margot. All six would have been surprised if they could have seen the amount of information about themselves which was written up in French's looseleaf book—a page to each person.

Directly French heard of the disappearance, he wondered if indirectly it might help him. His long experience of matters criminal made him suspect that this was no accident or careless failure to make known a change of plans. If a crime had been committed, its reactions might to some extent upset the routine of the ship, and some relaxation of precautions to keep the gambling within the law might not impossibly take place. It behoved him to miss nothing that was going on. French settled down to his work with a fresh ardour.

13

The Activities of Nugent

During the couple of days following Stott's disappearance, French did his best to find out details of what happened, but without success. On the first day no particular interest was shown in the affair. But on the second morning rumours began to circulate, increasing to a veritable flood by evening. Stott had gone off with a barmaid. He was lying drunk and incapable at the house of a friend. His wealth was a myth and he had been guilty of fraud and had fled the country. He had been crossed in love and had committed suicide. And then, at last, he had been murdered.

In the extraordinary way that rumours approximate to the truth, this last was repeated more and more generally until it ousted the others and held the field. Why or how he had been murdered was not suggested, but the smoking-room had made up its mind as to the fact.

On the third day the flying boat brought a letter for French. It was in the square envelope of the private correspondent, and was addressed to the ship's London agents in a lady's old-fashioned and somewhat spidery hand: the hand French's aunt would have written, had he possessed one. But within he found no suggestion of aunts. It read:

> '14, Guye's Lane,
> S.W.5.
>
> 'DEAR JOHN,—Just a line to say that my friends, the Northerns, are staying at Portrush—you can find out where—and to express the hope that you will call on them if you can manage it while in the neighbourhood. They were very kind to me when I was ill, and I am sure they would like to meet you.
>
> 'We are all well here, except that Jane has a cold.
>
> 'Hoping you are enjoying your trip, as I am sure you must be,
>
> 'Yours affectionately,
> 'ROBERTA LINDSAY.'

More than a little thrill titillated French's nerves as he read this epistle. He could almost hear the ribald laughter of the writer as he read it to his colleagues. 14, Guye's Lane was the address of Robert Lindsay, Sir Mortimer Ellison's private secretary. Here in the A.C.'s own inimitable way were his instructions. Sir Mortimer was sure that the Northerns in Portrush—the Portrush contingent of the police of Northern Ireland, or Royal Ulster Constabulary—would like to meet French, and he hoped that he would call on them. Clearly, they had applied to the Yard for help in the Stott affair, and this was the result. Fine! It was what he, French, had wanted, but had not dared to hope for.

He re-read the letter. At first sight, its form seemed childish and melodramatic, but it was not really so. If by any chance his true role on board were suspected, his correspondence might be tampered with. It would not do for an official letter from the Yard to fall into the hands of the people who were running the ship. But this epistle looked harmless enough and without the clue of the name and address would pass as the letter of an elderly lady. Well, here were orders. He wondered how he could best carry them out.

Taking out his maps, he looked once again at their position. They were now off Inishmurray Island in Donegal Bay. That morning a party had gone ashore at Bundoran and were motoring through the Lough Gill and Sligo districts to Killala, where they would come aboard in the evening. There was a railway from Ballina which could be reached by bus from Killala, but a time-table showed him that the journey to Portrush was long and involved many changes. If he could catch the night mail at Ballina, it might be better to go to Dublin and then north.

He had just decided on this plan when he was called to the telephone. A man's voice was speaking.

'That Mr John Forrester? I'm Northern. Miss Lindsay told me you were on the *Hellénique* and that she had written to you about me. I happen to be coming aboard tonight for a short cruise, so I hope we'll meet.'

This was not at all what French wanted. If he were to help in the case he should prefer to see everything for himself: the body, where it was found, any traces which might have been near it. He supposed he was only wanted to do the enquiries aboard, which in all probability would be neither so easy nor so profitable as those ashore.

That evening he watched the boats returning to the ship and noted that a stranger was with the party: a tall, bronzed man in grey tweeds, with a military carriage and a strong intelligent face: obviously 'Northern'. The newcomer did not, however, ask for French, but vanished in the wake of a steward.

Some half an hour later French's summons came—from a somewhat unexpected source. 'The Captain's compliments, sir, and if you are not engaged, could you step up to his cabin?'

When French entered, Hardwick and the stranger were seated together. They rose and Hardwick smiled at him. 'This is District Inspector Nugent of the Royal Ulster Constabulary,' he said, going on in a rather dry tone, 'Mr Forrester, or should I say Chief Inspector French of New Scotland Yard?'

French was amazed. He looked questioningly from one to the other.

'You mustn't blame me,' Nugent said quickly. 'I didn't tell him.'

'No,' Hardwick smiled again. 'No one has been indiscreet. As a matter of fact, my First Officer recognised you—only yesterday. He was a friend of Captain Hassell's of the *Jane Vosper*, and he and Hassell happened to be at home at the time of the trial which arose out of that case, when—what were their names?—Cruttenden and Henty were sentenced to death.'

'Cruttenden and Hislop,' French said heavily. 'Henty got fourteen years.'

'Ah, of course. Well, the First Officer was interested and attended the case with Hassell. He saw you there. When you came on board he thought your face was familiar, but it was only yesterday that he remembered where he had seen you. You need not be alarmed, however; he has not mentioned it to anyone else.'

French's annoyance was profound, but he crushed it down.

180

'Well, sir,' he said as evenly as he could, 'you've got my name.'

Captain Hardwick hesitated. 'That is true,' he said presently, 'but except that I'm always glad to meet a distinguished man, I'm not interested. I have no official knowledge of why you should be here under another name than your own, and with regard to the ship, I am concerned only in her navigation. But I am interested'—his face changed and grew more purposeful and eager—'in bringing to justice whoever killed John Stott, and if you, Chief Inspector, can give us the benefit of your help, we shall both be grateful. Isn't that it, Mr Nugent?'

The tall man nodded. 'That's it, Captain,' he answered in a pleasant, cultured voice. 'You have, so to speak, said it.'

'We'd better put our cards on the table, I think,' Hardwick went on. 'Apart from Mr Stott being my owner and the director of this cruise, we can't afford to have an unsolved murder mystery connected with the ship; At best—by which I mean if the murderer is quickly discovered, tried an executed—the affair will injure us seriously. It will keep a lot of people away who might have otherwise come. But an unsolved crime would kill us. People mightn't exactly fear that it would be their turn next, but they would decide to run no risks of getting mixed up in that sort of thing. Therefore I and all in charge on board will do everything in our power to get it cleared up: which means, I take it, helping you two gentlemen in every possible way.'

'Speaking for myself,' Nugent declared, 'that is entirely satisfactory. You've put your cards on the table, and I'd better be doing the same.' He turned to French. 'This case, you know, Chief Inspector, is very unusual: in fact, I never came across anything like it before. The trouble is the nationality of the ship. In my official capacity, I'm informed that I haven't any right aboard, except when she is actually in British territorial waters. I take it you're in the same boat, so to speak, but you'll know that. Now we've had a murder on British soil—in Northern Ireland territory. The clues to the murderer are more than likely to be found on board and nowhere else. We can, so I'm told, hold an enquiry on board by keeping the ship in British territorial waters, but we're not wanting to alter the itinerary of the ship, nor to do anything that the French Government would object to. So that our enquiries present some difficulty.'

'I am aware of that,' French agreed drily.

The others smiled and Nugent went on. 'For various reasons'—he looked at Hardwick with a twinkle in his eye—'I assumed that the question of police interference with this ship had been gone into by Scotland Yard. As you know, we don't consult the Yard on Northern Ireland cases, but we did consult them on the question of procedure on this French ship. They replied confirming our view of our rights, and added that you, Chief Inspector, were on board and that you might have information helpful to us. They authorised me to approach you and ask for your help.'

French nodded. 'I had a letter of instruction to put myself at your disposal if called on.'

Nugent was obviously pleased. 'Now, that's very decent of both you and your people. Thank you very much. I needn't say I'll gratefully accept any help you can give me.'

This seemed nebulous and French wondered what he was being let in for. 'What do you wish me to do?' he asked.

'The enquiries on board, Chief Inspector. You know the ship and the people. I don't. I mean, of course, to do

182

everything ashore, but the work aboard'—he shrugged—'well, it wouldn't be easy for me to do anything about it.'

'You mean,' interposed Captain Hardwick with a dry smile, 'that you want to unload your dirty work on someone else?'

The D.I. nodded emphatically. 'That's the idea, Captain. Again, you've said it. I see you know the ropes.'

French thought with some pleasure that he was going to get on well with these two. 'My job, sirs,' he said sententiously, 'is to do other people's dirty work, usually with abuse instead of thanks; though that's not a hint for you.'

'It's worth bearing in mind all the same,' Hardwick retorted. 'Very well, gentlemen, we seem to have cleared up the position. Suppose you two get together now and have a full and frank discussion, as the politicians say. I will be at your disposal when I'm wanted, and I needn't say I will do anything I can to help. What are your plans, Mr Nugent? You're coming along with us tonight, because we're already well out from the coast. When do you wish to go ashore again?'

'Where could I get ashore in the morning?'

'Tomorrow there's an excursion ashore at Mallaranny for Westport and the Killaries, returning to the ship from Clifden in the evening. You could go ashore at either of those places.'

'Thank you, Mallaranny'll do well.'

'Come to my cabin and we'll have a chat before dinner,' French suggested, leading the way.

He did not know what to think of this new development. It was almost as if his original case had been taken from him and that of Stott's murder substituted. Whether or not, it looked as if his original case was doomed to failure, since his identity was known and, he felt sure, his purpose aboard suspected. It had always been unlikely that the ship would have gone inside the three-mile limit with her gaming-rooms open, but now this was quite out of the question. The same might be said about other breaches of the law. As long as he was on board, they simply would not occur.

But this was not the time to think such matters out. Arrived at his cabin, he produced cigarettes, and rang for drinks. Then when his guest was entertained, their conference began. There was a good hour till dinner, and in an hour much can be done.

'I'd better begin by telling you of Morrison's visit,' said Nugent. 'He turned up at the police barracks at Portrush about lunchtime on Wednesday, two days ago. He told us about the cruise and so on, much of which we knew, then said that John Stott, the owner of the ship, had gone ashore on the previous afternoon and that nothing had been heard of him since. This was unlike Stott, and his Captain had become anxious and had sent him to report to us.'

The D.I. then repeated Morrison's story, continuing: 'After the interview I started to register my impressions, and the first was about Morrison himself. There was no doubt the fella was nervous. And there was no doubt he was glad to get the visit over. I couldn't see why, but I just noted the point.'

'Many people, as you know, are nervous about paying a visit to the police.'

'I know they are. But this seemed something more than that. I got the length of wondering whether he knew more than he was saying. Maybe I shouldn't mention this, for there's no what you might call actual evidence for it, but I want to tell you everything I can.'

'It's a valuable hint,' French said politely. 'Those sort of impressions are sometimes wrong, but not often.'

184

'I asked him the usual questions; got a description of Stott, and so on. Morrison had brought one or two photographs, so that was right enough. I issued a Missing Person sheet and then began enquiries in the usual way. I sent men round the hotels and boarding houses, to the Golf Club, the railway station, the various buses, the garages and so on. But I didn't get anything.

'Then I thought of the man's photographic hobby. If he was interested in old buildings, Dunluce Castle was the place he would naturally go. Besides, he had been seen heading towards the East Strand, which is on the way. There were other old ruins here and there. I sent men to them all, with instructions to examine the ruins and ask in houses nearby if anyone like Stott had been seen.'

'Good work,' French commented.

'Aw, now.' Nugent shook his head. 'There was one thing that stood to me, and that was the lateness of the season. If I'd had to work, we'll say in August, I likely wouldn't have got anything with the crowds. But now there are only a few people about, so a stranger is noticed. Well, we tried all the ruins, but the man who went to Dunluce struck it lucky.'

'You deserved it.'

The D.I. laughed. 'We usually get our deserts, don't we?' he ventured. 'But, whether or not, we got something useful. When the constable made his enquiries at a house close by he found a boy of about twelve who'd seen Stott. I'd better show you on a map.'

Nugent unrolled a six-inch Ordnance map and pointed as he spoke.

'Here is the Portrush–Bushmills road, and here is the East Strand. Portrush is here, just off the map. Here, about two miles from Portrush, is a rough footpath, a track only, leading up from the end of the East Strand to the road. Just opposite where this path comes up there's a strange saucer-like depression called McArtt's Hollow. Because of the shelter its rim gives, it's overgrown with scrubby bushes and small trees, the only trees along the coast hereabouts. Here, by the way, is Dunluce Castle, further along the road from Portrush.'

'That's all very clear,' said French.

'Now about four o'clock or a little later on that afternoon—the boy hadn't a watch and wasn't sure of the time—he started from his home, here near Dunluce, to walk into Portrush. He went along the road and then turned to the right down the track to the East Strand, opposite McArtt's Hollow. A couple of hundred yards down, at this point marked X, he met a stranger going up the path to the road. These country boys aren't always what you would wish about manners, but they're often sharp enough, and this one had kept his eyes open. He described Stott accurately enough and picked his photograph out of a dozen others. If the boy was right about the time he left his house, Stott ought to have reached the road about four-fifteen.'

'Though you deserved it, that certainly was lucky,' French put in.

'Lucky wasn't in it. Well, the next step was clear. I sent out some men to comb the area and in less than half an hour they had the body found and me notified. I drove out with the photographer and saw it before it was moved.'

The D.I. turned again to his map.

'It was lying here,' he pointed, 'at the Point A, near the middle of McArtt's Hollow, and hidden by shrubs and bushes. It lay twisted up on its face, with its arms beneath it. Here are some photographs.'

'Admirable work,' French said. He really meant it. The photographs would not have disgraced the Yard's best expert. There were two distant views of the body and four close-ups, giving its appearance from every direction. A seventh picture was a very near view, showing the injury to the back of the head. French pointed to this last.

'I see the skull was fractured,' he said. 'Was the skin not broken?'

'No, a soft weapon had been used: a sand-bag or something like it.'

French handed back the views. 'Yes?' he questioned. 'This is very interesting. What did you do next?'

'Keep them: I brought them for you,' Nugent answered with a lordly gesture. He tossed off the remainder of his sherry.

'You'll have another?' French invited, picking up his telephone.

'Thanks; if you'll join me.'

'Always glad of an excuse.' French was lying, as he didn't care for wine, but he thought this admirable tale deserved encouragement. 'Take another cigarette, or will you have a cigar?'

'A cigarette, thanks.'

They chatted about the cabin and ship's service till the steward had brought the drinks, then the D.I. went on.

'You can well imagine our next step: a careful search of the Hollow. The place was unpromising. The ground was covered with a coarse grass that wouldn't take prints, and the bushes had no thorns that might have collected fragments of wool or cloth. However, on odd patches of earth we found two footprints.

187

'One was here at B.' Again he referred to the map. 'As you see, it was inland of the body, and pointing inland away from the body. It was a good print, sharp and clear though not deeply marked. It wasn't easy to see unless you looked at it closely, and I gave a good mark to the man who found it. We made, of course, a plaster cast.

'The second one was here at C, just beside the body. It was partly on a patch of earth, but mostly on grass, and only the middle part of the sole was clear. Unfortunately there wasn't enough edge for it to be any use as an identification. We really wouldn't have bothered about it except for one thing.

'In the middle of the flat impression there was a hole about three-quarters of an inch or less in both diameter and depth. The upper half, about three-eighths of an inch deep, was roughly cylindrical, but the clay was broken and torn and gave no accurate impression. But the lower half was as clear as you'd wish it. It was semi-spherical in shape, and covered with a queer kind of irregular pattern. It bothered us all for a bit, and then we saw what it was.

'One of those round buttons covered with plaited leather strips that you'll see on sports coats had been trampled into the ground and then removed. The bottom half of the hole represented a true cast of the button, and the top half was broken by its being pulled out.'

'You didn't see the button itself?'

'I did not. I took it that someone had dropped it, trampled on it, missed it, looked for it, pulled it out and taken it away. It wasn't so easy to get a cast of this, but we managed it, and afterwards we made a positive of the button—or rather of half of it.'

188

'Excellent,' French approved.

'Unfortunately, that was all we could find. Since then we've been scouring the district for people who might have seen anyone near the Hollow that afternoon. But so far we've had no luck.'

'There were no footprints on paths approaching the Hollow?'

'There are no paths approaching it except at the entrance from the main road. This was grown over with grass and there were no traces on it. We searched right round the Hollow, but there wasn't a mark that we could see.'

'That's extremely interesting,' French declared. 'Yes?'

The D.I. shrugged. 'I'm afraid that's about the end of the story,' he answered. 'What I've told you has taken up all the time of our small staff. But I doubt we're not likely to get more.'

'You mean the gentleman with the sports coat was not a local man?'

'That's what I mean, Chief Inspector. It's only guesswork, of course, but I think someone from this ship went ashore and murdered Mr Stott.'

French considered the point. 'At first sight, it certainly looks like it. Tell me, did you form an opinion as to what the deceased was doing there? Are there any ruins in the Hollow?'

'No, none. None nearer than Dunluce Castle, on the sea side of the road.'

'There was nothing helpful in his pockets, of course? But I shouldn't ask questions like that. You would have mentioned it if there had been.'

'As a matter of fact, there wasn't. But ask away as much as you like. I'm not above overlooking something.'

'Well, then, here's another. I see from the photographs

that Stott had a camera with him. What about exposed films? Did you get any such developed?'

'I don't think he'd taken any photographs. The camera was filled, but was set to the first space. However, our photographer has instructions to develop the entire reel, so if there's anything there, we'll get it.'

'What about giving me details of the footprint and button?'

'The photographs weren't ready when I was starting. I'll send them to you at once with all dimensions. If you wish I'll make you a duplicate casting.'

'No need for that, thanks; the photos will be enough. You don't seem to have left much to be done, I will say.'

Nugent smiled. 'Not so much, except maybe to find the murderer.'

'And,' French ticked off his points on his fingers, 'you think, one, that he's on board this ship and, two, that you should do the work off the ship and I the work aboard?'

Nugent laughed a little uneasily. 'I suppose that's about the size of it—if you'll agree.' He paused, then went on: 'You see, it's unlikely that we'd get much by a formal enquiry when the ship was in territorial waters, which is all I could do. The thing'll want private enquiries that wouldn't break international law. To make them, I'd have to come aboard, incidentally leaving my end of things. You've a tremendous pull over me, anyway, in that you've been on board for several days. You probably already know several people with motives for doing Stott in.' He smiled. 'I know it's damned cheek of me suggesting all this, but there it is. What about it, Chief Inspector?'

'As far,' French returned, 'as my giving my help is concerned, I've already been told from London to do what

I can. Therefore, that's settled. If you ask me, and you have, I will act.'

Nugent sat back as if to indicate a relieved mind. 'I'm tremendously obliged,' he declared. 'I can't say how grateful I am. Then if you will look into things here, I'll do the local work. That's great'.

'By the way, has there been an inquest?'

'It was to be today. We kept over your quartermaster to give evidence of identification. We were going to apply for an adjournment after that.'

They had a little further talk, arranging among other matters a short code by which they could discuss the case by telephone without mentioning names. Then Nugent went on:

'I think I'd be as well away from that dining-saloon. No use in starting talk. What about sending a snack to my cabin?'

To this French agreed. He dined in the saloon as usual, but until the D.I. left with the morning excursionists, he was seen no more on board. And when he did leave, it was Captain Hardwick who saw him off, with detailed messages to a hypothetical family.

14

French Gets Busy

It was with mixed feelings that French settled down to consider the results of his interview with District Inspector Nugent. Firstly, and in a small personal way, he was disappointed at having been unable to go on that day's excursion, which was reputed to be one of the best on the list. From Mallaranny the party were to drive through Westport, past the sombre Doo Lough and round the head of Killary Bay to Lenaun, ending with magnificent views of the Twelve Pins Mountains, which they would skirt on their way to Clifden. He was sorry to miss all this charming scenery. But this was a comparative trifle. A much more profound disappointment was the fact that practically all hope of success with his original case had vanished. Captain Hardwick on his guard meant that all the ship's activities would be strictly legal.

His new case, however, was more promising. If Nugent were correct that John Stott's murderer was on board the *Hellénique*—and French was inclined to think so, too—it should not be difficult to identify him.

For the moment therefore, French realised that he must dismiss the gambling from his mind, and he turned to the steps he should take in connection with the murder. What lines of enquiry suggested themselves?

There were three to begin with. First, there was the general situation. Who wished Stott to be dead? Stott was a man of wealth: who was his heir? Would many people benefit under his will? Who had hated him? Whom had he injured? Who might be jealous of him? These questions must be answered and to answer them would require an immensity of detailed and tedious investigation.

Then he must make a note of all those who could have met Stott at McArtt's Hollow at the time of the murder. Names which were common to both categories would form his first list of suspects.

Thirdly, there were the actual clues found on the ground: the footprint and the button. Could he make anything from these?

Taking the footprint first, and assuming for argument's sake that the murderer was on board, it would follow either that the shoe in question was now also on board, or that the owner had thrown the pair away after the murder. He wondered which was the more likely.

No doubt the murderer had been careful not to tread on soft clay in the Hollow. But no matter how careful he had been, he could not be *certain* that he had left no print. Therefore surely his first thought would be to destroy the shoes he had worn? It could be done so easily. All that would be necessary would be to weight them and at night drop them overboard.

French saw therefore that a twofold enquiry lay before him. He would have to slip into the cabins of his suspects

193

and examine their shoes, and he would have to find out if a pair of shoes had recently disappeared from anyone's collection.

This latter could only be learnt from the cabin stewards. French wondered how he, an ordinary passenger, could put such a question without raising suspicion.

This baffled him for a little, then he thought he saw the way. He rang up the Portrush police and asked them to send by return a pair of second-hand shoes of the kind which might have made the print. Till these arrived, further work on this matter must stand over.

With regard to the button, the procedure was easier. He had simply to observe who wore buttons of the kind in question and see if a button was missing from any of the coats.

This seemed to be all that he had to go on, and then he remembered Nugent's statement about Morrison's nervousness. Was there anything in the D.I.'s suspicions.

Obviously there was enough to make him add Morrison's name to his list of suspects, though he doubted if the man would prove guilty.

Satisfied as to where he should begin, French telephoned to the Captain for an interview and was told to go up to his cabin then and there.

'I want to start by going through the late Mr Stott's effects,' he told Hardwick. 'Do you authorise the search?'

'Of course,' the Captain returned. 'I'll get you the spare key of his suite.'

'You needn't. Mr Nugent gave me the keys found on the body.'

French was going out, but Hardwick motioned him to stay. 'Sit down for a moment, Chief Inspector,' he said with the nearest approach to uneasiness that the captain of a great liner should show. 'I'm in rather a difficulty and I want you to help me out.'

French, surprised, reassured him.

'The matter concerns two of my passengers, and is therefore, of course, strictly confidential. There are, in fact, certain facts which I think you should know. I wish to make it clear that I am not suggesting that these facts have any connection with the murder: I merely say you should know them.'

'I appreciate your reservation, Captain.'

Hardwick nodded. 'It's about an incident which took place when the cruise was being considered. I have to explain that I personally know nothing about it: it was before my time. But you can get first-hand information from Bristow and Morrison. What occurred was this,' and in guarded language he told of Malthus's journey to Calais and its sequel.

'Were these two gentlemen ashore at Portrush?' French asked.

'Yes. I've seen the landing sheets.'

'You don't know how they spent their day?'

'No, and I've not asked them.'

'No: quite so. Well, I'm grateful to you, Captain Hardwick, for this information. I'll consider it carefully and I assure you I'll not jump to conclusions.'

French was interested, though not greatly impressed by the story. Hardwick apparently thought that these two men had committed the murder because of that eighteen-month-old dispute. But at first sight this did not seem likely to French. For one thing, if they had been going to kill Stott, they would surely have done it much earlier and, for another, he was sure that they would have acted more secretly. They must have known that to come openly aboard the ship would mean instant suspicion, as it had: a thing which they would certainly have avoided.

All the same, French headed his list of suspects with Malthus's and Mason's names. Hardwick was at least correct in suggesting that the matter must be investigated.

Ten minutes later French had locked himself in Stott's rooms. He was impressed with their size and luxury and for a few minutes moved about in sheer wonder that any individual could reserve such a place for himself alone. Then with a shrug he set to work.

A general inspection revealed nothing of interest and he presently settled down to go through the papers in the man's office. The desk was locked, but the key was also on the deceased's bunch.

There was a vast deal of stuff to be examined and it took French practically the whole day. Hour after hour he worked, taking out papers and books, glancing through them, putting them away again, and occasionally—far less often than he would have wished—making a note. He did not find much that he thought would be helpful, but there were some items.

First, he learnt the name of Stott's solicitors, Messrs Granger, Hill and Granger of Chancery Lane. This was important, as there was no will or indication of where the deceased's fortune was to go. Next he found a number of letters abusing Stott on various counts, mostly for sharp business practice which had caused loss to the writers. These he put aside for subsequent study, should this prove necessary.

There were a number of family letters, irrelevant in

themselves to his quest, but containing enough general references to shed a good deal of light on relations between the members.

First, from the genealogical point of view, it was clear that the connections assumed in the smoking-room gossip were correct, but some dates were given of which the smoking-room was unaware. John Stott was the uncle of Wyndham, and Margot, Wyndham's daughter, was therefore John's great-niece. Margot was born in 1910, making her now twenty-eight. In 1912 her mother died, and it was evident that as the girl grew up, she and her father had been devoted companions. Then in 1933, when Margot was twenty-three, Wyndham had married for the second time. Elmina Luff was a widow with a nineteen-year-old son, Percy. It was evident that Elmina was jealous of Wyndham's affection for his daughter and that Margot resented having to give up to Elmina the first place with her father. Also it was evident that from the first Percy had been a thorn in the flesh to all concerned; except to his mother, who appeared to dote on him. French came on the carbon of a letter from John Stott to Wyndham, complaining of Percy having disgraced the family in a drunken row and threatening to allow Wyndham only the life use of his money, so that he couldn't leave it to his wife or stepson. How this particular episode, which was recent, had ended, French could not discover, but he could find no instructions to John's solicitor as to the altering of his will.

It was clear that not a single member of the family liked John and his feelings towards them were equally cold. In the case of Percy Luff, it looked indeed as if there was real hate between the two. All the members, therefore, went down on French's list of suspects, with Percy's name underlined as a first choice.

Curiously enough, there was less among the papers to indicate the deceased's relations with the personnel of the *Hellénique*. There were three notes from Captain Hardwick, couched in increasingly stiff terms, about various semi-nautical matters in which Stott had apparently interfered. The Captain had summarily refused the freedom of the navigating bridge to Stott's friends, and had turned down equally forcibly suggestions that officers should be allowed to dance with passengers when off duty, and that engineer officers should be excluded from the dining-saloon. From Bristow there was a rather sadly worded complaint that his agreed percentage of the ship's profits was overdue, the answer to which French couldn't find, and from the Chief Engineer an indignant refusal to dismiss his Fourth Officer, because that young man habitually abstained from saluting Stott when they met. Altogether relations between Stott and the staff seemed slightly strained, though there was no evidence of a feeling likely to lead to murder.

Lastly, there were private ledgers giving the man's financial dealings, or some of them, as well as the profits of the cruise. French was astonished at the figures. He had known the deceased to be wealthy, but he had not realised to what extent. John Stott had been either a millionaire or a colourable imitation of one.

Particularly surprising were the figures of the *Hellénique* venture, which, apparently, Stott had kept to himself. Paying was scarcely the word for it: the profits were absolutely enormous. By the time it had been running for a year its entire original cost—purchase and alteration of the ship, gambling installation, flying boats and subsidiary services—had been paid off. For the past six months every penny earned, less the comparatively small cost of running, was profit. Stott, indeed, had been making a second fortune on the top of his first. More than ever important, French thought, became the matters of his will and heirs.

When that evening, with a sigh of relief, he replaced the last of the papers and relocked the suite, French's tentative list of suspects had been opened. Already it bore ten names: Malthus, Mason, Wyndham Stott and Percy Luff, with Elmina and Margot as secondary figures, Captain Hardwick, Mackintosh, the Chief Engineer, Bristow and Morrison, and his further enquiries into the writers of aggrieved letters would probably add to the number.

Before turning in, he wrote to the Yard asking for a man to be sent to Stott's solicitors, Messrs Granger, Hill and Granger of Chancery Lane, to try to obtain from them the terms of Stott's will.

Next morning when he went on deck the ship was still cruising between Innishark and Slyne Head. A party was going ashore at Clifden to drive south through the Joyce's Country, Galway and Lahinch, and he told himself that observation of that landing party might be helpful.

Accordingly, he took up an unobtrusive position above the ladder to the boats, from which he could watch the embarkation. It was some little distance down to the ladder, but still he could see all he wanted.

Sports coats, he noted with some embarrassment, were fairly common, and a good many had leather-covered buttons. He noted eleven men who wore the latter. Ten of these caused him no quickening of the pulse, but the eleventh did. It was Percy Luff. Luff's was the last boat for the shore and French, suddenly changing his mind, raced for the lift and joined it. He was just in time, and as luck would have it, was able to find a vacant seat opposite his quarry. As long as Luff sat still, he could not see what he wanted, but when presently the young man took a cigarette case from one side pocket and a lighter from the other, each sleeve became exposed in turn. None of the buttons was missing.

French experienced a sharp disappointment. In principle, he hated to find anyone guilty of murder, but when he became engrossed in a case he no longer considered personal implications—only the efficient carrying out of his work. It would have been gratifying on this second day of the enquiry to have identified the owner of the dropped button, though, of course, he couldn't expect to have miracles arranged for him.

His thoughts reverted to the other ten leather-buttoned jacket wearers. Now it would be necessary to go into the history of these and find out where, if at all, their lives had touched that of Stott. A long job and tedious, especially working under the confounded handicap of the *Hellénique's* ownership.

He happened to glance again at Luff, and as he did so, he felt once more that little thrill of excitement with which he was so familiar. The man was looking at something ashore and had raised his arm to shade his eyes. His sleeve and its buttons were more clearly visible than before, and now French noticed that the end button was slightly smaller and slightly lighter in colour than the others. A new button or he was a Dutchman!

While continuing to chat with his neighbour, French's thoughts were busy. If Luff had lost a button at the Hollow, where could he have obtained a new one? At Portrush? At Derry? At Sligo?

Possibly, but more probably at the ship's own shop. As sports coats were so much worn on board, it would be almost certain to keep these buttons. If, on taking off his coat after the day at Portrush, Luff should have missed the button, so elegant a young man would surely have had another put on at the earliest opportunity.

Once ashore French drifted away from the party, and as soon as the others were out of sight, he returned on board. Presently he strolled to the shop and began to chat to the pretty attendant. She would, he thought, have been even prettier had her face been less white, her hair less golden and her lips less red, but this evidently was not her opinion, and she regrettably had the final say. She seemed a good sort of girl and he enjoyed talking to her.

'I've lost,' he said, when the time of day had been leisurely passed, 'one of those leather-covered buttons off my sports coat, and I understand you've got the very thing. Can you give me one the same as Mr Luff got from you two or three days ago? Or is it asking you too much to remember that?'

It worked better than he could have hoped. 'No,' she answered, opening a drawer, 'I remember quite well. As a matter of fact, I've had a dozen of these buttons ever since the cruise started and Mr Luff was the first person who bought one.' She handed out a button. 'This is what you want?'

'That's it,' French returned; 'exactly right. Funny how these things happen. You've not made a sale for a year and a half and now in—what, three days?—you get rid of two.'

'Three days, yes. It was on Tuesday evening that Mr Luff came round.'

'You'll sell another inside the week,' French assured her solemnly. 'Things always run in threes.'

'Go on,' she returned; 'a man like you stuffing me up with nonsense of that kind.'

They chatted of superstitions and he gave her instances he had known of mishaps coming in threes, while she ridiculed his seriousness. Presently, clutching his button, he passed on.

So Percy Luff had bought the button on the evening of the Portrush call! This certainly was progress, and positive progress at that.

Negative progress French also made that day while the ship slowly passed the Aran Islands in the mouth of Galway Bay: namely, the discovery that neither Captain Hardwick nor the Chief Engineer had gone ashore at Portrush. While, therefore, Luff's name remained underlined on his list of suspects, Hardwick's and Mackintosh's were deleted.

His thoughts reverted to the button. Someone had picked it up and he had at first assumed that this had been the man who had lost it. Now he was not so sure. If Luff had picked it up, why had he not replaced it on his sleeve instead of buying a new one? Was it damaged from being tramped into the ground? French thought this unlikely. Then had two people been present and had the other one retrieved it?

French did not know, but it occurred to him that it might be well to obtain another button from Luff's coat, so that if the first should later be found, they might be compared.

Accordingly that evening after dinner, when the stewards had finished with the cabins and had vanished to their own place, he went in search of Luff. He found him seated at the tables and decided that the moment was propitious for his venture. Carrying a hat and light overcoat as if going for a stroll on deck, he went to Luff's cabin, easily discoverable from the sailing list and plan of the ship, and, after a quick glance round, he entered. In ten seconds he had found the jacket and wrapped it in his overcoat, and in another thirty he was back in his own cabin. There Mrs French was waiting, and soon the corresponding button from the other sleeve lay on his table, together with a lot of the thread which had been used to sew it on. Five minutes later the new button French had bought was in its place, and he was starting back with the coat. He replaced it unseen and continued on his way to the deck.

Next morning there came a parcel from District Inspector Nugent, apparently sent from Dublin, containing a rather well-worn pair of men's rubber-soled, tan shoes. Another package from the police at Portrush contained photographs of the footprint and of the hole from which the button had been pulled. There were two of the latter, one showing the hole as it had been found, and the other the bottom portion with the broken sides removed. This latter formed a mould of half the button, and on comparing it with his trophy from Luff's coat, French was satisfied that it had been made by a button of similar type.

The photograph of the footprint next claimed his attention. A glance showed it had been made by a man's shoe, rubber-soled, of medium size. Probably it belonged to a man of medium height and build, though, of course, this was not certain. At first sight he could find nothing distinctive about the trace, which might separate that particular shoe from the thousands of others of identical pattern.

With rubber soles, however, wear was the thing to look for, and closer examination brought out an important fact. The inner side of the shoe was more deeply worn than the outside, as was the rear end of both sole and heel compared with the forward position.

French knew that this was unusual. Most people wear away their shoes on the outer sides and at the front. He remembered having read that examination of the boots of soldiers had showed that 98 per cent were worn in this way, only 2 per cent being as in Nugent's photograph. Of course, the soldiers' marching walk might have affected the result. However, the point was suggestive.

The next thing was obviously to examine the shoes of his men suspects. On this day the shore excursion was from Dingle to Tralee, Cahirsiveen and Valencia, and it happened that all the remaining suspects had taken it. French had stayed on the ship and, watching his chance, he slipped into each cabin in turn.

In each his procedure was the same. He quickly reversed the most worn shoe he could find, laid a two-inch rule across the instep, and with a powerful torch took a photograph of the sole. His luck held and he got back to his own cabin unseen.

But though he had persisted with the photograph in each case, observation alone had given him both a surprise and a thrill. Luff obviously had not made the print; his foot was too long and too narrow. Nor had Wyndham Stott; his was too short and too broad. Nor had Bristow; his was too large. But Morrison's seemed exactly the size, and, moreover, Morrison's shoes were more worn on the inside, just as in the photograph. Immediately French made a rapid search of the cabin, and saw that the original shoe of the photograph was not there. Morrison might, of course, be wearing it; but then he might not.

French wondered if Morrison could be his man, and thought he might make a further test. A little observation indicated the steward who attended to Morrison's cabin and he called him over.

'Can you help me in a small matter?' he began. 'I'm asking everyone if he has lost a pair of shoes. An extra pair was left in my cabin by mistake and they should go back to their owner.'

'Yes, sir,' the man answered, to French's delight. 'Mr Morrison lost a pair last Tuesday. I asked him about them and he said for me to make enquiries.'

'What were they like? Tan shoes with rubber soles?'

'Yes, sir; that's them right enough.'

'Then come along to my cabin and see if these are they.'

French carried out the little farce to the end. He showed the steward the shoes he had obtained from Nugent, was suitably surprised to learn that they were not Morrison's, told the man to let him know if he heard of any others which were missing, and let him go with a word of thanks.

French was really surprised at this development. It looked as if not one, but two of his suspects had been in the Hollow. Had Morrison and Percy Luff conspired together to kill Stott? Or was one only the murderer, the other having come on the ground through some accident? To find this out must be his next step.

While satisfied with his progress, French realised that he

was only at the beginning of his enquiry. He now had an indication of what must have happened and a pointer in the direction in which his researches must continue. Not much in a way, and yet for the third day of the enquiry not too bad.

He moved a deck-chair into a sheltered position behind a boat, and settled down to think out his next step.

15

Family Tales

The more French thought over his new case, the more satisfied he became that he had learnt all that secret investigation could tell him. Up till now the method had proved valuable, but he could not hide his identity for ever, and he thought the time had come to reveal it.

He therefore sought out Captain Hardwick and put his views before him. 'If you, as an interested party,' he suggested, handing over a paper, 'would call together the people on this list and introduce me and suggest that they help me, it would be useful. Apart from easing my approach to them, I might learn something from watching their expressions during your announcement.'

Hardwick raised his eyebrows as he read the names. 'Bless my soul!' he exclaimed with something like indignation. 'You're surely not going to accuse Mrs or Miss Stott of the murder?'

'I didn't say I accused any of these,' French returned mildly. 'I want their testimony as to where they were when it was taking place. They may make alibis for other people,' he added, as the Captain continued to frown.

'Oh, very well,' Hardwick said at last. 'It's your pigeon. I'll do what you want.'

As various persons were leaving the dining-saloon that evening, stewards confidentially offered them the Captain's compliments with a request that they would give him the benefit of their company in his cabin at 9 p.m.

Hardwick's cabin was a large room as captains' cabins go, but it was taxed to its utmost at the meeting. Hardwick was at his desk, with French at his right hand. Ranged on the remaining four chairs and the settee were Elmina, Margot, Wyndham, Percy Luff, Malthus and Mason, while Bristow and Morrison stood beside the door.

Hardwick was official in his manner and rather curt in his remarks. He briefly thanked those present for attending and expressed regret that he had had to trouble them. They would see, however, that their summons was not without cause.

'I asked you to come,' he went on, 'in connection with the death of the late Mr Stott. All of you are concerned in the matter either as relatives or as former or present business associates. You are aware that foul play is suspected, and an enquiry has therefore been ordered.'

Malthus's brow darkened. 'I've never been associated with the deceased gentleman,' he interrupted. 'I don't know why you should have included me.'

'Nor I,' added Mason. 'In fact, I had never even seen him till we came on board.'

'In that case, some mistake has probably been made,' Hardwick returned smoothly. 'Perhaps you'll kindly speak to our friend here about it. I was just about to introduce him. You have known him as Mr Forrester, but that's not his name. He adopted it to avoid publicity, if I may so put it'—Hardwick's voice was dry—'so that on his holiday he might have a real change and avoid conversations on professional matters. He has not succeeded in this, for his headquarters officials have just asked him to undertake this enquiry. Ladies and gentlemen, allow me to introduce Chief Detective Inspector French of Scotland Yard.'

A good deal of surprise, considerable interest and some indignation showed on the faces of the little audience, but before anyone could speak, French got up and bowed.

'As Captain Hardwick has told you,' he said, 'I have been instructed to make an enquiry into this unhappy affair. I was chosen to do it owing to the fact that I happened already to be on board, and therefore could get to work sooner than if a man were sent from London. I offer you unreservedly my apologies for masquerading under another name, the reason for which the Captain has explained and which I hope you will all appreciate.'

French looked around, but the indignant looks persisted. No one spoke, and with a shrug he continued.

'Those of you, ladies and gentlemen, who were either relatives of the deceased or business associates, will be as anxious as I am that the affair be cleared up quickly, and for that reason I confidently ask your help. I want to ask you questions about the deceased, and about everyone's whereabouts on the afternoon of his death. This does not indicate suspicion of you, but is simply following the routine laid down for us officers, and I have no choice but to carry it out. I hope, therefore, you'll all give me as much information as you can.'

'And where do we come in?' Malthus demanded harshly.

'I'll tell you, sir, in a moment, if you and Mr Mason will be good enough to wait with the others.'

For a moment he paused, and this time Wyndham Stott spoke.

'I think we all recognise that an enquiry is inevitable, and we are anxious to help with it. But, to be candid, Chief Inspector, I think you have prejudiced your personal popularity by coming among us under a name other than your own.'

'Thank you, Mr Stott,' French answered, 'I'm grateful for your promise, and, as for the name, I've already apologised. Now I must put my cards on the table, as I do not want any of you to say you were questioned under false pretences.'

He looked searchingly around, then continued:

'Owing to this being a French ship, I have no *locus standi* aboard except when we're in British territorial waters, which are roughly inside three miles from any part of the shore. Therefore, with our present itinerary, I can only question you with the authority of the law behind me, between the hours of, say, eight to nine a.m., and five to seven p.m. During these hours you will probably be busy, and I don't want to inconvenience you. What I ask is that you voluntarily agree to being questioned at other times suitable to yourselves, in order to avoid my using those inconvenient hours, or having to get the ship's itinerary changed. Will you do that?'

There was some muttering amongst the eight visitors, then Percy Luff spoke up. His tone was always slightly offensive, but now it was much more so than usual, and French thought he had had too much drink.

'That sounds all very nice and very fair, but how do we know that still you're not bluffing us? What authority have you to question us inside the three-mile limit?'

French kept his temper. 'Perhaps it's as well that you

should have raised that point,' he returned. 'I shall show you my authority.' He took his card from his pocket and passed it round. 'The Captain will tell you that the area inside the three-mile limit is the legal equivalent of British soil. And on British soil you probably know that the law empowers a police officer to question civilians, and if he is not satisfied with their answers, to take them to a police station and detain them there for further interrogation.'

'That's all very well,' Luff answered, his tone still offensive, 'but you've no power to ask us anything at all except in the presence of our solicitors, and I for one am not going to answer any questions without mine.'

Elmina Stott's shrewd eyes showed approval, but Wyndham made a gesture of impatience.

'I disagree with you *in toto*,' he declared, looking with disgust at his stepson. 'We're all anxious to get this affair cleared up and we should all help the Chief Inspector as he suggests. I'm going to for one, and so should you—unless you've something to hide.'

'I'd like to know what you mean by that,' Mrs Stott said tartly. 'Are you accusing my son of committing a murder?'

'I'm accusing him of nothing, as you know very well,' Wyndham returned; 'but I repeat that if he refuses to answer the Chief Inspector's questions, it will look as if he had something to hide.'

'Thank you for the suggestion,' Percy retorted angrily. 'I'll manage my own affairs without your help. I won't answer without my solicitor, because I know what these police are like when they're out for a conviction. He'll find my name's in the will and heaven knows how he'll twist the facts against me.'

'You might have saved yourself, Mr Luff, from making

211

that entirely false insinuation,' French put in quietly. The little interchange, though embarrassing, had not been without its value. From the appearance and manner of the participants, as well as from their words, he had obtained a glimpse of their characters. Wyndham he had already seen something of and he believed him to be both straight and kindly, while his daughter, Margot, who was looking heartily ashamed of the whole affair, he held to be of the salt of the earth. But Elmina Stott was a shrew: her every intonation proclaimed it, and Luff was undoubtedly a bad egg.

'Well,' he continued, 'that's satisfactory. All but Mr Luff are going to help me and I'm grateful to you. You, Mr Luff, will be subpoenaed to attend the Coroner's Court at Portrush and will be arrested if you don't turn up. You can have your solicitor there and there you'll be questioned in public instead of here in private.' He paused for a moment. 'That's all our business, and thank you very much. I shall ask for statements from you—except Mr Luff—as may be convenient.'

'I shall have to know more about it before answering questions,' put in Malthus, while Mason nodded approvingly. 'On general grounds, I agree with Mr Luff.'

'Mr Luff's remark about his solicitor is perfectly correct,' French returned; 'and as for telling you more about the affair, I have every intention of doing so directly. That's all, thank you, Captain.'

Hardwick briefly added his thanks for their attendance and the party filed out, all but Percy Luff seeming relieved. Luff indeed looked almost murderous, though French believed he was now sorry for the stand he had taken, and unless he really had something to hide, would presently change his mind. It was with this object that French had made his bluff.

He moved off with Malthus and Mason. 'I'd like to have my chat with you first, Mr Malthus, and then afterwards with Mr Mason,' he went on, as Mason kept closely with them. 'It's our routine, laid down for us by authority.'

Rather unwillingly, Mason gave way and French followed Malthus to the latter's cabin.

'Now to give you the explanations you require, sir,' French went on briskly. 'Our instructions are that in the investigation of a suspected crime, the movements of everyone who *might* possibly be involved, must be gone into. This does not mean that we suspect these people. It's a matter of routine. For example, I don't suspect Mr Stott, still less Mrs or Miss Stott, but they benefit under the will, and I must therefore find out where they were at the time of the crime. I don't suspect Mr Bristow or Mr Morrison, but both have been heard inveighing against the deceased, so that brought them on to my list. I don't suspect you or Mr Mason, but owing to that business at the time of the purchase of the ship, you might have had a serious grudge against him. Hence this interview.'

Malthus seemed slightly taken aback. 'You're candid at least,' he returned, 'but all the same you really mean you do suspect me.'

'No, sir. As a reasonable man, you'll understand my position. I'm telling you the exact truth. With my present information it's theoretically possible that you may be guilty. I want more information from you which will prove your innocence and get your name off my list of possible suspects.'

'And if I refuse to give it?'

'You're entitled to do so, but, of course, that would arouse my suspicions in earnest, and I shouldn't stop till I got the information elsewhere.'

For a moment Malthus didn't reply and French could see that he was thinking intently. Then he shrugged. 'Well, since you're taking up a reasonable attitude, I'll answer your questions—with this reservation: that I may defer the answer to any question till I have consulted my solicitor.'

This was what French had been working for, as, if Malthus had insisted on his rights, it would have held up the enquiry.

'That's quite all right,' he agreed. 'Then I'll go ahead. I've really only one question to ask, though its answer may involve others. Tell me, please, in detail, all you did on the day the ship called at Portrush.'

Malthus seemed surprised. 'But you've got some bee in your bonnet about the purchase of the ship. Wouldn't it be well to clear that away before we go any further?'

'If you wish to make a statement about that, I shall be glad to hear it.'

'Oh, well, I see what's in your mind and I'd like to say that, though there might have been a little feeling about that affair at the time, it's long since dead. And there wasn't any real feeling either. We tried a little business trick to outwit Mr Stott, but he was too smart for us. We didn't expect him to bear malice for our action, and we didn't bear any for his. Do you think Mason and I would have come on board if the thing was rankling?'

'Since you've raised the question, why did you come on board?'

'I can tell you that. When we thought of doing this steamer stunt, it was for cruising for the small man as Bristow originally intended. And I may tell you incidentally that if we had pulled it off, we'd have offered Bristow a share. However, that's another matter. What I want you to understand is that we had no idea of the gambling.'

'I follow.'

'When Stott adopted this luxury gambling it left the small man's cruising scheme still unexploited. We still wanted to try it, but there was no ship available. Now, the *Yosemite Valley*, a big American boat, is to be sold and she would just do the job. We thought of buying her and came aboard to see first just what the cruising amounted to: I mean, what we could offer as to scenery and shore excursions and so on.'

'You met the deceased?'

'Yes, we met him and had a laugh over our experiences and formally buried the hatchet.'

'I see, sir. I'm glad to know that. Now perhaps you'd answer my original question?'

Malthus seemed annoyed. Evidently he had imagined that his explanation should have removed the need for an alibi. But French thought otherwise.

It seemed that a cousin of Malthus's, a widow named Hetherington, lived with her friend, a Miss Dormer, at Dungiven, a small town some thirty miles from Portrush. On going ashore on that eventful Tuesday, he and Mason had hired a car and driven by a roundabout route to Dungiven: up the Valley of the Bann and through Magherafelt and Draperstown and over the Sperrin Mountains. This had taken them till lunchtime. They had stayed with the ladies for tea, leaving in time to catch the ship's boat from Portrush just before six.

French realised that if this were true, it constituted a complete alibi for his first two suspects and he began to try for more details. As Stott was alive till after four, he was interested only in their return journey.

'You say you left Dungiven at half-past four, Mr Malthus. Have you any way of checking the time?'

'Well, we had reckoned that we should leave at half-past four to give us plenty of time to catch the boat. You see, we had to take back and square up for the car.'

'Quite. Did anyone else but yourselves note the time?'

Malthus considered. 'I think so,' he answered, 'though I couldn't really be certain. The ladies wanted a walk, and we took them with us for two or three miles and they walked back. I remember Miss Dormer had to go out that evening and she was fussy about the time they'd be back. She might remember.'

French thought this was all he needed for the present. The validity or otherwise of the alibi would depend on its confirmation by Nugent. He therefore thanked Malthus and went to Mason's cabin, where that gentleman was awaiting him.

Mason's story agreed in every material point with that of Malthus's, but he said further that he had discussed the time of departure with both ladies and he was sure both remembered it. They had had tea specially early, which he thought would fix it in their memories.

Wyndham Stott's was the next name on the list, but as it was now getting on to twelve and people went to bed early on board, he decided to postpone his interrogation till the following day.

Next morning the *Hellénique* was in Bantry Bay and the excursion was to Glengariff and Killarney. As it was such a good trip French had been reluctant to ask the Stotts, Bristow and Morrison to abandon it so that he might obtain their statements. However, he had no alternative, and all more or less willingly agreed to stay on board.

He began after breakfast with Wyndham. Wyndham appeared anxious to dissipate any suspicions his stepson's manner might have aroused in French's mind. 'He's an ill-mannered young ass,' he exclaimed, 'but you mustn't take him too seriously. I think he has an inferiority complex and feels he must bounce and swagger to keep his end up. But he's not really a bad sort. You'll find he'll come round presently and do all you want.'

'He's right about the solicitor, you know,' French pointed out. 'You can all follow his example if you want to.'

'I'm aware of that, but as far as I'm concerned I have nothing to hide and I feel that a man who has reached your position would not twist facts. I'm sure the rest of us take the same view, even Luff, though he did talk like a fool.'

'I'm grateful for that, sir,' answered French, and chatted on the cruise till they had settled down in the deserted music-room.

'Now,' he went on, 'I'll be glad of information of any kind which you think might be useful to me. Secondly, I want to know the relations which existed between all of you and the deceased, particularly whether anyone was on bad terms with him or had cause to hate him. Lastly, I have to ask you and the others to account for your time on the afternoon of the cruise. Now, sir, perhaps you'd start off.'

Wyndham was quite ready to speak, but he had nothing very interesting to tell. Generally speaking, the deceased was not popular. He had, or could have when he chose, an unpleasant manner, and he seldom curbed it or went out of his way to smooth the way for others. He was also a keen and successful business man, and, as the Chief Inspector

217

knew, one man's gain meant another's loss and there must be many financial casualties who had no cause to love him.

Wyndham made no bones of the fact that neither he nor the rest of the family liked John, but in no case was there active ill feeling between them. The general attitude was illustrated by his own. While he saw as little of the deceased as possible, when they did meet they were always friendly. John's feeling towards him was shown by the fact that he had—so Wyndham believed—made him his heir.

'That's a point I forgot to mention,' French put in. 'I wonder if you could tell me the provisions of the will?'

Wyndham shook his head. 'I couldn't,' he replied. 'I know that he told me some time ago that I should be his heir, as I was the only close member of his family left. He said there would be several legacies to other people, but that I should have the larger portion.'

'You can't give an idea of the amounts?'

'Not with any degree of accuracy. John was usually supposed to be worth about a million, and if I were to get the larger portion, I should have, I suppose, not less than six hundred thousand. But I can't stand over any of these figures.'

'Quite so, sir. Then your own will? I don't know that I'm in order in asking, but if you don't mind, I should like to know its provisions.'

Wyndham hesitated. 'I don't quite see what that has to do with the affair,' he protested, 'but I don't mind telling you. I have divided what I die possessed of into three parts: two go to my wife and one to my daughter, both absolutely.'

'Thank you very much. Now for the formal question as to your movements on last Tuesday afternoon. Perhaps you'd kindly account for the whole time you spent ashore.

Particularly mention. the names of persons you met. We always have to check up alibis.'

'I understand. All the family except my uncle—myself, my wife, my daughter and my stepson—spent the morning at the Salmon Leap at Coleraine. We lunched at Portrush with some friends, the Atkinsons. They live in a house, "Mera Maw", not far from the Ladies' Bathing Place, but they entertained us at the Northern Counties Hotel.'

'Good,' said French. 'That provides an excellent start. Yes?'

'We stayed with them for a little time after lunch and then the party broke up. The Atkinsons were driving to see some cousins at a place called Castlerock, a few miles along the coast, and they wanted us all to go on with them. However, I didn't particularly want to do so, and they were strangers to my wife and Percy. Margot was different. She had stayed with them a couple of years earlier at Capri and they had been kind to her, and she felt she couldn't turn the invitation down. So she went along with the Atkinsons. The other three of us separated at the hotel.'

'And what did you all do, sir?'

'My wife left me to have a round of golf on the Ladies' links and Percy disappeared; he didn't say where he was going. I went for a walk. I don't play golf, but I'm fond of walking and I walk when I can.'

'Quite so. And where did you go?'

'I took a bus to Portstewart and walked out along the strand to the mouth of the Bann. I'm interested in rivers and currents and I knew that a lot of money had been spent there with moles and training banks and so on, and I wanted to see the work. I followed the bank of the river for a mile or two up towards Coleraine, then turned back across sand-dunes and fields to Portstewart. There I got a car back to Portrush.'

'Where did you get tea, sir?'

'I didn't have any. At tea-time I was out on the sand-dunes and when I reached Portstewart there was only time to get over to Portrush and catch the last boat to the ship. The walk took longer than I had anticipated and I had to hurry back.'

'The last boat left about six?'

'Yes, at six nominally—actually at five minutes past. I got to the slip at five minutes to and had to wait ten minutes.'

'Did you meet anyone on your walk?'

'No one that I knew. There were people at Portstewart, of course, and I think I met people on the strand beyond it, but I don't remember anyone along the river.'

'Where did you get your car?'

'At a garage in the main street. I don't remember its name, but it was about half-way round the bay.'

French considered. 'Thank you very much, sir,' he said at last. 'That's all I want at present. Some other point may arise later, but there's nothing more in the meantime. I wonder if you'd ask Mrs Stott to come here if she's not engaged?'

Though French had not suspected Wyndham of the crime, he had hoped to have been able to eliminate him entirely from doubt. Now he could not do so. He believed that the man could, so far as time went, have committed the murder. He unrolled a one-inch Ordnance map which Nugent had also brought him and scaled the distances. Yes, he felt sure he could have done it. If Wyndham had reached Portrush at 5.55, he would not have left Portstewart till nearly 5.50, the distance being only three and a quarter miles. If, further, the murder had been completed by, say, 4.30, as seemed likely, there would have been ample time for him to walk from the Hollow to Portstewart, using the route past Portstewart Station and Magherabuoy, which would have kept him in the country and out of Portrush. And the same applied in the opposite direction. There would have been plenty of time for him to have reached the Hollow after his luncheon party, even if he had first taken a bus to Portstewart. For the present, therefore, Wyndham must remain on the list of suspects.

French's further cogitations were brought to an end by the entrance of Elmina Stott. French had only met her on the previous evening and he had not taken to her. Now she was strongly on the defensive and her manner was brusque and unhelpful. Indeed, she seemed to be taking a leaf from her son's book. French chatted a little on the general situation before coming to actual business, trying to obtain her reactions to both people and events.

He did not learn very much except to confirm his ideas of her character. She spoke critically and rather slightingly of her husband and French felt that Wyndham could not have too easy a time. Also, he was sure she hated and was jealous of Margot, probably partly for her looks, and partly for the fondness which evidently existed between father and daughter. Altogether Wyndham's second marriage could not have proved an unmixed blessing either for him or Margot.

As to her movements on the Tuesday, these were simple enough. After the luncheon party—which began at one and ended at a quarter to three—she walked directly to the Ladies' Club House, played a round of golf, had tea, and returned to the boats about half-past five. All the afternoon she was in the presence of several other people, who could vouch for her.

Margot came next on the list. The more French saw of Margot, the more he admired her. He had liked her when they had first met in the flying boat, and she had since been unfailingly pleasant to him, as well as really friendly to Mrs French. Mrs French had quite fallen in love with her, proclaiming her delight in meeting any young person so good and kind and unspoilt.

From his preliminary discussion with her, French learned little that he had not already known. Margot was deeply attached to her father and had evidently deplored his marriage. It looked as if she did not care for Elmina, though French doubted if her feeling amounted to actual jealousy. But of her dislike of Percy there was no doubt whatever. She could not keep the distaste out of her tone when she spoke of him.

On the Monday she had lunched at the Northern Counties Hotel and there had learnt from the Atkinsons that their cousins, the Donnellys, with whom she had stayed in Capri, were at Castlerock and were hoping to see her that afternoon. It was inconvenient, as she had meant to go to the Causeway; but the Donnellys had been so kind to her abroad that she felt she could not refuse. There was another reason which weighed also with her. Clara Donnelly, the daughter, had been offered a job as private secretary to a man Margot had known in Egypt and she wanted some confidential advice as to whether acceptance would be wise. This also Margot felt she could not refuse.

French was puzzled by her apparent eagerness to justify her visit to Castlerock. 'But did it really matter to you which you did?' he therefore asked.

'Well,' she answered with some hesitation, 'it did in a way. You see, Mr Morrison had asked me to let him show me the Causeway and I had agreed. He had been there before and knew what to look out for. So I had to ring him up and say it was off.'

'Did you ring to the ship?'

'No, to the Causeway Hotel. He lunched there.'

Her slight unwillingness to speak tended to confirm a rumour that French had heard from many sources. It was the general opinion on the ship that she and Morrison were in love and that an engagement might be announced at any time. If so, French sincerely hoped he was mistaken about Morrison's shoes.

That was the only point of interest he learnt from Margot. She had gone to Castlerock, returning with the Atkinsons to Portrush just in time to catch the ship's boat at six o'clock.

French looked at his watch. It was getting on for lunchtime. He thought he had done enough for that morning and that Morrison and Bristow could wait till the afternoon. He would go for a breather on deck before lunch.

But on his way he ran into Percy Luff. The young man stopped him. His aggressiveness had largely evaporated. French had expected it would, though not so quickly.

'I say,' he accosted French, 'I think I was a bit short last night. I've been hearing what you asked the others, and if that's all you want from me, I don't mind answering your questions.'

From Luff this was an apology and a handsome one. French took it as such, replying in a friendly way: 'That's all right, Mr Luff; it's all the same to me. But what about your solicitor? You were quite right about that, you know.'

Luff seemed surprised. 'I didn't do the old boy in, so I don't mind about it,' he replied. 'All the same I don't want anything said about where I was. I don't mind telling you, you understand, provided it goes no further.'

French shook his head. 'I can't promise that, I'm afraid,' he returned seriously. 'If it's not material evidence in connection with the case, I'll keep it to myself. If it is, it may have to come out in court.'

Luff seemed relieved. 'It has nothing whatever to do with the case, but it concerns a lady aboard this ship and I don't want her name dragged into it.'

'That's all right. But I warn you I shall require you to sign a statement that you gave me your information of your own free will and without any compulsion on my part.'

'All right. Haven't I told you I'm willing?'

'Fine,' said French. 'Let's meet in your cabin after lunch and get it over.'

Delighted to find he was not to be held up here either, he went for his breather.

16

Retort to Nugent

Luff's statement, when French presently obtained it, confirmed those of the other members of his family as to the period up to the end of the lunch on the fateful Tuesday, except that his comments about the Atkinsons were not so parliamentary. The party had broken up outside the Northern Counties Hotel and he had gone for a short stroll on Ramore Head.

A question brought out the reason: it was not for the sake of the scenery, but to let the others get away. He had then returned to the town and taken a bus to Coleraine, some five miles distant. There he had hung about till 4 p.m., at which hour he was to meet his friend from the ship. But she hadn't turned up. He had waited about for over an hour, then had returned to Portrush and had taken a boat aboard, leaving the shore about a quarter to six.

This was exactly the kind of tale French would have expected to hear, were Percy Luff guilty. Here was the incipient alibi, which would be strengthened later, but which would eventually turn out incapable of verification. However, he could but continue his questions.

He suspected the lady—if she existed at all—to be Mrs Mercer, a flamboyant dame with a *penchant* for loud dresses, whiskies and sodas and smoking-room stories. He had seen the two together on many occasions and the bar considered that a promising flirtation was in progress. A little bluff might settle the point.

'That's all right, Mr Luff,' he responded easily. 'Now if you don't mind, just a little more detail. Where in Coleraine were you to meet Mrs Mercer?'

Luff seemed taken aback. 'Damn it all, Chief Inspector, I mentioned no names,' he said huffily.

'I know,' French returned sweetly, 'but it's easy to visualise happenings if you know the actors. It was Mrs Mercer, of course?'

'I think this is a dirty trick. I particularly wanted to keep her name out of it.'

'Yes, but you can't. However, it's most unlikely that it'll go any further. Where were you to meet?'

Luff glowered at him, but finally answered, 'We were to have tea in a small shop in New Row.'

French nodded. 'Discretion? I understand. Where did you have tea yourself?'

'I didn't have any. I walked about waiting for her and then, when I finally gave her up, it was too late for tea.'

'Quite so. Now, Mr Luff, when was this meeting arranged?'

Luff seemed more and more unwilling to proceed. 'Damn it all,' he repeated, 'what has that got to do with the murder?'

'Nothing that I know of,' French returned, 'but a lot to do with your alibi.'

Luff gave him a look of positive hatred. 'She wrote to me that morning,' he said unwillingly.

'Oh,' French gave a nod of understanding. 'Got the letter?'

'Yes, damn it. But I don't suppose even you want to see it.'

'Oh, but I do,' French assured him brightly. 'I'm not suggesting that I doubt your alibi, but we have to test such matters, and once it is established I need give you no further trouble.'

Unwillingly Luff took a paper from his pocket and handed it over.

The note was written on *Hellénique* paper, and was a model of propriety:

'DEAR MR LUFF,' *it read,*

'I am going to Coleraine this afternoon to see an old family retainer and hope to have tea at the Corona in New Row at four o'clock. If you happen to be in the neighbourhood, I should like to show you the strange epitaph to my ancestor in the churchyard, which I told you of. It is really worth seeing, and if you would bring your camera, perhaps you would take a photo of it for me?

'Yours sincerely,

'EDITH MERCER.'

'Had she told you of an epitaph in the churchyard?' French asked.

'No,' Luff muttered with another look of hatred.

French smiled easily. 'Well, that's all right and quite normal. It was just to give you the opportunity to meet her if you wanted to. Nothing to criticise in that. Did she hand you the note?'

'No, a steward brought it to my cabin.'

'Did he say where he got it?'

'Yes. He had found it on the floor of the alleyway outside my cabin.'

French looked interested, but he made no remark except a non-committal, 'I understand.' He paused for a moment, then went on: 'Had you any conversation with Mrs Mercer about the letter?'

'Not then.'

'Not when?'

'Not that morning.'

'You mean that you didn't see her on the subject before the hour of the meeting?'

'That's what I mean.'

'Then when did you see her? Come on, Mr Luff, do let me have these details without my having to drag them out of you. Don't you know your statement is useless without them?'

Luff seemed to resign\himself to the inevitable. 'I spoke to her next time I saw her: that was after dinner that night.'

'Yes?' French's tone was impatient. 'What did she say?'

'I asked her why she had not turned up and she simply stared at me. Then I asked her about her letter and she denied having written it.'

'Oh,' said French. The alibi was developing on conventional lines. 'Knew nothing about it, did she?'

'Nothing. It must have been a forgery. But who could have done such a thing, and why? We thought it was an imbecile joke by some of those swine on board, but we couldn't think of which one.'

'Well,' suggested French, 'it's not so difficult to imagine an explanation. The murderer of Mr Stott might have wanted to fit you up with an afternoon without an alibi. You're a beneficiary under the will, aren't you?'

Luff seemed shocked. 'Damn it all, I never thought of that.'

French suddenly dropped his rather aloof manner and spoke seriously. 'That's the reason, Mr Luff, as you can see for yourself, why your alibi is so important to me. If someone forged that letter, it was probably the murderer. That letter may be the most valuable clue I have yet got. You can see that for your own sake you must give me all the help in your power.'

Luff was evidently much shaken. 'But I'm doing so,' he protested.

'I'm sure you are,' French agreed heartily. 'Now just another question and I have done. I noticed a new button on the left sleeve of your sports coat. Where did you lose the old one?'

Though French watched the young man keenly as he spoke, he could not be certain as to his reaction. That he was frightened by the question was obvious, but it was not clear whether this was due to guilty terror or to a vague fear that French must know damaging facts which he had not revealed.

'I don't know where I lost it,' he answered, and a more complete contrast to the former young man of bounce and brag could scarcely be imagined.

'Then when did you discover the loss?'

Luff hesitated, either thinking or pretending to think.

'It was that evening,' he replied almost in a flood of words, 'coming back in the boat. I remember now. I leant my arm

229

on the gunwale and saw the button was gone. It was my own fault. I had noticed it loose, and I should have had it tightened on. But I thought it was all right for a day or two. Why do you ask?' He was almost breathless.

'I saw that it had been replaced. Those sorts of things help sometimes, but apparently in this case, it's not going to. Well, Mr Luff, that's all at last. I'm greatly obliged to you for your statement and I'm sorry to have kept you so long.'

As he left the cabin French swore inwardly. Luff was his chief suspect and here, as in the case of Wyndham, he had not reached certainty. The letter, he took it, would prove to be a forgery all right and written in all probability by the murderer, but that got him very little further. Had Luff written it himself and dropped it outside his cabin, or had someone else done so? Perhaps examination of the letter would throw some light on this point, but the facts he had learnt so far certainly didn't.

Well, that could all be gone into later. The thing now was to get these blessed interrogations over. Bristow's was the next name on his list, and after ringing him up, he went to his cabin.

He did not hope for much from Bristow, as his grounds for suspicion of the man were of the slightest: merely that he had been overheard to express contempt and detestation for Stott. But he intended to examine him carefully, so as to prevent Morrison from realising that he was the real suspect. If they discussed the affair afterwards, as they certainly would, they must find that they had been treated alike.

'You're entitled, as you probably know, Mr Bristow,' French began, when they were seated, 'to refuse to reply to my questions except in the presence of your solicitor. I take it you don't wish to stand on your rights in the matter?'

'Thank you, but I do very decidedly,' Bristow returned. 'I'm a solicitor myself and I know very well what you can ask and what you can't. I'll look after myself.'

'Quite satisfactory to me,' French assured him. He had come across Bristow very little in his Forrester impersonation, though he had spoken to him once or twice. Now he saw that, were he guilty, the man would prove a hard nut to deal with. He had undoubted ability and strength of character and his solicitor's training would keep his answers discreet and innocuous.

French first obtained a brief history of the start of the cruise, learning that the original idea was Bristow's, that at first he could interest no one with money, that in despair he confided in Morrison, that Morrison introduced him to Stott, and that Stott proved to be the man for whom he was looking. Then how he had fixed up an agreement with Stott for the division of profits, how Stott bought the *Hellénique* through the French Company, refitted her, and developed the flying boat service. So far as French could see, Bristow told him all he wanted to know directly and without evasion.

'Now, that agreement you had with Mr Stott,' French went on, remembering the letter from Bristow he had found among Stott's papers, complaining that he had not been paid his share of the profits, 'was it carried out?'

'Absolutely,' Bristow returned. 'I admit that Mr Stott had not paid my percentage profits, but when I wrote reminding him about it, he said that when he had met one or two outstanding items, which would affect the amount due to me, he would settle.'

'And you had no doubt that he would do so?'

Bristow smiled rather unpleasantly. 'None,' he answered grimly. 'There could be none. I had drawn up our agreement myself and if he had refused to pay I could have taken him into court and recovered the money. He knew that as well as I did, though I'm not suggesting the knowledge was needed to make him pay.'

'Very well, Mr Bristow. Now can you tell me anything about personal relations on the ship? How did you all get on?'

Bristow's reply was typical. He considered that they got on as well or as badly as any ordinary crowd of people would do under similar circumstances. There were on occasion misunderstandings and bickerings, but nothing was seriously amiss. Taking them by and large, the men aboard were a very decent crowd, and so far as he, Bristow, was concerned, he got on well with them all.

'But you didn't like the deceased?'

'No,' said Bristow, 'I didn't. Nor did anyone else, if it comes to that. But I found him all right to work with. He had an unpleasant, domineering manner which put people's backs up. But I don't think he meant to be offensive.'

'Then just one other routine question, which I put to everyone. Will you please account for your time ashore on the day of Mr Stott's death?'

For the first time Bristow seemed less self-assured. But he replied as directly as before. 'There,' he said, 'I'm afraid you have me. I haven't a satisfactory alibi, if that's what you want. Morrison and I were talking about it when we heard you wanted to question us, and neither of us have.'

'Too good an alibi often creates suspicion, Mr Bristow, as I expect you know. Never mind about proof; just tell me what you did, and put in plenty of detail.'

'I went ashore with the others and was met at the boat-slip by a couple of friends from the Golf Club: people I had known in London, but who were then staying at Portrush. I wanted some films, and after getting the camera charged, we had a round of golf. We lunched at the Club House and after lunch developed an argument on driving. I had my camera and I took a couple of snaps of one or two of the men in the middle of their swing. I could not play myself in the afternoon, as Mr Stott had asked me to take some photographs of a ruin a mile or more out of the town. So I walked with my party for a few holes of the round, as far as our ways were parallel, then I left them, went to the ruin, took my photographs, and returned to the Club House. They were at tea when I arrived and I joined them. They were still arguing about the driving and after tea I took one or two more snaps of swings. There wasn't time to begin another round, so after the photographing we went down to the boats and I came aboard.'

'That's very clear, Mr Bristow. Could you say at what hours you left your party and returned to it?'

Bristow smiled a little grimly. 'I can't answer that exactly,' he returned, 'but I can approximately. We had lunch at one-thirty, and it lasted for about an hour. Then we sat over coffee for perhaps half an hour more. We started play about three, as near as I can estimate. It would take, I suppose, forty minutes to reach the hole at which I left them, so that must have been somewhere about three-forty or forty-five. It was almost exactly five when I got back: they were half-way through tea.'

Once again French experienced that little wave of annoyance. It looked as if Bristow was entirely correct when he said he hadn't a satisfactory alibi. An absence during the hours stated would undoubtedly have enabled him to visit the Hollow. Moreover, he could have been there at the estimated hour of the murder. Was there to be no certainty about anyone in this exasperating case?

'Just show me those places on the map,' said French, unrolling his 6-inch Ordnance.

'There,' Bristow pointed, 'is the Club House, and some-where about there the hole at which I left the party. Up here'—he searched for a few moments, then his pencil halted—'that's the ruin I photographed.'

'Quite.' French scaled the distances. 'I make it a mile from where you left your party to the ruin, and a mile and a half or more from the ruin back to the Club House: say, two and a half miles altogether. How long would it have taken you to walk that, Mr Bristow?'

'About three-quarters of an hour, I expect. It was across the fields and there were some fences to be climbed.'

'Three-quarters of an hour, and you had about an hour and a quarter altogether. What about the other half-hour?

'Oh well, I spent at least that taking the photographs; I should have said even longer. You can't go to a place like that and simply let fly at once, you understand. You have to consider a number of points: what exactly you want to show, how many pictures will do it, where you should stand to include the required details and to get the best light. You'll find, if you try it yourself, half an hour isn't any too long for a job of the kind.'

French smiled. 'I'm not questioning it. How many views did you take?'

'Of the ruin? I took five. One roughly from north, south, east and west, and a detail of what looked like rudimentary carving.'

'Can I see the photographs?'

'As a matter of fact, I haven't developed them. Stott, of course, is no longer in a position to demand his, and in the hurry and upset caused by his death I let the matter slide. But I'll develop them for you with pleasure.'

'Perhaps you wouldn't mind my photographer doing them? He's a very good man.'

Bristow seemed surprised at the request. 'Of course,' he answered, 'I've no objection whatever. Save me the trouble. But I confess I don't get your idea.'

'Well, to put it bluntly, has it not occurred to you that if you were photographing this ruin at quarter-past four, you could not have been at McArtt's Hollow murdering Mr Stott?'

'I realise that all right, and if you think the photographs will establish it, I'm not likely to dispute your decision. Morrison and I discussed the point, and he was satisfied that they would.'

'But you don't think so?'

'You're no fool, Chief Inspector, so there's no use pretending to you. My spool of film will prove that the photographs were taken. Unhappily, they won't prove I took them.'

'You mean that you could have lent your camera to someone else during that hour and a quarter?'

Bristow hesitated. 'As a matter of fact, I don't think I could. But you'll think it.'

'Well,' French decided, 'let me have the undeveloped spool, at all events. I suppose, Mr Bristow, since you did not murder Mr Stott, you've no idea who might have done so? Any theory would be gratefully received and kept confidential.'

But Bristow was not to be drawn, and after a few more questions French left him.

Though the photography made a kind of alibi for Bristow, French was not interested in it. So far as he could see, the matter of motive settled Bristow's case. Bristow had no motive for killing Stott, but he had a very strong one for keeping him alive. If Stott were to die, the whole continuance of the gambling cruise was jeopardised. If, as seemed likely, the venture would pass to Wyndham, no one could say what would happen to it. Wyndham might be a pleasanter character than John, but he was no business man. He would almost certainly let the affair down. And if so, neither Bristow nor anyone else in it, so far as French knew, had the cash to set it going again. John Stott's rule undoubtedly meant security for all concerned.

His thoughts turned to Morrison. Because of the footprint, Morrison was his first suspect. But were not Morrison and Bristow in the same boat with regard to motive? If Bristow had everything to lose by Stott's death, was this not true of Morrison also?

At once French saw that he was wrong. Morrison's position and Bristow's were as different as day and night. For Bristow John Stott's death meant insecurity; for Morrison, if he could pull off marriage with Margot, it meant the approach of a fortune. And everything that French had heard tended to the belief that he would pull it off. Morrison, if he were sufficiently callous, certainly had an ample motive for the crime.

All the same, Morrison scarcely seemed to be of the stuff of which murderers were made. He was a very ordinary young man, unlikely, French would have said, to adopt drastic measures even were his situation desperate, which it certainly was not. However, bitter experience had taught French that appearances were the last foundation on which to build a theory. It was with an open mind, therefore, that he presently called at the young man's cabin.

'Now, Mr Morrison,' he began cheerily, 'it's your turn, if you please. I've had statements from Mr Malthus and Mr Mason and the family, and Mr Bristow has just given me his. Will you please tell me what you did while ashore on the day we were at Portrush?'

It was evident that Morrison was acutely nervous; much more nervous than could be accounted for by mere interrogation by the police. French watched him surreptitiously.

'I had an appointment before lunch with the manager of the Causeway Hotel, and to fill up the time while waiting for it I had a look at Dunluce and the Causeway. I lunched at the Causeway Hotel.'

'Yes? And then?'

On the whole Morrison told his tale well. Lunch over, he had found himself somewhat at a loose end. He had, however, wanted exercise and had walked the eight miles into Portrush, where he had caught one of the earlier boats to the ship.

'A negative lie,' thought French. 'He's trying to keep Margot's name out of it.' He unrolled his map.

'Point out your route on this,' he directed. 'It doesn't show the Causeway, but here's the road from it to Portrush.'

Morrison did as he was asked, indicating the path to the shore up which Stott had passed.

'Now I want the times of all that fixed up,' French demanded, and after working it out, he continued: 'Then you must have passed this place here, marked McArtt's Hollow, at about quarter past four?'

Morrison could scarcely speak. He nodded shortly.

'Why does that upset you, Mr Morrison?' went on French, keeping his eyes on his victim.

Morrison made a gesture of impatience. 'Well, you might know that,' he retorted. 'We understand that Mr Stott was supposed to have been killed there some time in the afternoon, and I'm not such a fool as to miss the direction of your questions.'

"If you think my questions objectionable, Mr Morrison, you have only yourself to thank for it,' French said harshly. 'Why can't you be open with me and tell me the truth?'

Morrison's jaw dropped. 'But that is the truth,' he stammered.

'Half the truth perhaps,' French went on inexorably. 'Did you go into the Hollow as you passed?'

For a moment Morrison could not reply. Then feebly he shook his head. 'No,' he returned. 'Why should I?'

His manner showed that he was lying. French was satisfied that he was normally honest, and normally honest people make bad liars.

'We'll see about that in a moment,' French went on. 'Now tell me, did you receive a telephone message at the hotel?'

Morrison hesitated as if thinking over his reply. Then with a helpless gesture he answered, 'Yes.'

'Then why did you not mention it?'

'It had nothing to do with my movements, which were what you wanted.'

French sympathised with his effort to keep Margot's name out of it and accepted this.

'Very well,' he agreed. 'But you've mentioned it now. Who rang you up?' Then as Morrison still remained silent, he went on: 'I know all about it, as well as about some other things you haven't mentioned. You can't keep Miss Stott's name out of it, so you needn't try.'

Morrison's nervousness passed for the moment and he spoke earnestly. 'But why not, Chief Inspector? Miss Stott had no connection with the affair. Why should she be dragged in?'

For the first time during the interview French admired the young man. 'I don't say she'll be dragged in,' he returned more pleasantly. 'What I want is a truthful account of your own movements.'

'Very well,' Morrison agreed, as if giving up the struggle. 'She had promised to come out to the Causeway in the afternoon and she rang up to say she was prevented.'

'What exactly were your plans?'

'To walk together round the Causeway and Heads and to return to Portrush in time for the last boat.'

This answer frankly puzzled French. He had no doubt it was true, not only from the man's changed manner, but because it had been practically confirmed by Margot. But if it were true, Morrison would not have passed the Hollow at the time of Stott's death. He would not have been able, except in the presence of Margot and the driver of their vehicle, to visit the Hollow at all. More significant still, he could not then have had an appointment with Stott.

French wondered where this was leading him. If Morrison had had no appointment with Stott, could he have murdered him? His meeting Stott—if he did meet him—would have been an accident, and it was most unlikely that a quarrel involving murder could have arisen so suddenly. Indeed, there had not been a quarrel. Had such obtained, the ground would have been trampled up and traces would have shown on the body.

It looked as if Morrison were innocent: and yet what about the shoes?

'Tell me, Mr Morrison,' French said suddenly, 'why did you get rid of the shoes you wore that afternoon?'

Morrison stared speechlessly and his face slowly whitened till French thought he was going to faint. But French did not withdraw. 'I want to know that,' he said impressively, and, deciding on a bluff, added: 'And I also want to know what you did with Percy Luff's button.'

It was a knock-out blow. Morrison gave a groan and sank his head in his hands. French said nothing. Silence would increase the effect.

At last Morrison looked up. 'I see you know everything, Chief Inspector,' he said in shaky tones, 'so I must tell you the truth. I was in the Hollow and I did pick up the button. But I didn't murder Mr Stott. I swear that.'

'I'm not saying you did,' said French. 'All I want is the truth.'

'You shall have it;' and he told exactly what had happened. 'You must see why I wanted to hide it,' he went on piteously. 'I was afraid that if I told you you'd suspect me. And now probably you do suspect me, and I can't do anything about it. I can't prove my innocence.'

For some moments there was silence, then French asked for the button. Morrison took it from a drawer and handed it over. Fortunately there was some thread attached to it, enough to settle the question of whether or not it had come from Luff's coat.

To say that French was satisfied as to Morrison's innocence was putting it too strongly, but he was disposed to believe the story and that for three reasons. First, there was the point he had already considered, that it was by accident that

Morrison reached the Hollow when he did. Second, there was his manner, now completely different and French believed that of a truthful man. Third, had Morrison been the murderer, it was not easy to account for the position of the footprint. It would surely have been leading towards or away from the body, but it was not. It indicated a direction passing well away from where the remains were lying. But the position was exactly in accordance with Morrison's statement.

Now he saw, so is the wish father to the thought in even the most logical of us, that the motive he had been attributing to Morrison was really not so satisfactory as he had imagined. He doubted if a man of Morrison's apparent character could have murdered a relative of the girl he hoped to marry, so that she would eventually obtain money of which he would have the use. Morrison, he thought, was of too good a type for this, and in any case he was strongly of opinion that he had not the nerve.

It looked more and more like as if Luff was his man. However, he reminded himself that he must avoid leaping to conclusions. A good many points required further investigation before he could reach a decision.

The first was that of the letter Luff said he had received from Mrs Mercer. French took it from the desk in his cabin and examined it with a lens.

At once the opinion he had formed from a cursory glance was confirmed. The letter was a forgery. It was full of those tiny shakes which showed it had not been written boldly, but had been carefully drawn in.

Unfortunately, this proof of what he had already suspected got him no further. It was reasonable to suppose that the forger was the murderer, but there was nothing to show whether Luff was or was not the man.

French next saw Mrs Mercer, who luckily had not gone ashore on this day. She denied absolutely having written the letter or knowing anything whatever about it except what Luff had told her. French then got her to rewrite the note from his dictation, and was interested to find that the hands were dissimilar. The murderer therefore had not had access to her handwriting. But again this did not help. Luff had not known it either.

But the letter evidently *had* been copied. Probably not from a complete draft. It would have been dangerous to have such a thing made, as, had it been read in court, the writer might have heard of it and come forward. It was more likely to have been built up word by word from the other writings of some women, for the hand was undoubtedly feminine. Certainly the writing could not have been assumed or designed. It was a natural hand.

Was there not here a clue? If he could find this woman, he would be on the track of the murderer.

However, that must wait. His first job was to prepare a surprise packet for Nugent. He put in copies of all the statements he had received, asking for local checking of details. He enclosed the Mercer–Luff letter (having first photographed it) suggesting that Nugent might find someone who wrote a similar hand. He sent Bristow's roll of films, demanding enlargements of the critical views and a check-up on the sites. He asked for interrogations of the staff of the Causeway Hotel as to Morrison's movements, of the drivers at the garage half-way along the Portstewart main street for the man who drove Wyndham to Portrush, of after-lunch bus drivers from Portrush to Portstewart, of people who had been to the mouth of the Bann on that afternoon, if any could be discovered, and of shopkeepers and others in

New Row, Coleraine, who might have seen Luff hanging about.

'That'll be tit-for-tat,' French thought with satisfaction. 'When they get this those folk won't be so pleased that they unloaded their beastly job on me.' He went down to dinner with the consciousness of good work well done.

17

Complete Elimination?

French didn't think that there was much that he could do on board until he received Nugent's answers to his questions. Indeed, he knew of only one enquiry which he might usefully make. The pattern for the Mercer–Luff letter had probably been written by someone on the ship. If he could find the handwriting, it should prove a clear pointer to the murderer.

Having missed Killarney on the previous day, he was strongly tempted to postpone this not very urgent job and go ashore. The excursion was from just inside Roche's Point up Cork Harbour, past Cobh and Ringaskiddy and Monkstown and Passage West to the city, then from Blarney to Lismore by coach and by river steamer down the Blackwater to Youghal.

Duty, however, prevailed, and when the shore party had left, he began work by a visit to the purser. From him he was able to obtain samples of the handwriting of practically every woman on board, and in the few instances in which this source failed, queries about bills or other small subterfuges quickly produced the needful. The result was negative.

After a lot of work, French became satisfied the writer was not on the ship.

It was on that same evening that he received his first openly official letter from the Yard, Sir Mortimer having evidently realised that Forrester was dead and that French had come to life in his place. It contained two interesting items of information. First, it gave a *précis* of John Stott's will, obtained (with difficulty) from his solicitors. This showed that French's previous information was correct: that John was worth about a million, and that, subject to the payment of a number of small legacies, including a not unsubstantial remembrance to each other member of the family, Wyndham was his heir.

The second item cleared up a point which had puzzled French. It was not usual, of course, either for the Royal Ulster Constabulary to apply to Scotland Yard for help nor for the Yard to give it. In this case apparently, the R.U.C. had not asked for it, but only for information as to the status of the *Hellénique*. But Sir Mortimer had immediately offered French's help, and that with the utmost cordiality. Now came the explanation. 'I hope,' wrote Sir Mortimer, 'that you will prosecute your *Hellénique* enquiries into this murder to good purpose.' To anyone who knew Sir Mortimer, the meaning was clear. It was to give French a better opportunity to investigate the shipboard life and the gambling that he had been pitchforked into someone else's job.

French felt he had a distinct grievance in the matter. He now had two cases to worry over instead of one. Sir Mortimer's action, he believed further, had been a profound mistake. It had not helped him about the gambling. On the contrary, all that it had done had been to put the ship's officers on their guard against him.

However, that was not his pigeon and he must not look at the dark side of the affair. The bright side was pleasanter, and the bright side was that, until he heard from Nugent, he could with a clear conscience go ashore.

This blissful state of affairs lasted for three days. On the first they landed at Dunmore at the mouth of Waterford Harbour and drove to Howth, through Waterford, New Ross, Woodenbridge, Glendalough, the Wicklow Hills and Dublin. Next day was spent in Dublin and its surroundings, while on the third they went from Dundalk through Newry and round the Mourne Mountains to Belfast. All were charming excursions and luckily the weather was excellent. French enjoyed every minute of the time.

On the next morning came a voluminous reply from Nugent. The *Hellénique* was off the Isle of Man and the excursion was from Peel to Douglas, going practically round the island. Having seen his Em off, French pulled a deck-chair into the secluded place he loved between the two boats, and proceeded to digest his despatch.

It was at once evident that the D.I. had spared neither himself nor his staff. Indeed, French was astonished to receive so much information at such short notice, even though he had not forgotten what he had noticed on his earlier cases in Northern Ireland: how closely the local constables keep in touch with the people of their districts. If information is required, they usually know where it is to be found, and, unless political considerations forbid, they can generally obtain the hint they need. Here Nugent had drafted his replies separately about each suspect and French took the reports in turn.

The first was about Malthus and Mason, and as French read it he saw that the theory of their guilt must be abandoned. Their statement, it appeared, was true and their alibi sound.

Nugent's men had visited Dungiven and seen Mrs Hetherington and Miss Dormer. Malthus and Mason had called with them for lunch and tea on the day in question and the ladies had accompanied them for a couple of miles on their way back to Portrush.

The police had gone carefully into the question of the hour at which the party had left Dungiven. It was half-past four. Lunch had been taken in the house, but, owing to the specially fine day, they had had tea in a summer house in the garden. After tea they had started almost immediately. Both ladies had looked at the sitting-room clock before going out to the car and it pointed to half-past four. The clock was right that evening with the nine o'clock time signal.

Nugent's men had driven back from Dungiven to Portrush at a high rate of speed—an average of over forty miles an hour—and found that it had taken them forty-four minutes. This was only six minutes less than Malthus and Mason had claimed to have taken. Further, their statement as to their time was correct, as they really had reached the garage in Portrush at 5.20. They had complimented the proprietor on the running of his car, telling him where they had come from and at what hour they had left. He had noted the time of their arrival particularly, in order to work out their speed. Lastly, if they had done all this—which was unquestionable—it was utterly impossible for them to have visited the Hollow and committed the murder.

Though this was not what French had hoped to learn, he was at least glad to achieve certainty on some point in the case. With a sigh, he turned to the next name on the list—Wyndham Stott's. Here also he soon found that the man could not possibly be guilty.

The conductor of the Portrush–Portstewart bus did not remember him, but two of the passengers did. These were a young married couple who had recently come to stay at Portrush. The husband was recovering from a nervous breakdown, and as they were not golfers, they took long walks on fine days. These two had noticed Wyndham on the bus, and had walked behind him to the Strand. They had seen him continuing on his way towards the mouth of the Bann, though they had not themselves gone so far. In addition to this evidence, the officers had found the man who had driven Wyndham from Portstewart to Portrush to catch the boat, and he confirmed the hour of the trip. Both the married couple and the driver had picked out Wyndham's photograph from a number of others.

This was proof positive. If Wyndham had walked to the Strand, he could not have committed the murder. Once more French was pleased at reaching certainty.

Of Elmina and Margot there had been no real suspicion, but the next two reports cleared them equally decisively. There was ample evidence that Elmina had played golf all that afternoon, and that Margot really had been with the Donnellys at Castlerock.

The information about Percy Luff caused French both surprise and misgiving. He had practically made up his mind that Luff must be guilty, not only from the unsatisfactory nature of his story, but also by the method of elimination. But now it looked as if he had been telling the truth after all.

It appeared that three or four doors from the Corona teashop in New Row was a haberdashery presided over by a young lady with a strong interest in well-dressed young representatives of the opposite sex. Trade was slightly below normal on the afternoon in question, and the lady was reduced for her entertainment to observation of the somewhat restricted traffic of New Row. As a rule she knew all, or nearly all, of those who passed—which had the advantage of enabling her to speculate as to their business—but on this afternoon there swam into her vision a stranger: just such a youth as she had often pictured, but had never yet met. This young scion of the nobility, as she considered him, appeared just before four o'clock, and at intervals during a solid hour he was to be seen pacing up and down, a growing disillusionment on his face. These facts she had disclosed to a youthful and good-looking member of Nugent's staff, and had finally clinched her story in the time-honoured manner—by picking out the wanderer's photograph from the usual dozen. Needless to say, it was Luff's.

Certainty once again! The murder had been committed between four and five, and if Luff was at Coleraine during that period—well, there was no more to be said.

With growing anxiety, French turned to the next lot of papers, those concerned with Bristow. Here, in the nature of the case, there could not be direct evidence of the type obtained in connection with the others. He examined with considerable interest the information Nugent had amassed.

First came a strip of cinematographic film with twelve tiny pictures and then twelve large photographs, enlarged from the others and all admirable views. Seven were of various people in the act of driving and all of these had immortalised interested spectators; the other five were pictures of a ruin, four taken from a distance and one a close-up. With them was a report saying that all the golfing pictures contained residents of Portrush as well as members of the cruise. All the residents had been approached and all had agreed that the photographs numbered 1 to 4 inclusive had been taken near the Club House after lunch on the Monday in question, while those numbered 10 to 12 inclusive had been taken later on the same afternoon, immediately after tea. No. 3 contained Bristow himself, it having been taken for him by another of those present.

Bristow's statement as to his having been met at the boat-slip by two temporary members of the Golf Club, his purchase of the films, his game of golf, his lunch at the Club, and the times and places at which he had left and rejoined the party, had been amply corroborated.

Of the photographs of the ruin, numbered 5 to 9, Nos. 5 to 8 were taken from about 20 feet away from south-east, south-west, north-west and north-east respectively. No. 9 was from about 3 feet away, and represented some carving on the north-west side. French could see for himself that all the views occurred on the strip in the order which Bristow's story required: first, the four golfing ones taken after lunch, then the five of the ruin and, lastly, the three golfing ones taken after tea.

There was here as much corroboration of the man's story as could possibly be expected. Bristow's entire day was vouched for except the time during which he left his golfing friends. The photographs were taken during that time. It was, in fact, a complete alibi for Bristow except for the one point—whether or not he himself had been the photographer.

French frowned. He would have accepted the alibi without question had it not been for the fact that Bristow was becoming very nearly his last hope. Though he had found no motive, there might, of course, have been one which so far he had missed.

He picked up and re-examined the photographs and suddenly his attention focused on something which he had seen before but had dismissed as immaterial. On No. 6, that of the ruin taken from the south-west, there was stretching across the level foreground a shadow—the shadow of the photographer. It was a blemish to the picture, but if on a sunny day a man takes views from all round a given object, he cannot prevent his shadow from showing in one of them. Here was unexpected evidence: could he identify the man from his shadow?

It stretched, long and narrow, across the smooth grass area around the building, which the Ancient Monuments Department of the Government of Northern Ireland had levelled and enclosed. It showed the operator from the waist up, bending forward over his camera. On the left of the picture was a bit of the surrounding railing with a stretch of flower bed inside it. This latter looked about 2 feet wide.

French thought for a while, then got up and strolled about the deck. The ship was almost, though not quite, deserted. The Isle of Man excursion had proved popular and most of those who had remained on board were down in the gaming-rooms. The day was perfect, warm and calm and sunny. They were moving gently along the coast, about six miles out.

One of the deck-tennis courts supplied French with what he sought—20 feet of clear space, with a deck-house in one direction and the sun in the other. He paced various short distances, made a few chalk marks on the deck, and walking to the nearest telephone, rang up Bristow and Morrison.

By a stroke of luck both were on board, and they agreed to join him immediately, Bristow promising to bring his camera. Meeting the purser, French pressed him also into the service. Five minutes later the four men had assembled, and French was delighted to find that Bristow was wearing the identical suit and hat shown in photograph No. 3.

'I want your help, gentlemen,' French explained to his little audience, 'in trying a small experiment. You'll perhaps be good enough not to ask questions at this stage, though I promise that if anything comes of it you'll hear the whole story.'

'Delighted to do anything we can,' the purser assured him and the others nodded.

'I want four photographs of this deck-house, if you please,' French continued; 'one to be taken by each of us. The photographer to stand here'—he pointed to a chalk cross— 'and the picture to include the whole height of the house and the deck back to this chalk line.'

'Do you mean you want us all to take the identical same view?' Bristow asked, with some show of incredulity.

'That's the idea. It sounds mad, but it isn't really. Will you start, Mr Bristow?'

'Oh, all right,' said Bristow, 'anything for a quiet life.' He moved to the chalk cross, focused for some little time, operated his shutter, moved the film, and stepped back.

'Thanks,' French returned. 'Now, if you please, Mr Morrison.'

Morrison, Grant and French himself took their turns and French then intimated that the proceedings were over.

French's luck held, for when he went to the photographer's cabin with the camera, he found the photographer had not gone ashore either.

'There are four exposures on this film,' French told him.

'I'd be grateful if you'd develop them and print me four enlargements. Could you possibly do them at once?'

'It just happens that I can,' the photographer replied. 'You've come at a good time.'

'Please don't cut the views apart on the film,' went on French. 'Their order is important and no doubt of it must be allowed to creep in.'

Later that evening the four prints and the piece of film were delivered. French shuffled the prints, and without looking at their backs spread them out on his desk. At once he was interested to find that the four shadows on the deck displayed marked variations. Clothes, shape of hat, way of standing, type of figure: all were different. To a much greater extent than he had imagined possible, each view was characteristic.

His eagerness increased as he reached the last stage in the test. Taking the view of the ruin with the operator's shadow, he compared it with the others.

The conditions under which the two sets had been taken were not identical. The grass round the ruin was smooth and level, but naturally neither so smooth nor so level as the deck. Nor had French achieved his angles with absolute precision, while the sun was higher over the ship than over the ruin. But these factors diverged but slightly, and French believed adequate allowance could be made for them.

But even without making any such allowances, the result was clear. The ruin shadow matched that of one of the four deck views in every essential and differed in important points from the other three. And when French turned over the prints he found that the likeness was with No. 1.

The shadow on the ruin photograph was therefore Bristow's beyond doubt or question. As French considered what this meant, his heart sank.

It meant that Bristow, like all his other suspects, was innocent. It meant that a fortnight's hard work had left him exactly where he had started, not only having failed to discover the murderer, but being entirely unable to suggest his identity. It meant more: it meant that the outlook was less hopeful now than previously, that for two reasons: first, he had eliminated all his suspects, and secondly, the scent was now cool.

There were, of course, Nugent's notes on Morrison's statement still to be examined, but French no longer suspected Morrison. And when he read the notes he suspected him still less. Morrison had had a genuine appointment with the manager of the Causeway Hotel just before lunch. He had walked round the Causeway before it, and had had lunch at the hotel after it. He had been called to the telephone and had left the hotel and arrived at the ship's boat, all exactly as the man himself had stated.

The last item on Nugent's report concerned the buttons. 'The two buttons,' it ran, 'Exhibit 37 handed to you by Morrison and Exhibit 38 cut by yourself from Luff's sleeve, are identical. They are, however, turned out by the hundred, and this similarity alone might not be convincing. But the thread attached to each is also identical, which makes the presumption that they came from the same coat overwhelming. Further, Exhibit 37 contains between the leather plaiting traces of the same kind of clay as is to be found at Point A in McArtt's Hollow.'

This matter of the button had worried French a good deal. At first it had seemed clear proof of Luff's guilt. Then when the Mercer letter had proved a forgery, it began to look less convincing. If the letter were a trick, why not the button also? Its position, after all, was suspicious; it had been deposited where there was no chance of its being overlooked.

Now that Luff's presence in Coleraine during the critical period had been established, it followed that the button had been planted, presumably by the murderer, to throw suspicion on Luff. French wondered if this fact might not prove a clue.

He began to work out in his mind how the thing might have been done. As the button could not have been removed while the coat was being worn, someone must have slipped into Luff's cabin to secure it. And he had not simply cut it off: this might have aroused suspicion. Luff had noticed it loose. It was unlikely that it had conveniently loosened itself. Therefore the murderer had probably visited the cabin twice—once to loosen it and once, probably the evening before the crime, to remove it.

Immediately French began a new enquiry to find out whether anyone had been seen entering or leaving Luff's cabin and before long he obtained some information. Luff's steward had on two separate evenings noticed a man leave the cabin, in both cases in a secretive way.

'Did you recognise the man?' French asked.

'On the second occasion, yes,' the steward returned, 'not on the first.'

'Who was he?' went on French, with obvious interest.

'Yourself, sir,' was the answer.

French stared, then broke into a shout of laughter. 'That's rather a blow,' he grinned, 'I thought I had been extra careful. I was, as you can now guess, after the first man. What was he like? Can you not describe him?'

Except that he was tall and in evening clothes, the steward could not. Nor could French obtain any further information.

He began pacing the deck, pipe in mouth and head bent forward, as he sought for light on his problem. Surely, *surely*, with all he knew, he should be able to find the solution. Though his work up to the present had been unproductive, he had still learnt facts which he felt must be vital. He now knew positively what he had only suspected before, that the murderer was on board the ship; the button episode alone proved that. Further, he must be either a passenger or one of the senior officers, firstly, because he knew details the crew could not know, proved by the Mercer–Luff letter, and, secondly, by the fact that he was ashore at Portrush, for which the crew had no leave. Next he must be one of the narrow circle who had come into personal contact with John Stott, and who wished his death, presumably either from hate or in hope of gain. And, lastly, he must have the necessary selfish, cruel and determined character.

There could not be many persons who fulfilled these four conditions, and that was what made the affair so tantalising to French. The murderer must be within his reach, probably within his sight in the dining-room, and yet he could not identify him. It was exasperating beyond words.

Slowly his thoughts swung back to Malthus and Mason. In their cases there was at least a satisfactory motive. They had tried to do Stott in the eye and had been bitterly discomfited. And hate resulting from a blow of this kind, which would so severely have hurt their pride, would be of a serious and lasting type. They had, moreover, not only the motive, but the other three requirements as well. They had been on board for some time, and either could have cut the button off Luff's sleeve. They had every chance to know the ship's gossip and of Luff's infatuation for Mrs

Mercer, and they probably were aware or could guess the relationships between the various members of the Stott family. Finally, French imagined from his contacts with them, that neither was the type to hesitate about murder, if it would suit his purpose or gratify his craving.

But their alibi was good. No use in going into that again. Nugent had been quite satisfied.

But had he himself been? He began checking up on his own mental processes. Had he not been rather ready to accept the alibi because of an idea which he had since learnt was entirely false? Practically all concerned—Wyndham, Bristow, Morrison, even Margot—had told him of the Malthus affair, and the idea they might be trying to divert his attention from themselves had lurked in his mind. Had he allowed this doubt to cloud his critical faculty?

Pacing up and down, he reviewed the alibi in detail. Malthus and Mason had left Mason's cousin's house near Dungiven at 4.30 and arrived back at Somerville's garage in Portrush, where they had hired their car, at 5.20, catching a boat to the ship at 5.40. Nugent had had the route driven over at a high rate of speed, and found that his man had only been able to do the run in six minutes less time. That meant that the suspects had driven fast, as indeed they had stated.

It followed absolutely certainly they had not had time to visit McArtt's Hollow; or, conversely, if they had visited the Hollow and committed the murder, they must have left Dungiven earlier than 4.30. How much earlier it was impossible to say, but his previous estimate, which he saw no reason to doubt, had been half an hour.

Once again French considered the means by which the hour of that departure had been established. Malthus and

Mason had stated that it was the time at which they had decided to leave, and that they had left at it. Mrs Hetherington and Miss Dormer had each confirmed the hour, saying that they had noted it on their sitting-room clock. The clock, they further stated, was correct by the time signal of the Third News that night.

The hour seemed unshakable, and French felt that his former conclusion had been justified. The point, however, was crucial; his whole case depended on it. If he could discover any trickery about it, he had as good as solved his mystery.

He went down to his cabin for the dossier of the case, and turning to the pages in question, re-read them carefully. Then a point which he had forgotten was brought back to his memory.

Mrs Hetherington and Miss Dormer had accompanied the men for a couple of miles along their road, on the ground that they would enjoy the walk back. Was anything to be learnt from that?

French felt his excitement grow as he grappled with the problem. For some unaccountable reason the conviction was growing in his mind that the solution was there, within his reach, if only he could grasp it. He continued puzzling over it, then suddenly a possibility occurred to him.

Suppose that earlier in the afternoon one of the men had on some pretext got the ladies out of the sitting-room, while the other advanced the clock by half an hour. It would then be by the altered clock that they had timed their start. Suppose, further, that when they were in the car, just on the move, one of the men had declared he had forgotten his gloves. Naturally, he would not trouble the ladies to get them for him, he would borrow their latch-key, and run in for them himself. What then easier than to put the clock back?

This seemed feasible to French provided the clock was not of the striking variety. It was a point he had omitted to ascertain. He would do it now.

What other points, he wondered, might throw light on the affair? Methodically he checked them up. There seemed to be nine altogether:

1. Had the men, or either of them, had an opportunity to put on the clock?
2. Had they had an opportunity to put it back?
3. Was the clock a striking one?
4. Did the ladies, or either of them, think that half-past four had come unexpectedly quickly?
5. Did they think they had returned early from their walk?
6. Had anyone noticed the car start from their house, and if so, at what hour?
7. Had anyone seen it along the road to Portrush, and if so, at what hour?
8. Had anyone seen men or car near McArtt's Hollow?
9. Had anyone seen the car entering Portrush, and if so, from what direction?

Another job for Nugent, French thought with a smile, as he drew out a sheet of notepaper and began to write.

18

French is Worried

French posted his letter to Nugent that evening in Douglas, then metaphorically sat back and surveyed the world with complacence.

He felt he had reason for his satisfaction. There could be no doubt that he had found the solution of his problem and that the clearing up of details and amassing the necessary proof for the Public Prosecutor would follow in the normal way. The work, furthermore, had been done quickly. Less than a fortnight had elapsed since the murder, which was not too bad, considering the divided control.

His certainty was due to several considerations. First, elimination proved his case: no one but Malthus and/or Mason could be guilty. Then their alibi was of the constructed kind: an attempt to prove that they were in their car far from McArtt's Hollow at the time of the crime. Further, they had called attention both to the time of leaving Dungiven and of arriving at Portrush, so as to have these established by other witnesses. And finally, the trick of altering the clock was old and well-tried and fitted the situation exactly. Confirmation and the necessary warrants should arrive in two days, and the arrests could then be made on the first occasion on which the men went ashore.

French felt he had done so well that he deserved a holiday, and as no further step could be taken till he heard from Nugent, he decided to join the shore party next day. They were to land at Maryport and drive through the northern part of the Lake District, returning for the night to the ship at Whitehaven. On the following day they were to do the southern half of the Lake District, rejoining the ship at Heysham.

He found Mrs French strangely unenthusiastic when after dinner he announced his intention of accompanying her. Rather hurt, he asked what was the matter.

'Well,' she said after some hesitation, 'I had promised to sit with Margot Stott. It appears Mr Morrison can't go, and she's like a fish out of water without him.'

'What of it?' French returned. 'My going won't prevent you sitting together.'

'No, I suppose not,' she answered doubtfully.

French swung round. 'Look here, Em, what's the trouble? You've got something on your chest. Get it off.'

'Well, if you must know, Joe, Margot's afraid of you. She thinks you're an enemy. She thinks you suspect Mr Morrison and she can't forgive you for it.'

'Oh?' French turned away. 'She does, does she? And why does she think that?'

'You ought to know. I don't. At all events, I'm certain she'll not come if she hears you'll be there.'

French grunted. 'Not very fair that. I've only been doing my job.'

'She knows that and she bears you no malice. It's just that she can't stand you for suspecting her young man.'

'Huh!' French was slightly testy. 'And what does she expect? That I should stay in my cabin all the time?'

For a moment Mrs French did not answer. Then she spoke in a lower tone. 'You know, Joe, I never interfere in your cases. But this time I'm going to ask you a question: Do you still suspect Mr Morrison?'

French hesitated. 'As a matter of fact, I don't,' he said presently. 'But I can't say so. If I began that sort of thing, people would put two and two together and guess where I stood.'

Mrs French nodded. 'I see that—as a general rule. But in this case I want you to make an exception. The girl's worrying her soul out. You must stop it: since you can.'

French, cautious man, was unwilling to commit himself until everything was cut and dried beyond possibility of revision. But after all, he told himself, this *was* a special case. If he could properly ease the girl's mind, he should do it. Besides, he liked Margot personally, and to cause her unnecessary suffering was the last thing he would wish.

'Very well,' he presently agreed. 'I'll tell her if you like. Or you can.'

'No, it wouldn't be worth anything from me. Just stay where you are and I'll find her and you can do it now.'

The evening had turned chilly and they had been sitting in the music-room. French opened his novel to discourage the advances of the sociable, but before he had read many pages, his wife returned with Margot.

'Mrs French tells me you've something very pleasant to say to me?' Margot began as he pulled over a chair for her.

'Well,' French answered cautiously, 'I hope so. My wife tells me that she thinks Mr Morrison is worrying because he imagines he is still on the police list of suspects.'

'I expect you're being tactful and that she said that I was,' Margot interrupted. 'You know so much, Mr French, that you must know that we hope to be married as soon as this affair is over.'

'Of course I said it was you,' Mrs French put in. 'Don't try to be clever, Joe.'

'Very well,' French admitted sadly; 'it was you. Now you know, Miss Stott, we were bound to suspect everyone concerned—technically even yourself. It doesn't mean anything, but it's the regular routine—we have to check up on *everyone*. I had to check up on Mr Morrison.'

'Go on,' Mrs French said, in exasperated tones. 'Can't you say what you mean without all this beating about the bush? It's like when he makes a joke, my dear. You can see it coming ten sentences ahead.'

'She wants me to say that Mr Morrison is no longer under suspicion,' French explained, ignoring this flanking attack. 'I hate doing it till the case is ended and nothing can be reopened. But, subject to that reservation and for your ear alone, I may say that I'm satisfied that Mr Morrison is innocent.'

'It took you long enough to get to it,' Mrs French grumbled.

Margot's eyes shone. 'I can't say,' she declared in low tones, 'how thankful I am to hear that and how grateful I am to you both. I don't deny it has been a ghastly worry.'

'I'm more than sorry,' French protested; 'but, you know, things did look suspicious at one time. He was actually at the Hollow when the murder took place.'

Her eyes grew round. 'Does he know that you know that?'

'Oh, yes. I put it to him and he admitted it.'

'He never told me. He told me he was there, you understand, but not that you knew it.'

'Wanted to save you worrying,' suggested French.

She looked at him gratefully. 'I think you're the nicest man I ever met. And so clever as to be uncanny. How *on earth* did you know that he had been there, and when you did know it, how *on earth* did you clear him in your mind? But I suppose I mustn't ask questions of that sort. I can only repeat how grateful to you both I am.'

A nice girl, this, French thought. Young, and yet not too modern. He loathed the hard-faced, loud-voiced, gin-tippling type of young woman. These he called 'modern', oblivious of the fact that they represented only an insignificant part of as fine a rising generation as this country has ever possessed.

'I'm glad to have been able to set your mind at rest,' he assured her, 'and, as the matter is past, I don't see why I shouldn't answer your questions. Someone left a footprint in the Hollow and Morrison was the only person we could hear of who had got rid of a pair of shoes at the time.'

'Yes, he told me he had done that as a precaution. He didn't know he had left a print.'

'Naturally, or he would have rubbed it out. The print, however, showed wear in certain places and his other shoes were similarly worn. There was no doubt that he had made it.'

'How extraordinarily clever. I can't imagine how you thought of it all. But that only makes the other mystery the greater. In the face of that, how ever did you prove his innocence?'

'Through your action principally.'

She stared. 'My action?'

'Your action,' he insisted. 'There were several indications that he was telling the truth, the chief being that he couldn't have had an appointment with Mr Stott, as he expected to be at the Causeway at the hour of the crime. It was your unexpected action that altered his plans.'

'But—it seems almost too dreadful to joke about—but couldn't we have had a conspiracy about that?'

French smiled. 'No. The Atkinsons made a statement, like everyone else, and after that it was impossible to believe that when you went ashore you had intended to go to Castlerock.'

'Nothing about my admirable character,' Margot gurgled happily. 'I may tell Harry, mayn't I? I'd run now, but he's with the Captain.'

'Oh yes, you may tell Morrison. But he must keep it to himself.'

'I think all that's simply marvellous,' she went on. 'Then there have been tales about Mr Bristow and photographs. I suppose I mightn't ask about that?'

'What is being said?'

'Just that he was suspected, but that he took some wonderful photographs which cleared him.'

'Well, that's true in a way,' French admitted. He wondered whether he might properly show this delightful girl the prints: to make up to her as far as he could for the suffering he had caused her. After all, why not? They were ancient history so far as the case was concerned. 'I'll show them to you if you like, but, again, it must go no further.'

'Oh,' she breathed, 'I promise that. I'd be simply thrilled.'

A little uneasy in his mind, yet assuring himself that he had no need to be, French went to his cabin and brought the photographs.

'There,' he explained, handing over that of the ruin from the south-west, 'is a photograph taken near Portrush at just about the time of the murder. Whoever took it must therefore be innocent. You see?'

She nodded.

'And there,' he handed over the four he had taken on deck, 'are experimental views taken by four different photographers. Can you make anything of them?'

For some moments she looked blankly at the views, then suddenly clapped her hands. 'But, of course,' she exclaimed, 'you don't know who this is'—she pointed to the shadow on the ruin photograph—'but you do know these?'— touching the deck views.

French agreed.

'Clever!' she declared. She looked over the prints and picked out No. 1 of the deck pictures. 'That's the one, isn't it?'

'That's the one,' French admitted. 'Mr Bristow.'

'I see how you do it now! I call that just fascinating.'

'You've said enough,' Mrs French put in reprovingly. 'He'll get swelled head and be impossible to live with.'

French indeed was enjoying himself. This was an intelligent girl and it was interesting to hear her comments.

'Wonderful the way the Government of Northern Ireland look after their old ruins,' she went on, picking up the Portrush view again. 'I could understand a railing and even grass, but I must say that flower-beds are doing the thing proud. What do you think, Mrs French?'

266

French's Em looked over her shoulder. 'Yes, and good flowers, too. Delphiniums and clarkia, those are, and good plants.'

'Yes. Don't they bloom late in that northern climate? I am a bit of a gardener, you know. Did you see the garden on that island in—Bantry Bay, wasn't it? We've seen so many bays I get them all mixed,' and she ran on so light-heartedly that French grew more and more pleased with what he had done. Presently she excused herself and went off to look for Morrison, who, as she put it, 'must have finished with the Captain by this time.'

The next day's excursion through the Keswick and Ullswater areas was such a success that French felt he must at all costs join that of the following day also, to Coniston, Windermere and on to the south. That following morning was as fine and clear as its predecessor, and everything seemed propitious for the drive.

French had struck up a mild friendship with Carrothers, the Galashiels stockbroker, and they had booked seats on the coach behind those of Mrs French and Margot. French was in great form. He had missed so many of these shore excursions that he was feeling pleasurably excited and talked more than usual, cracking not a few somewhat elderly jokes.

Then the whole thing was suddenly spoilt. Half an hour before the boats were due to start he was called to the telephone. It was Nugent.

'I thought I'd better ring you up,' came the D.I.'s voice thinly, 'to save you going any further with that theory you put in your last letter.'

French's heart sank. 'What exactly do you mean?' he asked, trying to banish any feeling from his voice.

'Just that the Malthus-Mason idea is a washout. The alibi's sound.'

For a moment French remained silent. Then, 'Tell me,' he said in the same steady voice.

'Firstly,' came the answer, 'neither Malthus nor Mason had an opportunity of tampering with the clock. They went out with the ladies to the garden after lunch, and apparently it might then have been possible for one of the men to have hung back and put it on half an hour, though neither of the ladies noticed this. But it would have been impossible for them to put it back again.'

'How so?' French asked as the other paused.

'The only time it could have been done was just before starting back in the car, when the ladies went upstairs to put on their things. But it wasn't done then. It's a striking clock, and it couldn't have been put back half an hour. As you know, it would have to be put on eleven and a half hours. But this would have been heard. It has a loud chime which sounds through the house.'

'That seems pretty conclusive,' French admitted.

'There's more in it than that,' Nugent's voice continued. 'Mrs Hetherington went to the sitting-room and looked at the clock before they started and it was then half-past four. She was the last to leave the sitting-room and neither of the men returned to it after her.'

'I give up the idea.'

'There was still another check,' the D.I. went on inexorably. 'Miss Dormer was going to some function later in the evening, and, being nervous about the time, she checked the hour of leaving the house by her watch. It was four-thirty, and her watch was correct later on and was not altered. Neither lady, furthermore, noticed anything unusual about the time of arriving back.'

'In short, it's established the men left at four-thirty.'

'Yes, absolutely. And it's equally established that if they did that they couldn't have called at McArtt's Hollow.'

'Quite; I see that. Well, that's one matter settled at all events. Thank you for ringing me up.'

To French this information was a knock-out blow. He had been satisfied that at last he saw his way through the case, and now instead of the success he had counted on, failure was staring him in the face. And it wasn't as if he had made some small error, some revision of detail, some modification of theory. His failure was fundamental. Not only was he unable to prove the murderer's guilt; he had now, after an exhaustive investigation lasting almost a fortnight, no idea who the murderer was.

It looked as if he must be someone outside his circle of suspects. No doubt, Stott's character having been what it was, there were many who had wished him dead. But how were they to be discovered? French had made a list of those whom Stott's correspondence showed as potential enemies, and compared it with that of the ship's company. The only names common to both were those whom French had already considered and found innocent. What more could he do? It was not possible to investigate the life of everyone on board. One could deal only with those against whom there was some shred of suspicion.

It looked as if the criminal must have been someone ashore; someone who had been in Portrush when the *Hellénique* called. If so, the affair was Nugent's, not his. Fortunately, there was no doubt as to Nugent's competence.

One thing, however, was unhappily certain. If the problem were not solved, it would not be considered Nugent's failure, but his own. From the matter of the button, it would be argued that the murderer was on board, and unless the contrary were proved, he himself would get the blame for his escape.

French did not see what he could do about it at the moment, but with his case in such a state his conscience would not allow him to go off on a whole-day excursion. With genuine disappointment, he made his apologies and watched the shore party set off. Then drawing a chair into his favourite position between the two boats, he lit a pipe and settled down to think the thing over.

First, was his list of suspects exhaustive?

Presently he went back to John Stott's cabin, which had remained sealed since the tragedy, and spent some time in another examination of the deceased's papers. But in spite of the greatest care, he found nothing more than on the first occasion.

But if the murderer were on board and if his list were complete, it followed that the murderer was on his list. Could this be so, after all?

Once again he went over the evidence for each person's innocence, and gradually as he did so, he came to see that of them all, only one had not produced direct proof. The Captain and engineer were on board, Malthus and Mason were at Dungiven, Wyndham was at the mouth of the River Bann, Luff at Coleraine, Elmina playing golf, Margot at Castlerock and Bristow at the ruin. But Morrison? Where was Morrison?

Morrison at the time of the murder was at McArtt's Hollow. And Morrison had denied it until the truth was forced from him. Moreover, of all concerned, Morrison perhaps had the strongest motive. Firstly, he hated Stott and had been heard breathing forth threatenings and slaughter against him. Secondly, Stott's death would bring his money nearer to Margot. It would prevent him from making a new will and perhaps diverting his wealth from Wyndham.

French felt really horrified at the direction his thoughts were taking, particularly when he remembered his interview with Margot on the previous evening. He had been wrong to give an opinion on the case. He had known at the time that he was wrong and he had allowed himself to be persuaded. If he now had to arrest Morrison, could he ever lift his head again in the presence either of Margot or his own wife?

With an unhappy frown he went down to lunch as the ship crept down the low-lying Cumberland coast, and after lunch he tackled his problem again. But it was not till after he had taken a smart walk, played some deck tennis and had tea that light occurred to him. Then an idea shot into his mind, suggested by a phrase that had been used incidentally on the previous evening.

For a moment he thought he had solved his problem, then he saw that he had done nothing of the kind. All the same, the point was suggestive. He considered it with growing doubt for an hour, then just as the boats were preparing to go ashore to Heysham Harbour to pick up the excursionists, he reached a decision.

Jumping up, he hurried to his cabin, wrote a short note to Mrs French, tumbled some clothes and the dossier into a suitcase, gave a hurried message to the purser's assistant at the ladder, and caught the last boat for the shore.

19

French is Delighted

French waited about Heysham till he was able to go on board the Irish steamer, then turned in and read himself to sleep. In the morning he went on deck to find they were coming up Belfast Lough. The charming, early morning views of the rich, well-wooded country on the County Down side and of the more austere but equally beautiful hills on the Antrim shore, brought back vividly that other morning when he had sailed up the estuary to take part in that worrying case of Fred Ferris and the inert patrol.

An hour later he stepped down on Donegall Quay, glad to renew his acquaintanceship with the district. Having rung up Nugent, he went down to Portrush by the 9.15 express. The D.I. was waiting for him at the station.

'You've got a new idea?' Nugent asked after greetings.

'No,' French returned, 'I've not got so far as that. But when one is at a deadlock one is ready to turn to anything. I was showing No. 2 of the photographs Bristow took of the ruin to my wife and a girl friend, and the girl dropped a phrase which has made me think. In the absence of anything else, I decided to pass the remark on to you.'

Nugent raised an eyebrow.

French took the photograph from his case. 'You see,' he went on, 'a bit of the surrounding flower bed has been included. My wife, who is a gardener, but not an archaeologist, spoke of the flowers. They were good plants, she said, of delphinium and clarkia. It was then, the girl made her remark. "Don't they bloom late," she said, "in that northern climate?"'

For a moment Nugent did not reply, then as French also kept silence, he said: 'Well, what of it? I suppose they were late. I don't get you, Chief Inspector.'

'I'm a little bit of a gardener myself,' French answered, 'though you mightn't think it, to look at me. And it occurred to me that the girl was right. It was late for these flowers.'

'I'm not a gardener,' Nugent admitted, 'and I'm afraid I don't get your point. What does it matter to us whether they were late or whether they weren't?'

'Well,' French returned easily, 'I was interested. In fact, that's what I've come about. For my own curiosity, I'd like to settle the point. Is there a first-rate gardener in Portrush whom we could consult?'

French could see that the D.I. thought he had gone mad, but an Irish police officer is always polite, and Nugent kept his idea to himself. Instead of answering, he called his sergeant.

'Who looks after the gardening side of the ancient monuments enclosures?' he asked.

'Mr Jackson, sir. Him that does the Urban Council flowers. He has the both jobs.'

'Can you get hold of him for us?'

'Surely, sir. He'll be in the house at his dinner now. I'll send M'Gonigle for him.'

'When he's finished his dinner, you know.'

'Maybe we'll get him before he starts,' the sergeant returned confidentially as he withdrew.

Ten minutes later a fresh-complexioned man of about fifty was shown in.

'Mr Jackson?' Nugent asked affably, pointing to a chair.

'That's me, sir,' returned the man, sitting down and crossing his legs as if to indicate willingness to take part in a conference.

'You look after the flowers in the beds round the old ruin up at Ballywillan?'

'I do so.'

'Have you much experience of gardening, Mr Jackson?'

'I have that. I was brought up till the work at M'Quaid's Nurseries at Port-e-down. You've heard tell of M'Quaid's Nurseries, I make no doubt?'

'I know the place well. I've friends in Portadown.'

Jackson smiled genially. 'Have you so? Well, that's where I was. And then I was an assistant gardener under the Belfast Corporation. I put in ten years in the Botanic Gardens, so I did.'

The D.I. was genial in his turn. 'Well, you're the man to give us a piece of information. You've got some delphiniums and clarkia in those beds round the ruin up at Ballywillan. What would you say was their period of flowering?'

'When would they be in flower?' Jackson paraphrased the question as he gazed earnestly at the speaker. 'Well, now, you couldn't just say that, not till a day, don't you know.'

'I understand that all right. But couldn't you give us an idea?'

'Oh, aye, I could give yez an idea. I mind rightly the delphiniums were out at the same time as the orange lilies.

The lilies were a wee bit late this year for the Twelfth,* and the delphiniums lasted on a while after them.'

'And the clarkia?' prompted the D.I.

'Aye, the clarkia. Well, I bedded them out in June and they were just coming into flower when the delphiniums were going over.'

'If I might interrupt,' said French, foreseeing no early end to this dissertation, 'perhaps one question would settle my point. Could Mr Jackson tell us if the delphiniums and clarkia were in flower about the twenty-seventh of September, that's a fortnight ago?'

Jackson transferred his gaze from the D.I. 'A fortnight ago?' he repeated. 'They were not. Nor for three or four weeks before that again. No, no; they wouldn't last as long as that.'

Once again the familiar thrill of excitement had titillated French's nerves. The look of incredulity on Nugent's face strangely delighted him. But he controlled himself and handed the photograph to Jackson.

'There are the flowers we're speaking of,' he pointed out, trying to preserve the atmosphere of the meeting. 'Can you tell us about what date that might have been taken?'

Jackson gazed at the print for some moments, then shook his head. "Deed if I could,' he replied succinctly.

This was evidently a negative and French tried again.

'Well, can you tell us when it could not have been taken? Could it have been taken on the twenty-seventh of September?'

Jackson again shook his head. 'F'ith, it could not,' he returned with emphasis. 'Them flowers was away long before that date, so they were.'

---

* Orangemen's Day, July 12th.

French, jubilant, returned the burden of the conversation to Nugent. After long efforts with Jackson, a cautious man who clearly did not wish to commit himself rashly, he learnt that only during the first two weeks of August were the flowers at just that stage.

'I think we might try the hotels,' French suggested, when after cordial leave-takings the gardener had disappeared.

A short investigation revealed the fact that Bristow had stayed for two nights at the Northern Counties Hotel—August 6th and 7th. He had been, so he told the manager, making arrangements for the call of the *Hellénique* in late September.

When they were once more in the street the D.I. indulged in an unexpectedly lurid oath.

'This is a triumph for you, Chief Inspector, and no mistake,' he went on generously. 'I never would have thought of it. But I'm damned if I understand it even yet. How did the beggar do it?'

'I have an idea, but I can't prove it as yet,' French answered.

'Come on, then, back to the barracks and we'll have a go at it.'

French followed with eagerness. Though as yet he was far from clear as to everything which Bristow had done, he believed that they had reached the last lap of the case. Surely, he told himself, with what they had now learnt, a little further thought would solve all their remaining problems.

'Take the easy chair,' began Nugent, indicating one with wooden arms drawn in to the desk. 'Not that it's so very easy,' he added, a rather unnecessary qualification for anyone with eyesight. 'What'll you smoke?' He held out his cigarette case.

'My pipe, I think,' French returned. 'More satisfying if we're going to take our time over it.

'Far better,' Nugent approved politely, though lighting a cigarette. 'But I've got used to these things. Well, we've got a bit of a puzzle now and no mistake.'

'We've got something more than that,' French said, with but slightly concealed jubilation. 'We've got our man. The only explanation of that photograph is that Bristow's guilty.'

'You've got him,' Nugent corrected. 'It was your idea. But there's a deal to be cleared up before you can make the arrest. How did the fella do it?'

French nodded. 'That's it,' he agreed. 'That's the first thing we've got to find out. And the second is, Why? What was the motive? I've discovered none.'

'Well, let's stick to the how for the present. What are your ideas, Chief Inspector?'

French settled himself in the 'easy' chair and drew slowly at his pipe. 'Well,' he suggested, 'I think we ought first to make sure we are absolutely clear about what he did. He came ashore on that Tuesday at half-past nine and went aboard again at six, and during the whole of that time he was in the presence of several people, except between the hours of three-forty and five o'clock. During that period we now believe he murdered Stott.'

'Agreed,' murmured the D.I.

'As a proof that he had spent the time in photographing the ruin he put forward an undeveloped film. I had that film developed and left uncut. The first four photographs, as you know, were of golfers, and definitely were taken just after lunch on that day. The last three were also of golfers and equally certainly were taken after tea. The intermediate five were of the ruin and were taken about six weeks earlier,'

Nugent nodded slowly. 'It would look like it,' he admitted hesitatingly, 'but it's not easy to see how.'

'It isn't,' French agreed. 'I simply don't see it.'

Nugent looked up and spoke with more animation.

'How would it be if, when he was here six weeks ago, he put a fresh roll of films in his camera and twisted it on to the fifth space, leaving the first four blank? Then after taking his five ruin photographs he would take out the film and put it on one side. Then on the Tuesday he would put it back, expose the first four pictures, turn the film through five more, and take the other three golf views. Wouldn't that do it?'

French shook his head. 'Very ingenious, but you've forgotten your own evidence,' he declared. 'Don't you remember that Bristow brought his camera ashore empty that morning and the first thing he did was to buy a new film? More than that, the photographer put the film in the camera for him. Don't you remember? You gave me the man's name.' He turned back the pages of his book. 'McAfee, it was.'

'Be damned but you're right,' admitted Nugent. 'There was no hanky-panky about that either. Two of the men, temporary members of the Club, Martin and McBride, met Bristow when he came ashore and they were with him in the shop. And you're right, too, about McAfee putting in the film. He remembered it because it was the only one of that kind sold that morning. And he remembered Martin and McBride being in with the stranger, too.'

'And Bristow had no chance of changing it?'

'Right again. Divil a one.'

'Then the photographs of the ruin were definitely taken between the time he bought the film on the day of the murder and some four or five days later when your people developed it.'

'But they couldn't have been, because of the flowers.'

'They must have been, because of the purchase of the film,' French insisted.

Nugent moved uneasily. 'Damn it all, the thing's impossible.' He paused, then continued: 'But, look here, he could have done it in one way. He could have had an accomplice.'

'He couldn't have had an accomplice, because his own shadow showed in the photo. It's inconceivable that anyone could have made up to give exactly his shadow.'

'That certainly seems right.'

'And what's more,' went on French, 'I don't believe he ever thought of the shadow. You see, he wasn't a super-man. He never thought of the flowers.'

'That's right again. It does seem as if he'd taken it himself. And if so, he's innocent.'

'He's guilty because of the trick about the flowers,' French declared firmly.

'Then he'll have had an accomplice to take the photographs, shadow or no shadow. But see here, there's another thing we haven't considered, and it confirms your view. It was Bristow started the talk about the driving.'

French glanced at him keenly. 'I didn't know that.'

'Well, it was. It's only just this minute that I've seen its significance. He started the subject and he suggested the photographs. In fact, he insisted on taking them.'

'There you are,' retorted French. 'That's pretty strong. I tell you he's as guilty as sin.' He paused, then as Nugent didn't speak, went on: 'Suppose we have another look at the photographs. If they contain that evidence of the flowers, they may contain something else that we've missed.'

'If they do, I'll eat my hat,' Nugent declared. 'But, by all means, we'll try again.'

They spread the five views of the ruin out on the table, and stood for some moments gazing at them. Then with lenses they went over every inch of their surfaces.

'No good,' French admitted at last. 'We've seen everything about them.'

Nugent stood back and drew at his cigarette. 'There's not another thing in them,' he declared. 'Sure, they've been examined till there couldn't be. It's no good, Chief Inspector. There is only the accomplice for it.'

French did not reply. He stood gazing from print to print, his face growing gradually more eager.

'What is it?' Nugent asked, seeing his expression. 'Got something? '

'I don't know,' French said presently. 'Look at those photos again. Do you see anything about the lighting?'

'The lighting?' the D.I. repeated, staring at the pictures.

'Yes.' French's manner now showed keen interest. 'Any part of them better lighted than any other?'

Nugent made a gesture. 'You're right, by George; I see what you mean. In all five views there's more light in the upper right-hand corner than anywhere else. That it?'

'That's it,' French nodded.

'But wait a bit: don't be in too big a hurry. It's only very slight. Something about the lens maybe?'

'No, it's nothing about the lens,' French retorted. 'I've got it at last,' he went on in delighted tones. 'I see what was done!'

'By the hokey! It's more than I do,' Nugent declared. 'Explain yourself.'

'Well, look here.' French no longer tried to hide his

satisfaction. 'All those five ruin photos are better lighted towards the top right-hand corner, but that is not true of the seven golfing ones taken with the same camera. Therefore it's nothing about the lens or camera.'

Nugent nodded slowly.

'And it has nothing to do with the light at the ruin, because if so it would vary on the different photos. If there was extra light on the right of a view facing north, it would be on the left of one facing south.'

'You're right there. But what do you get from it?'

'That they're the photographs of photographs!' French declared triumphantly.

Nugent stared, then slapped his thigh. 'You've got it!' he exclaimed. 'You've got it this time right enough.'

'As I see it,' French continued, 'Bristow came here early in August and took the photographs and made enlargements of them. Then he came here again with the ship, bought his new roll, took the first four views of the golfers, screwed his film round for five spaces and took the other three golfing pictures. When he went back to the ship, he took out the roll of films, rewound what was used, put it in again, and screwed it round to No. 5. Then he fixed up his enlargements somewhere in his cabin and photographed them on the proper spaces. All he had then to do was to make sure the original film and enlargements were destroyed and there he was.'

'Good for you, Chief Inspector.'

'But he made his mistake all the same. He overlooked the fact that the light was stronger on the right side than on the left.'

Nugent was enthusiastic. Bristow was a clever ruffian, but he had met his match in French. French was right, they had got their man, though the case still wanted further proof.

'I hope we'll get it through the enlargements,' French returned. 'It's not an easy thing to make enlargements secretly. The apparatus is clumsy and couldn't be hidden. I don't believe Bristow would have attempted to do it himself. And if he got it done for him, we should be able to find out where.'

'Not in Portrush, anyway,' Nugent believed.

'I shouldn't think anywhere in Northern Ireland,' French returned. 'The ruin would probably be recognised. London, I should think, is the likely place. They'll go into that at the Yard.'

'If that could be proved it would end the case.'

'As far as method is concerned, yes. But we've yet to find motive.'

'You thought he had a motive at first?'

'Yes, for two reasons. First, because he had been heard blackguarding Stott, and second because of his letter complaining he hadn't been paid his percentage.'

'But he agreed that Stott was going to pay him?'

'Yes, and I thought that was an answer to the thing. But now, of course, it might have been a lie, told to cover that very suspicion.'

Nugent thought deeply. 'It'll be the money,' he pronounced presently. 'The old fella'll have been cheating him out of it.'

'He couldn't. They had an agreement.'

'How do you know that?'

'I've seen it.'

'Could they have gone into court in England? A French boat, you know.'

'It was drawn up and signed and witnessed in England

and stamped with an English stamp. I don't think the boat could affect it.'

Nugent shook his head sagely. 'He's got round it somehow, old Stott has,' he insisted. 'Try it again, Chief Inspector. Let's have the agreement out and see if we can find a hole in it.'

Among French's notes was a copy of the document. He now read it clause by clause. When he came to that giving the percentages each man was to get, Nugent called a halt.

'Read that again, Chief Inspector,' he demanded.

'"The nett profits of the said undertaking shall be divided between the said three partners to this agreement in the estimated proportions that their ideas, money and help shall have contributed to its success, this being at present estimated as follows: to the said John Mottram Stott, forty-five per cent, to the said Charles Bristow forty-five per cent and to the said Harry Morrison ten per cent."'

Suddenly Nugent slapped his thigh. 'There you are,' he exclaimed with animation. 'There's the thing at last! Don't you see?'

'Got it, you think?' French's manner was tense.

Nugent seemed equally excited. 'Well, see,' he returned. 'It says, "this being at present estimated at so and so".'

'And if it does?' French's manner was slightly testy.

'Well, couldn't he have got out of that? It means that those percentages were liable to revision if the respective contributions of the three partners were altered. Suppose Stott put in another hundred thousand after the concern had been running a while; under that he could claim a larger percentage.'

'Yes, that would be a reasonable provision. But we don't know that he did put in anything extra.'

'Don't we?' Nugent returned. 'What's the date of that agreement?'

'October the first, 1937.'

'There you are. That was after they had begun their negotiations and before Stott had decided to buy the ship. Now what happened—if I'm not greatly mistaken—between these dates?'

French moved impatiently. 'I hope I'm not being half-witted, but I don't see what's in your mind.'

Nugent made a gesture of horror at the idea. 'Well, wasn't it this?' he exclaimed. 'Wasn't it between those two dates that Stott thought of the gambling?'

French sat quite still thinking this over. 'You mean that as a result of putting in the gambling idea, Stott would demand a larger percentage?'

'I mean that Stott might have argued that the entire profits came from the gambling and that as a cruise the affair would have been a washout.'

'Not easy to prove that.'

'If you have the books under your own control you can prove a whole lot.'

'Then you think he might have refused Bristow any share at all?'

'I do. I think it's what he's done.'

French considered this again. 'But, look here,' he said at last. 'Even if you're right, I don't see how it would lead to murder. How would killing Stott alter the percentages?'

'Revenge, most likely. If Bristow couldn't enjoy the cash, he'd take damned good care Stott wouldn't either.'

French was far from satisfied. Murders for revenge did take place about women, but seldom, he thought, about money. Even if Bristow had lost some of what he expected, he could not complain, provided the profits really did come from the gambling. The man, moreover, had a good salary and an extraordinarily interesting and comfortable life. No, there was not enough motive here.

Then suddenly French saw. If John Stott would by a legal quibble evade payment, Wyndham Stott would not. Even if Wyndham thought of the scheme, which was doubtful, he would never adopt it. He might be a gambler, but he was both straight and generous. With Wyndham in control, Bristow would get his money.

Here was ample motive, and when French considered it further he found corroboration. Wyndham was generous and straight, but Percy Luff was neither. Suppose Wyndham should die and the control go to Luff? Would Bristow not then be as badly off as ever?

Here seemed to be the explanation of the button and Mercer letter episodes. If Luff were executed for the murder, it would not only meet this difficulty, but it would ensure Bristow's own escape from suspicion. To arrange matters that Luff should be convicted would be a very important part of the scheme.

Nugent was enthusiastic about the idea. To the D.I. it seemed to clear up the entire case. 'In theory,' he added after a panegyric. 'But it hasn't been proved yet.'

'I'll get the proof all right,' French returned optimistically, 'but what I want help in is an arrest, and that's your pigeon.'

Nugent thought an arrest premature, but French was insistent, and eventually he carried the day. The *Hellénique* was then moving down the coast from Aberystwyth to Swansea, while the excursionists drove through the Welsh hills. The warrant could be got that day, and he and Nugent could cross that night to Liverpool, making the arrest at

Swansea on the following evening. It could be carried out either ashore or on board inside the three-mile limit, according to whether Bristow had or had not taken the excursion.

This programme was carried out. Armed with the warrant and accompanied by a stalwart Northern Irish constable, French and Nugent took the night boat from Belfast. When the coaches arrived at Swansea on the following evening, Bristow was among the first to alight. French went up to him, while the other two closed in.

'I'm sorry, Mr Bristow,' he greeted him, 'that we have an unpleasant duty to perform. It had better be done privately. Will you come away from the others, please? No,' he went on, as an ugly light showed in the man's eyes, 'these are police officers from Portrush: you can't do anything.'

Bristow's face went a dead white and for a moment French thought he was going to faint. But he pulled himself quickly together. French, indeed, admired his coolness. With a curt nod he turned and went with them.

20

Proof

French found the further working-up of the case easier than he had anticipated.

First he dealt with the photographs. He went into Bristow's movements after he left Portrush early in August. The *Hellénique* was then off the Channel Islands and Bristow had returned to her via Belfast, Liverpool, London and Southampton. On the whole, French thought, it was more likely that he had dealt with the photographs personally, and therefore he began by concentrating on these places. Reproductions were circulated to the local police, with the gratifying result that a photographer was found in Southampton who had made the enlargements. When this man stated that he had been given the order on the date on which Bristow passed through Southampton on his way to the Channel Islands, and when further he picked out Bristow's photograph from a dozen others, French felt that the foundation-stone of his structure was well and truly laid.

This foundation was still further strengthened by his discovery of twenty tiny perforations, such as might have been made by drawing pins, in the wooden panelling of the wall of Bristow's sitting-room. These were distributed in four lots of five each, and spaced just where the four corners of an enlarged photograph would come. When he found that the ceiling light shone most brilliantly on the upper right-hand corner of this parallelogram, he felt he knew what had happened. No doubt Bristow had changed the bulb for a more powerful one when making his exposures, but no proof of this need be looked for, as that larger lamp would now no doubt be overboard.

Among Bristow's papers, French came upon the next course of the structure he was building. The file labelled 'Claims' contained several letters from a lady who had had her left hand crushed between the boat and the ladder when coming aboard. These, he saw at a glance, bore the handwriting of the Mercer–Luff letter, and he was able, after a good deal of work, to find in them the exact model for every word or letter of that work of art.

In connection with this find was the further one of a book of Bristow's pen-and-ink sketches—not of a very high class perhaps, but showing that he had quite enough skill to carry out the forgery.

The third major discovery could not be placed in the category of proof, but it was so suggestive as not to be far removed from it. In a folder marked 'Personal', locked carefully in the safe, were a lot of figures showing that Bristow had been trying to estimate the relative returns from the cruising and gambling sides of the undertaking. It was interesting to note that he had begun this work—the sheets were methodically headed, numbered and dated—just one week after he had written to Stott complaining of his failure to pay the percentages. Doubtless in that week he had had Stott's reply.

Another important find among Bristow's papers was a carbon copy of a statement which at first puzzled French, but which, when he had grasped its significance, threw a flood of light on a side of the case which up till then had been completely beyond his grasp.

It was locked away in the same 'Personal' division of the safe and was headed 'Proposed Hotel at White Rocks'. Obviously it was a summary of the arguments for building such an hotel. There was a sketch map attached, and as French glanced at it and read the paragraph labelled 'Site', he felt he understood how Bristow had managed to lure his victim to his end. The paragraph read: 'The hotel should be built on the small plateau immediately at the back of the saucer-like depression named "McArtt's Hollow", as this ground is of a suitable size and commands admirable views of the sea and coast. The Hollow itself, protected from the winds by its lip, would make a charming and sheltered garden or small park.' A further paragraph near the end of the statement was also significant: 'This matter should be treated as absolutely confidential. If you are even seen approaching the place, two and two will be put together and the price of the land will soar.' Well done, Bristow, thought French. With all this ingenuity, you ought to have succeeded. He could imagine the man saying: 'It's a marvellous place, Mr Stott, and there's a fortune in it. Don't take my word for it, but come and see it for yourself.' And Bristow might well have gone on: 'The first idea I put up to you has brought you in money and this one will too,' until Stott agreed to meet him there at 4.30 on that fatal day.

Why, French wondered, had the man not destroyed so compromising a document? He puzzled over this for a while, then presently saw the reason. Bristow must have something to account for his own presence at the Hollow, should he unluckily be seen there, and it would be less dangerous to show the document than to be unable to offer an explanation.

Such were the main items of the case which French, in association with Nugent, later handed to the Public Prosecutor of Northern Ireland. In his able hands they proved sufficient, and at the next assizes Bristow was found guilty and sentenced to death. A point which told heavily against him—though incidentally inducing some sympathy with him—was the establishment of the motive. Meaker gave evidence that John Stott had consulted him on the question of whether he could avoid paying Bristow any part of the profits, on the ground that cruising without gambling was a dud scheme. He had had to advise that this would be legal and Stott had decided not to pay.

When Bristow learnt that there was no chance of a reprieve, he made a statement which showed that French's theories were substantially correct. One point which French had been unable to explain was that he had made a sandbag and carried it folded in his pocket from the ship. On his way to the Hollow he had filled it with sand, emptied it after the murder, taken it back to the ship and that night thrown it overboard.

For Bristow the arrival of Malthus and Mason had been a splendid accident, and he had at once decided to make his attempt while they were on board. He did not go so far as to try to prevent them having an alibi, but he thought their presence would at least cloud the issue, while investigation into their movements would give time for the scent to cool.

Incidentally, he would have preferred to murder Stott on board and throw his body into the sea, but he realised that, owing to the legacy, the body must be found.

Bristow also explained that when he had first visited Portrush it was a showery day, and he had taken two sets of photographs, one while the sun was shining and one while it was cloudy, so as to be able to use whichever would suit the weather on the second visit.

French had every reason to be satisfied with his part in the affair, but he was still profoundly conscious of his failure in his original job: somehow to get the gambling stopped. Then suddenly it occurred to him that it was just possible that he was in a position to accomplish this also.

While going through Bristow's papers he had come on another file labelled 'Casualties'. It was not connected with the murder, and at first he had not imagined it could be of any value to him. It contained some rather dreadful reading. 'Casualties' were people who had come to grief through the gambling. In the seventeen months during which the ship had been running, there had been nine cases of more or less complete ruin. Three men and one woman had committed suicide, three had gone abroad and disappeared, and two had been reduced to beggary at home; besides which there were many letters telling of serious loss, and either begging for help or protesting that the rooms should be closed. Now, it occurred to French that an experiment might be worth trying.

He invited Wyndham Stott to his cabin, handed him the file and asked him to read the contents. 'That's what these rooms are doing, Major Stott,' he said quietly, 'and they're yours now.'

Wyndham Stott had been a different man since Margot had asked Morrison's help to get him from the tables. He had never again taken too much drink, and had practically given up gambling. Apart from these small failings, he had always been decent and kindly, and it was on his better nature that French had decided to play.

Here again, perhaps slightly to his surprise, he was successful. Wyndham read the documents with a deepening frown, and at last exploded.

'Damn it all, French! This is a hellish business! I had no idea of this side of it. I'm not going to be responsible for this kind of thing. I'll shut it down.'

So, strongly backed by Margot, eventually he did. Quietly he approached the firm of shipbreakers who had originally wanted the *Hellénique*, and the first thing the public heard was that she had already been sold for breaking up and that her cruising would be discontinued as soon as existing bookings had been worked off.

A couple of months later French and his wife received an invitation to the wedding of Margot and Harry Morrison—one of the few occasions on which French had become a real friend of former suspects.

'The murder case was a legitimate win, French,' Sir Mortimer Ellison said in closing the affair, 'but getting the gambling stopped—don't talk to me of flukes! However, we'll keep that dark. The P.M. will never know we're not as brainy as we seem.'

French glanced at him. The twinkle was in his eye. It was all right. French smiled happily.

By the same author

Inspector French's
Greatest Case

At the offices of the Hatton Garden diamond merchant *Duke & Peabody*, the body of old Mr Gething is discovered beside a now-empty safe. With multiple suspects, the robbery and murder is clearly the work of a master criminal, and requires a master detective to solve it. Meticulous as ever, Inspector Joseph French of Scotland Yard embarks on an investigation that takes him from the streets of London to Holland, France and Spain, and finally to a ship bound for South America . . .

'Because he is so austerely realistic, Freeman Wills Croft is deservedly a first favourite with all who want a real puzzle.'
TIMES LITERARY SUPPLEMENT

By the same author

Inspector French
and the Cheyne Mystery

When young Maxwell Cheyne discovers that a series of mishaps are the result of unwelcome attention from a dangerous gang of criminals, he teams up with a young woman who is determined to help him outwit them. But when she disappears, he finally decides to go to Scotland Yard for help. Concerned by the developing situation, Inspector Joseph French takes charge of the investigation and applies his trademark methods to track down the kidnappers and thwart their intentions . . .

'*Freeman Wills Crofts is among the few muscular writers of detective fiction. He has never let me down.*'
DAILY EXPRESS

By the same author

Inspector French and the Starvel Hollow Tragedy

A chance invitation from friends saves Ruth Averill's life on the night her uncle's old house in Starvel Hollow is consumed by fire, killing him and incinerating the fortune he kept in cash. Dismissed at the inquest as a tragic accident, the case is closed—until Scotland Yard is alerted to the circulation of bank-notes supposedly destroyed in the inferno. Inspector Joseph French suspects that dark deeds were done in the Hollow that night and begins to uncover a brutal crime involving arson, murder and body snatching . . .

'Freeman Wills Crofts is the only author who gives us intricate crime in fiction as it might really be, and not as the irreflective would like it to be.'   OBSERVER

By the same author

Inspector French and the Sea Mystery

Off the coast of Burry Port in south Wales, two fishermen discover a shipping crate and manage to haul it ashore. Inside is the decomposing body of a brutally murdered man. With nothing to indicate who he is or where it came from, the local police decide to call in Scotland Yard. Fortunately Inspector Joseph French does not believe in insoluble cases— there are always clues to be found if you know what to look for. Testing his theories with his accustomed thoroughness, French's ingenuity sets him off on another investigation . . .

'Inspector French is as near the real thing as any sleuth in fiction.'   SUNDAY TIMES

By the same author

Inspector French: Found Floating

The Carrington family, victims of a strange poisoning, take an Olympic cruise from Glasgow to help them recover. At Creuta one member goes ashore and does not return. Their body is next day found floating in the Straits of Gibraltar. Joining the ship at Marseilles, can Inspector French solve the mystery before they reach Athens?

Introduced by Tony Medawar, this classic Inspector French novel includes unique interludes by Superintendent Walter Hambrook of Scotland Yard, who provides a real-life detective commentary on the case as the mystery unfolds.

'I doubt whether Inspector French has had a more difficult problem to solve than that of the body 'Found Floating' in the Mediterranean.'   SUNDAY TIMES

By the same author

Inspector French
The End of Andrew Harrison

Becoming the social secretary for millionaire financier Andrew Harrison sounded like the dream job: just writing a few letters and making amiable conversation, with luxurious accommodation thrown in. But Markham Crewe had not reckoned on the unpopularity of his employer, especially within his own household, where animosity bordered on sheer hatred. When Harrison is found dead on his Henley houseboat, Crewe is not the only one to doubt the verdict of suicide. Inspector French is another...

'A really satisfying puzzle ... With every fresh detective story Crofts displays new fields of specialised knowledge.'
DAILY MAIL